Blood Vengeance

A Mitch King Mystery

Sam Waas

Blood Vengeance

By Sam Waas
© 2016 Blood Vengeance
Swartz Creek, MI 48473
Cover design by Clarissa Yeo

Published by Tell-Tale Publishing Group.   A Casablanca Imprint

First of all, Wow! Second of all, I miss Mitch King already. The novel starts off quite well, with a bang, bloody as it is. The images the author paints throughout the book are easy to imagine, with information registering, or rather, dissolving into one's mind like sugar in a hot cup of coffee. "Dissolving" isn't exactly the word I'm looking for here. What I'm trying to say is that the settings the author paints are easy enough to almost see, touch, and sometimes, even smell. And that in itself is expert writing right there.

There are some very loveable characters, each one unique and realistic in their own way. The man with the no nonsense attitude, Captain Joe Duggan. The thoughtful friend and my favorite character in the book, David Meierhoff. The man with the amazing guns, Tony. The mafia boss with her sights set on legitimacy, Julie Cards. Julie's bodyguard Angel, everyone else, love them all. Good job!

About *Blood Vengeance*, not the writing, but the story, I think it's amazingly well balanced. The book has just enough murdering going on to remind the reader that he/she's reading a detective novel, just enough humor to lighten the reader's experience, just enough twists to keep the reader turning pages, just enough sad moments for the reader to appreciate the characters a bit more, just enough culture to make Mitch's world seem more realistic, just enough of everything to make the book, overall, simply a great read.

-- Leon Durham

Appreciation to my pals for their support and assistance on such diverse minutiae as firearms, sailboats, law enforcement procedures and many other topics. Special thanks to "Orchidman" for persuading me to create my Kiwi trauma surgeon from hell, Dr. Alice Colhoun, and for helping me devise her biographical thread. And appreciation to "Teach" for his advice, and to Dan Chamberlain for his excellent recommendations and fine examples in his own novels.

Many thanks for the fine help from the folks at Tell-Tale for getting the Mitch King stories before the readers.

Kudos to Bill Pronzini and Robert Crais for their inspiration in setting targets to strive toward.

And always, to the one who provides love and joy for each day, the wonderful woman in my life

I am in blood
Stepp'd in so far that, should I wade no more,
Returning were as tedious as go o'er
— Macbeth

Chapter 1

An efficiency apartment, neat and spotless, maintained by a young woman who took student life seriously and felt pride in modest surroundings. Inexpensive bookshelves lined the walls, filled to capacity with paperbacks and collegiate texts. Stacks of notebooks were cornered on a pristine desk in an office-style cubicle complete with laptop, printer, and two framed family photos. The nearby bed was made up, bedding tucked military tight. An adjoined kitchenette gleamed, with the dining counter and two bar stools clear of even a single crumb. The bathroom was next, also clean, with bright colored linens adding a spark of cheeriness to the otherwise clinical sterility.

Unfortunately, the apartment was now an abattoir, every surface strewn with her body parts. A vile and perverted display, hacked-off fingers, random pieces of flesh, internal organs and intestines strung across shelves. Other things. Complete reproductive system cut out intact, arranged just so. A kidney. The obscenity of two breasts draped across a chair.

A diorama in blood, meant for us to absorb, for us all to bear witness.

I stood there a moment, stunned, unthinking. Then the stench and blasphemy and evil overtook me and I turned quickly, out the apartment door, choking, spitting up anything in my stomach onto the little lawn. Acidic coffee was all I offered, but the spasms persisted.

Hunched over and dizzy, I eventually regained my balance, deep breathing until I was fairly certain I wouldn't simply run down the street screaming, continue running and screaming until I was spent, spent of energy and spent of the sordid life in which I found myself this day.

Instead, I steeled my resolve and walked back inside where Homicide Captain Joe Duggan and Detective David Meierhoff were patiently waiting.

Chapter 2

Earlier that morning I was wakened by a rabid buzzing.

It disrupted my dreams, jumbled and hesitant though they were. I cautiously opened my eyes. I'd fallen asleep—fallen adrunk, actually—propped in my office chair, feet on the desk, face twisted sideways against the headrest. I straightened from the drooping slouch I'd wedged myself into, cheek stuck from a patch of dried drool, pulling away from the leather with a sickening rip. *Was I drinking myself into a John Bonham exit? Time to cut back, you think?*

If I could.

The external rattle ceased while the tumult inside my head continued. Cellphone snarkily atop my desk, silent now but proud to have exerted power over my feeble body and mind. No sooner than I breathed relief, though, it resumed the clarion summons, insistent that I obey. The cell from hell.

Sunlight streaming through the windows didn't help, stabbing rudely at my eyes, superheating my brain, making me want to hurl that nasty little ringing chunk of smartphone technology against the wall. Instead I calmly picked it up and checked who was intruding upon my stupor at, goddamn, six-forty in the fucking morning!

Lieutenant—*no*, I reminded myself—*Captain* Joseph Michael Duggan, recently promoted to Deputy Chief of Houston Homicide.

I considered slinging the phone anyway, but knew full well that the gadget would prove resilient to my luddite behavior, and in accordance with its superb Samsung design and manufacture, roll with the punch, bounce off the wall and lie there on the office floor, happily making electronic merriment and otherwise invading my personal solitude.

The phone already cycled into one pass-through to voicemail, but Duggan redialed and I knew he'd keep pushing his repeat button just to taunt and harass me further.

"Realize that you interrupted my beauty sleep?"

"For you to get beautiful, dickhead, you need a suspended goddamn animation chamber." A gruff voice. "Fuck that anyway, coming to pick your ass up. Half hour."

"How do you know I'm even home? I could be lying within the arms of some wealthy socialite at her sumptuous River Oaks estate."

"Fuck that, too," he said. "I know you're hanging out at the shabby pit where you live, pretending it's a home, plotting to jerk even more gullible clients into your shitty office."

"First it's shabby, then shitty. Make up your mind."

"Both. Shabby the living quarters at the back, shitty the office up front. Get over it. We'll cut by Starbucks and I'll let you buy me some real coffee while you indulge yourself in the usual latte-creamy-froth yuppie crap."

"Given up the yuppie lifestyle. I've now pledged allegiance to the hipster mantra."

"Go ahead, drink PBR outa cans and wear knit caps down over your friggin' ears if you want. I don't give a rat's ass. Just be waiting outside your shabby house in thirty minutes, or else I'm callin' the cops."

"You are the cops," I laughed. "But why choose me, Joe? It's not my birthday."

"Screw birthdays. We got work to do."

"Work?"

"Headed down to Montrose. Looks like he's back and left us another gift. If you could call it that—it's pretty bad, gotta warn you."

Back? Who? What gift? I was still coming up to speed, my tipsy and very foggy body doing its oxygenation thing. I tried to observe this quasi-educational reboot from a safe and detached location, distant from my own brain, impartial observer into my tumult and self-doubt. Hopeful also that the John Bonham images would soon fade.

"Who's back, Joe?"

"Who? Our old pal George Burgess. The Slicer."

The Slicer. God help us all.

* * *

I dove in and out of the shower, scraped away at my bristly face, found fresh clothes. I dumped breakfast into the cat's dish, my own a life-healthy and balanced repast of four Tylenol washed down by an Ensure, and then outside to wait for Joe.

It was humid and nearly eighty even though it was still an April morning, but this is Houston, where our four seasons consist of almost summer, summer, still summer and Christmas.

My neighbor across the street, Ernie Banks, namesake of the late great Cubs player, had just retrieved his *Houston Chronicle* and was headed inside. Ernie's a retired postman, a short, wiry black man with a pleasant visage and sterling sense of humor. He saw me and waved. I waved back, leaned against a handy tree and thought about George Burgess, aka The Slicer.

I'd screwed the pooch royally last year, allowing a smart and vicious serial killer to slip through my grasp. George Burgess, veteran cop, yes. But also a murderer and leaving a trail of clues that anyone should recognize, his hidden life clearly obvious. After all, I had my touted brainpower coupled with extensive practical experience as a private investigator. Easy? *You'd think.*

Instead, I seized upon George's younger brother Ray and by my intemperate and obsessive behavior, had driven the poor unbalanced fool to suicide. Meanwhile his more canny elder sibling ambushed and stabbed me, left me for dead and escaped.

Burgess had thus far avoided capture, using both his criminal cunning and law enforcement training to stay clear of police. And for months now, he'd slaughtered women with impunity all along the I-45 corridor, taking time to mail me cheery and bloodstained *Wish You Were Here* greeting cards after each murder, payback for his brother's death. Eight human beings I could add to my personal scorecard of guilt and despair. Eight. And now, according to Joe Duggan, a new one. Nine.

Despite well-meant support from friends, I'd taken more to drink, anesthetizing myself to find sleep. Which of course doesn't work because a drunk brain isn't a resting brain, REM sleep denied. A couple bourbons are okay, but a dozen? Nope. Nevertheless I kept up the boozing and now it was beginning to cut into my work and health. But I'd have to deal with those consequences in due time. Right now I was ramped up with nervous anticipation, waiting for Joe Duggan and the new murder scene he'd be dragging me to.

Life is such a treat.

I was coughing into my palm, sniffing to see whether I'd successfully Scoped away the whiskey breath when Duggan drove up in his unmarked Crown Vic, and clicked the door locks. "Get the fuck in. I need coffee."

While I hitched my seatbelt, Joe glanced outside, scowled. "When you gonna add a gun?" He pointed to the very modest and conservative signboard next to my front door, *Mitchell King,*

Investigations. "Least mebbe put a magnifying glass." Joe's a constant delight, consistent in his grouchiness to everyone, me especially. I'm apparently his chosen life project.

We took off with a little screech of impatience, quick coffee on the agenda and what next promised to be a lengthy and excruciating journey into the tenets of modern blood sacrifice.

Chapter 3

As he pulled from the curb, Joe Duggan shot a hard glance in my direction. "Christ on a crutch, Mitch, how much you drink last night? I can smell the fuckin' booze oozing from your goddamn pores!"

So much for the mouthwash camouflage. And so begins my day.

I looked at my pal Joe Duggan, a ringer for actor Ned Beatty. He was spiffily dressed, still a surprise to everyone. For years, Joe was awarded by default the imaginary but highly coveted *Worst Dressed Houston Cop* trophy due to his consistently wrinkled shirts, faded ties, unpressed slacks—your archetypal Dragnet-era TV tough-guy cop attire.

Whether urged upon him by HPD bigwigs after his promotion or a final victory by his wife Margaret (who I thought the true impetus), Joe suddenly appeared at the office one Monday morning in a new suit, stylish but conservative, finely-striped shirt with elegant, perfectly tied neckwear, gleaming loafers and over-the-calf socks sporting little *fleurs-de-lis*. A sartorial sea change.

Joe said nothing about this nor would he brook inquiry. He changed his spots and the evolution seemed a permanent mutation. It took getting used to.

Today I was severely down dressed by comparison, khaki Levi's, a maroon short sleeve sport shirt with enough overhang to conceal the compact Springfield .45 in my Crossbreed holster, and habitual Nikes to round it off. Certainly no match for Duggan's victorious Men's Wearhouse makeover.

* * *

Coffee acquired, a dark Brazilian roast for both, we headed toward Montrose, Houston's venerable arts and music neighborhood. My house is in the Heights, just north of the Montrose district, so Joe took Heights Boulevard south. He sidled to Yoakum, passed the Greek Orthodox church and school, continued by the campus of St. Vincent, a top-ranked Roman Catholic liberal arts college and finally booked it west on Richmond Avenue.

Four blocks after the campus we cut to a shady and once peaceful side street where police cars, the county coroner and CSI vans were parked all over, their indiscriminate hogging of the narrow lane generally blocking further access. A Channel 13 remote was also setting up nearby, making it impossible to find a spot.

Undeterred, Joe carefully squeezed through the maze, waved hello to a uniform cop directing traffic and pulled alongside an HFD ambulance, its roof lights quietly flashing. Our destination was a hundred feet further, a quaint eight-unit apartment building, tidy and well maintained. Joe stuck his HPD placard on the dash, as if a dark blue Crown Vic with three antennas sprouting from the trunk lid and parked square in the middle of the street could be thought anything else.

"Nice little place," Joe observed. "Mostly grad students, they told me."

"Yeah. Lived in an apartment just like this when I was at UT."

Joe frowned. "Your old man was loaded. He didn't put you up in some smarmy Austin high rise?"

I shook my head. "He covered major expenses, tuition, rent, but I had a strict lifestyle budget and he insisted that I work part time for my support. Four years, I think I flipped ten million burgers at the Nighthawk cafe."

"Smart thinking, good way to raise a kid," Joe said, smiled. "So what happened to you?"

"I was corrupted by hanging out with Houston's finest. Sad, but that's show biz."

Joe ignored that, apparently not considering it worthy of comment. We got out and walked to the police line.

The apartments were one story, a contiguous yellow stucco-fronted building, narrow lawn with evergreen shrubs and microscopic flower beds decorating a walkway that serviced the apartments, all surrounded by a chest-high wrought iron fence delineating the apartments from the sidewalk and street. A small reserved lot along one side of the property held a collection of economy imports.

Crime tape was stretched along the entryway to the complex, with cops, medics and CSI techies standing all about, talking and smoking and trying to make themselves slightly useful. Or slightly useless, depending on the individual's dedication to the task.

A half dozen civilians sat near the parking lot in lawn chairs, impromptu gallery, glancing surreptitiously at the cluster of cops concentrated around unit four, where CSI had set up a tall, translucent plastic three-sided screen across the open doorway. I guessed the watchers to be temporarily displaced residents, gathered out of mutual curiosity, shared anxiety or, more likely, because the cops had asked them not to go anywhere until questioned.

Joe handed me an HPD *Consultant* pass. "Here. Don't lose it."

I glanced at it and smiled as I clipped it to the front of my belt. The badge closely resembled the counterfeit ones I often use, cranked out with Photoshop, my HP color printer and a laminator. Actually, I think my designs are better.

Homicide Detective David Meierhoff was standing in front of apartment four, reviewing notes on his touchscreen with other investigators. Like Duggan, Meierhoff had been newly promoted, now sergeant and shift supervisor. And still my best friend.

David was once impetuous and brash, smart-mouthed, something of a square peg at Homicide. It was through Duggan's guidance that he'd matured, become more professional. Duggan himself had stabilized, grown into his leadership role, spending more time in administrative duties, fewer hours on the street.

And me? I think I've slipped back. Yes, I've increased my clientele and found steady retainers with local insurance firms and yes, I'm on more solid financial footing, but my personal life is nevertheless a morass of indecision and inaction. Yet this was no time for analyzing my psyche. Freud is dead and disavowed, I was among professionals and I needed to act the same. So I referred it to committee.

David Meierhoff finished his chat with the other cops, grinned at me, we shook. He's five-eleven, maybe an inch taller than I, definitely more athletic and handsome, resembling a rakish young Elliott Gould. David always dresses impeccably, today a blue dress shirt, deeper blue power tie, dark slacks and a soft tan sport jacket. For a long time, Joe Duggan's attire was no challenge to Meierhoff and although Joe was now knocking at fashion's door, Meierhoff still had everyone at the cop shop beat, like a stylish Kojak minus the little cigar and later, the more politically correct lollipop.

"Duggan tells me you're primary here," I said.

"True. It's because of my rugged good looks and kindly demeanor."

Duggan snorted. "Or maybe 'cause you're HPD lead on the Slicer task force?"

"That, too," David said, smiling. He looked at me. "Other team members were called, they'll be here this afternoon. Scudder is flying from Beaumont, Danforth driving down from Austin."

The whole gang, I thought. I'd met FBI Special Agent Ed Scudder and Texas Ranger Arvis Danforth last year when I was drawn into the Slicer case. Under better circumstances I'd enjoy seeing them both again. But now? Not so pleasant.

"And I'm square in the mix, right?" I asked.

"Yep. Joe and I talked, want you to see what we've found. We're certain the killer is George Burgess, which means that he's back in Houston."

"Or maybe just passing through?" Joe added.

Meierhoff nodded his assent. "Maybe. But I've got the impression that he's here for at least a long visit. This is his home base and he's been targeting Mitch all along. Could be he's amping the volume now. Or, as you said, just swinging by and wanted to leave another victim on the way."

We quietly considered the alternatives, whether to expect Burgess setting up Slicer Headquarters back in the Houston area or to wish him transient and visiting his bloody business onto a more distant population. Neither prospect was very enticing.

"What makes you think that Burgess is targeting me again?" I asked. "Were there any—"

"Hang on a sec." Meierhoff cut me off, turned toward apartment three, adjacent the murder scene. The door had opened and two women emerged, a tall, ascetic black female uniform cop and a stocky Anglo woman, short grey hair, fiftyish, blue slacks and jacket, yellow blouse beneath, a big fabric bag across one shoulder. The women were as unalike as possible except that each had been crying.

As they came over where we were standing, the older woman looked at Meierhoff. "Officer…?"

Meierhoff smiled at her then glanced to us. "Gentlemen, Sister Mary Frances Brookshire. She teaches at St. Vincent, lives in three."

We offered her a forced smile, best possible under the circumstances.

"And I'm Sergeant David Meierhoff, Sister, but please call me David. Did you get your laptop and books?"

"Yes, sorry for making a fuss with all this… this terrible…" Her head sank as she glanced sidelong at people coming in and out of apartment four, then quickly turned her eyes away. "Rennie, she… she was such a sweet girl, she…" Sniffling, she rubbed her hand across her eyes.

Meierhoff gently put his hand atop her shoulder. "We understand, Sister. This is traumatic for us all," he said sympathetically. "You've got my business card, right?" A nod. "My office and cell numbers, email, all there. I'll phone you later, stop by St. Vincent this afternoon with some follow-up questions. In the meantime, if you think of anything, no matter how unconnected or trivial, call me right away, okay?" She nodded again. "Now, Officer Jackson will see you to your car, ensure you're all right."

"Thanks for letting me get inside my place. I'm teaching this afternoon and I really needed the laptop. It's got all my notes." She turned to the uniform cop who escorted her. "Okay, Shawnelle, I'm parked just down the street. Let's go."

Jackson glanced at the heavy shoulder bag. "Carry that for you, Sister?"

"No, thanks. It's my laptop to bear." A brief smile and the pair strode away, tall rangy cop, short and well-fed nun, linked now as impromptu siblings on this dark and nasty day.

Meierhoff looked at me. "Sister Mary Frances is professor of history at St. Vincent, lives next door. She was out for an early walk, thought she saw what looked like, but couldn't be, copious blood splatter inside one window of the neighbor's apartment. Knocked, no answer. She had a spare key, took one glance and nearly fainted right there on the doorstep. She seems to be bearing up, but she's just running on vapor now, and will probably crash later."

One of the CSI techs, a guy named Kenny Phelps, was listening, and frowned. "Sister Mary Frances? A nun? Don't nuns, like…" He curved both hands around his head, pantomiming a coif.

"You watch too much TV, Kenny, and movies," I told him. "Nuns in the US haven't resembled penguins for years. Started during Vatican Two in, ah…" I drew a momentary blank.

Meierhoff immediately took up the slack. "Second Vatican council, nineteen sixty-two, convened by Pope John twenty-three."

"You're Jewish," I said. "How come you know that?"

Meierhoff winked at me. "Keeping up on the competition."

"So," Kenny asked. "Nuns now dress like Dana Scully?"

"But with longer hemlines," I said. "Some still maintain the traditional habit, pun intended."

There was a brief pause and Meierhoff sighed. "Dana Scully. I sure had a crush on Anderson."

"Ha!" Kenny laughed. "Tell me what nerd didn't?"

"I actually think she's better looking today," I offered. "Saw her in that *Hannibal* show on TV."

"Y'know who I thought was sexier, though?" Kenny remarked. "Mimi, whatzhername, you know, ah, played another FBI gal. Was in *Playboy*, too."

"Mimi Rogers, otherwise Mrs. ex-Tom Cruise," Meierhoff said.

Kenny chuckled. "Meierhoff's right, Cruise it is. Ya gotta keep an eye on Meierhoff here, Mitch. He's up to date on Hollywood, reads all the murder mysteries, downloads CSI episodes so he can compare what we do with TV. He's so very helpful that way." Kenny smiled, jerking Meierhoff's chain. "Ol' Sergeant Meierhoff's real smart, a regular Brainiac."

"Not a good analogy," Meierhoff said. "Brainiac is actually a malevolent alien entity that attacks the Earth, tries to kill Superman and other superheroes. In Frank Miller's graphic novel *Dark Knight Strikes Again*, Brainiac—"

"Whoa," Duggan interrupted, his arms raised. "Hold on. Can we back off the trivia a while and stop talking like we're in a Quentin fucking Tarantino movie? There's a murder investigation, in case you've all forgotten."

Joe was right. But this sort of random shop talk and diffident conversation occurs all the time. You see it with cops, firefighters, paramedics, doctors, most of whom will chat inanely about disconnected junk while confronted with a bloody event. It's a mechanism to release tension that outsiders often interpret as uncaring. It's not.

We quieted down anyway and approached the plastic curtain leading to four. A big floor fan was in the doorway, whooshing. I thought about what unholy and terrible surprises the forced ventilation was intended to dissipate and my reluctance genes kicked in. "I still don't know why you want me here."

"You're the closest thing we've got to a witness for how Burgess operates, how he thinks," David said.

"I only met him that once, when he…" I trailed off. *When he nearly killed me. When I forced his mentally ill brother into suicide.* One of my better days.

"But you did study him, watch him," Duggan said. "We still think you can help, even if only a little. Besides, Mitch, it was me who got you involved in the whole damn thing in the first place. Whatever input you can give is a plus."

I shrugged. "Sure, if I can."

I thought a bit more, recalling TV shows where the boyfriend of the lead cop takes an investigatory role, even though his presence as mystery writer, debunked psychic, or requisite hunk would get the bad guy's indictment tossed out in five seconds. But I was only blowing smoke. In all honesty, I simply didn't want to step inside that apartment, so I raised a final objection. "I'm not legally supposed to be here," I whined. "Won't that compromise evidence?"

Meierhoff smiled. "Good point, Mitch. But your badge says *Consultant* and that's technically true, were anyone to ask. And they'd have to get past Duggan or me first."

To augment what Meierhoff said, Joe Duggan employed his patented persuasion tool, holding up a meaty hand, four fingers spread wide. "Count 'em off," he said, pulling his little finger down to the palm. "One, you're a valuable witness." The ring finger. "Two, we can use your help on this." Middle finger and a wry smile. "Three, me and David love your ass so much that we're starving for your company." The forefinger. "Finally, the Slicer left you a message." The big fist formed and he swept it past my chin, grazing me with a sharp right, like Cagney's signature move from *Public Enemy*. I tried to pass it off, even though it jarred me down to the Nikes.

"You ready?" Joe asked. "Just make sure you don't touch anything."

I looked to Meierhoff. "Lead on, Macduff."

David's smile turned dour. "After you see inside, I don't think you'll be quoting The Bard of Avon much more today."

I knew what George Burgess was capable of as the Slicer, gruesome yet tenable. "What's the deal?"

Meierhoff glanced toward the horizon, searching for a way to prepare me. "Ever read about Jack the Ripper? How he escalated the murders, each time more graphic than previous?"

I wavered side to side, suddenly unstable. "Like…?"

Duggan said, "The Slicer's gone overboard. The worst."

And I was the special guest. Great.

We gloved up and slipped on disposable plastic booties. Then we passed the uniform cop guarding the door, our own private Cerberus, and descended into hell.

Chapter 4

After first glance at the horror inside apartment four, after heaving my guts in front of TV news crews and therefore auditioning for the lunchtime *Bleeds It Leads* feature, I considered checking out and heading home for more bourbon. But I persevered and tentatively braved the doorway again.

David Meierhoff proffered me a narrow, reassuring smile. "Don't sweat it, Mitch. Happens to everybody."

One of the CSI techs handed me a little jar of peppermint balm. I spread a ribbon on my upper lip, nodded thanks, handed it back. And yeah, I know it seems like a movie cliché but they really do use the stuff. It helps. A little.

Strobes were flashing everywhere as CSI took photos, quietly gathered samples, murmured among themselves, no laughter, no dark crime scene humor. This murder was so overwhelming as to shake even a veteran into quiescence. Or retirement.

CSI had asked for help bagging and labeling specimens, and a few uniform police volunteered their service, having stronger stomachs than mine. Some of the CSI wore full hazmat gear. These were the techs with the unenviable assignment of actually collecting strewn body parts. Others working the scene were dressed as we were, plastic booties and surgical gloves.

I was briefly introduced to a muscular linebacker-size black man, Doctor Frank Winger, Harris County forensic pathologist in charge of the medical investigation. With both of us wearing gloves, his bloodied, we simply bobbed heads at each other in passing, two dilapidated freighters at sea.

What remained of the young woman's torso lay partly on the bed and was draped off to the thinly carpeted floor. She had been viciously disassembled as by some inept but persistent butcher. Because the head was missing, torso eviscerated, legs and arms shredded, the angles were badly distorted from what was once a living person, and it took a moment for me to orient the body position in my mind, shoulders on the floor, hips toward the bed.

Fecal matter and other fluids were still dripping from her intestines strung across the bookshelves and furniture. Random body parts everywhere, sitting with fixated neatness, centered on countertops, tables and shelves. Pieces of her skin, bones, flesh, organs covered the room, the walls.

And with that, my brain locked out. It refused to further catalog, instead blurred it over like they do nude movie scenes for broadcast TV. I looked without seeing.

The human brain, its self-censoring mechanism evolved to protect us from immediate harm or trauma, generally prevents us from freezing in step and instead sends out adrenalin so we can fight or flee. But the evolutionary calendar hasn't yet flipped enough pages for our minds to become inured to tragedy. And so I knew that these images would rise from my subconscious and haunt my dreams for months to come.

Welcome to the real world, Mitch.

"For God's sake, who was she?" I finally managed to whisper.

Meierhoff glanced grimly around the room as if there were messages in the carnage. "Renata Martinez, twenty-three, El Paso. Professional parents, attorneys, fairly well off. Here on scholarship for her master's in comparative religion, honor student at St. Vincent." He grimaced. "We talked briefly to family, neighbors, some faculty. She's been in Houston a couple years, decent girl, hetero if you're wondering, nice guy boyfriend, smart and well balanced young woman, cheery but not overly, some nightlife. Essentially a perfectly normal grad student. Hoped to be professor of religion, teach at some good Catholic school." A deep sigh. "But not any more."

Not any more. Three words to encompass an entire life, now cut short, ripped away. Dreams torn like her poor shattered limbs, hopes asunder as was the body she once inhabited. Gone to blood and blood alone.

We were all silent a while. "No clues why she was picked?" I asked.

"None so far," Duggan said. "Why we're bringing you into this."

"Joe, you guys are good," I told him. "You've got a whole team of homicide and CSI at your disposal. There's got to be something else, asking me here."

Meierhoff pointed. "Watch where you put your feet. Glance in the bathroom."

With great trepidation and regret, I picked my way around the human debris and moved toward the small bath.

On the mirror, written in Renata Martinez' blood, *heres looking at you mitch*. And in the basin, her head, ears gone, lips cut off, eyes gouged out and staring at me from two bloody pools on the shelf below the mirror.

* * *

There's a point at which the mind simply clicks off. My protective instincts already shielded me from carefully observing specifics of the devastation and now my forebrain shut down totally, leaving behind a functioning, reactive, protean residue but minus a soul. I was no longer queasy or nauseous because I was no longer human. I rejoined Duggan and Meierhoff, beheld the remainder of the room with clinical and detached observation.

Doctor Winger came over where we were standing. "We looked for the Pflaugher clamp like you guys asked, but couldn't find it. Maybe he's abandoned that habit."

Meierhoff looked to me. "You remember, Mitch, Burgess would leave this big surgical clamp in his victims' vaginas. One of his signatures."

I'd carefully and intentionally forgotten that item from when I witnessed Burgess' frightening carnage last year. "Thanks for reminding me, David."

"Hey, it comes with the territory, something you gotta get used to, okay?" I nodded, accepting. "Anyway, we figure that his source for the clamps dried up when his brother died, he being a hospital worker. He's also stopped marking up the victim with the felt tip pens, too. But ritual killers often modify their schema anyway, sometimes to sidetrack an investigation, sometimes for unknown reasons. They aren't the robots you see on TV or the movies."

"Any other surprises?" I asked.

"Yeah," Meierhoff replied, seemingly not wishing to speak further. "We're still conducting a thorough inventory, but it appears that some of the body parts are missing."

"Trophies?" I asked, fearing worse.

And worse came. Winger consulted his notepad. "One kidney, a lobe of the liver, the heart." He looked at me, squinted. "We've seen this in his recent two victims as well, something we've not made general knowledge. He may have become a Lecter copycat. Eating his victims."

Behind us: "With some fava beans and a nice Chianti."

We all turned to see one of the uniform cops suppressing a laugh, his colleagues staring at him with considerable anger and shame. The cop's nametag read *P. Jenks.*

Crap, I thought, *Phil Jenks again.* I might have known. Meierhoff and I had a run-in with Jenks a year ago. Biggest screw job on the force, always getting written up, borderline for being terminated. Jenks is a tall athletic man who looks the part of a solid and trustworthy beat cop, but inside, pure slime.

Meierhoff stepped up to Jenks, glanced at his nametag, stared. "Officer Jenks, we've met previously. Did you say something? Share it with us, please."

Jenks stammered. "Er, y'know, just makin' a joke."

For a moment I thought that Meierhoff would unleash a typhoon of Shotokan karate onto Jenks. He'd done it that time before, when they got into it physically, Meierhoff bringing Jenks to his knees in about five seconds. But this was the more subdued and laid back version of Meierhoff, less impulsive.

Still, Jenks must have expected to be hit square on, because when Meierhoff pointed at him, he flinched. The impact was however verbal. "Jenks," Meierhoff spoke loud enough to gain the attention of everyone in the room. "You are a complete fuckup. You are a class one, premium grade, high caliber, dick-brained fuckup. You are a spherical fuckup because you're a fuckup from any direction. We all know it. Hell, even you know it by now, pigheaded as you are."

Jenks twitched nervously, wanting to be elsewhere but not having the will to leave amidst the ass chewing. Instead he just stood there, shifting from foot to foot while Meierhoff continued.

"You don't have any buddies on the force, no real partners, because you pissed off or alienated everyone you've been paired with. Word gets around, but you haven't. You've been handed from officer to officer like some rotten hot potato. You're as worthless as shrimp shit and about as low." Meierhoff pointed at

Jenks again and again Jenks flinched. "Now get the fuck out of here and let the real police do their jobs! Am I clear? Well?"

"Asshole!" Jenks growled. "I'm taking this to my union rep."

Meierhoff hesitated and I thought Jenks was going to be awarded a *nukite* jab to the solar plexus anyway, but Duggan raised his hand, intervening, glancing around the room. "You all know me. I'm Captain Joseph Duggan, Homicide Deputy Chief. I'm the senior officer present and witness to whatever. I just observed an act of blatant disregard for the murder victim, a rude and uncaring assault on her memory, something both the disciplinary committee and the TV news folks would be interested in hearing." He paused a moment for effect. "Detective Meierhoff expressed disdain at this remark. Now, if anybody has a gripe, they can run it past me first. And that includes you, Officer Jenks."

Everyone turned away, suddenly busy with the task at hand. Silence in the room. Jenks' face was red, angry, frozen with frustration. He spun on his heels and stormed out of the apartment.

"We finished here?" Duggan asked. Nobody spoke. "Done is done," he concluded.

The fix was in.

Chapter 5

Joe Duggan and I sat at the counter of James Coney Island, an upscale wienery on South Shepherd. He had two big Hebrew National hot dogs on wheat buns, the dogs now invisible because they were topped with thick layers of shredded cheese and chopped onion. And sliced jalapenos. And chili.

Myself, I wasn't eating, sipping a Coke instead, still upset from the murder scene. It wasn't the insane way Renata Martinez' body was desecrated, disturbing as this was and despite my initial reaction. Yes, I'd been blown away, but got my sea legs soon thereafter. What really set me off was that this horrific murder had been perpetrated on my account, George Burgess dedicating her body to me. That sent my mind into spirals and my whole body off kilter. What's the Hopi phrase, *Koyaanisqatsi*, a life out of balance? My whole existence was certainly out of phase and not likely to regain any semblance of stability soon. And today hadn't helped.

Joe picked up the first dog carefully, watching for drips. Last year he'd have likely used his ratty necktie for a catch bucket but the revised Duggan *Part Deux* exercised normal human caution about stray food. He bit off a piece, chewed thoughtfully. "Sure you don't want anything? My treat."

I shook my head. "I don't think I'll be eating much the next couple days, thanks."

Joe acknowledged with a brief nod, took another bite, set the dog back on his plate, and diligently wiped his mouth with a napkin. "It was a tough one, pal. That I understand."

"You guys sure you want me to work on this?"

"We appreciate your help, Mitch, honest. I remember you once told me that private detectives go places the cops cannot, ask questions they cannot."

I shrugged. "I suppose. But this is a primo murder investigation, all sorts of cop shops working on it, you guys, Texas Rangers, the Feebs. I'm low grade by comparison."

Duggan picked up the wiener, and took another munch. "You got contacts, is all. And you've also got a personal interest in the thing. That bathroom note would put the fear of God into anybody."

"Not the best thing to see before noon," I admitted.

I thought back to last year, all the death, the blood. And how I failed. It was my fault, the murders clearly on my ticket. If I'd been half as smart as I made myself out, I'd have quickly seen that Ray Burgess was no killer and looked elsewhere. Older brother George may have still gotten away but at least that sad and miserable Ray would be alive.

Ray's secretive behavior led me to mistakenly think he was hiding a string of vicious murders. Instead, Ray was simply concealing that he was addicted to autoerotic asphyxiation, that he was what's known on the street as a *space monkey*. And thanks to my harassment, Ray was driven to a miserable, lonely suicide. Were I his brother I'd want to kill me too. But there was no going back and perhaps I could somehow alleviate my burden of guilt by trying to help grab George. And so, "If you really think I can do something, anything."

"Attaboy," Joe said, around the hot dog. "Sure you don't want maybe a burger? Nachos? Fries?"

"No. After that… that nightmare, I'm surprised you can even look at food."

"Ten, fifteen years ago I couldn't. It's something you get used to. Or go nuts. But we hard-ass cops take it for granted after a while, murder scenes, the blood, the stink. Now Sister Mary Frances? She'll have nightmares for months."

Us versus them, I thought, there it was again. The dichotomy that normally surfaces at a crime scene, this time benevolently, but most often as a sharp and unfriendly chasm between those in the know, those connected, ones who are favorably ranked compared with others lacking access. And understandably, civilians in turn often view cops as thugs and crypto-Nazis.

Some kids are, of course, raised from birth to hate or distrust the cops, an attitude that takes but one generation to bestow yet many to dispel. A few cops also dislike civilians, see them trash or somehow as impediments to a good work ethic and need for them to just stay out of the way.

Most on either side don't see things that darkly, instead fall comfortably into the old terse and restrained mode of mutually assured suspicion, like two disparate animal species meeting at a water hole on the veldt. Regardless, the tension is always there, pulling and nagging and preventing any reasonable solution from alleviating potential harshness to the rule of law. Thus does the great karmic wheel cycle, grinding down the mind and soul. And dust always as the result. Always.

My phone tweedled. I pulled it out, checked. "Okay. Meierhoff emailed his preliminary notes." I scrolled. "Victim info, apartment management contact, her faculty advisor."

Joe took another bite. "I'll get you copies of the full case file. You got a spare thumbdrive? I'll dump it on that."

"At the house. Remind me when we get there." Then, "I'm supposed to go shooting with Meierhoff, maybe tomorrow, he can bring the other info with him."

"Shooting? Hopefully at the range and not at citizens, right?"

"Lucky for you and your department, not at John Citizen," I said, falling into the same old *us versus them* dialogue myself. Shows how sincere I can be, judging others, then speaking from the back side of my mouth. Anyway. "We've both got new pistols to try. Gonna drink beer and brag about it afterward. Typical gun owner bullshit."

"What you guys waste your money on now?"

"I got a Springfield XD forty-five Tactical, David bought a nice little mouse gun, mostly for plinking, Ruger LCP three-eighty."

Joe chuckled. "Talk about King Kong and King Can't."

"Want to come with us, poke random holes in paper?"

"I might just do that," he said, popping the last of the dog into his mouth, chewing. "'Course, I wouldn't want to show you boys up or nothin'." A sidewise smile, modestly chili imbued.

Yeah, right, I thought, *show us up*. Meierhoff took second place in tactical combat shooting at the *Coplympics* last November, losing only to one of the SWAT commanders. And I'd just won a friendly shoot-off at my local range, no trophy but two hundred bucks. Good luck to Joe Duggan on trying to top either of us. Great cop he might be, expert shot he ain't.

I looked to Joe, back on subject. "We've got to figure why George Burgess chose her. If he did. Might have been random."

"Maybe random. But even if it was, learning what led him to find her may lead us back to finding him."

"If and when we do?"

Joe glanced at his lunch ticket, plopped some bills on the counter, shrugged. "Depends on the circumstances."

I sipped the last of my Coke, pushed it away from me. "If I do the finding, I might do the rest of it, too."

Joe slowly wiped his lips, carefully folded the napkin in half, put it on his plate. "That could happen." He looked straight at me. "But if it did, vigilante stuff, which of course you'd never get involved in, but if it did, I don't want to know."

I nodded.

"One thing," Joe added. "Don't fuck this one up. Either quit while you're ahead or take it all the way. Like I always tell people, *Done is done*."

Another dutiful nod from me. I'd just been greenlighted.

Chapter 6

Joe drove me home. I ran inside, grabbed a blank thumb drive, and ran back out to his car. "I'll check the prelim info, chat with some of her neighbors, friends."

"Back off on contacting any of the wits for now," Duggan told me. "You're just a lowly consultant anyway." He grinned. "Better that you pick up on the second pass of interviews, fill in the gaps, stuff like that."

"Sure, Joe. Whatever. Just let me know when you want me to proceed." I gave him the thumb drive and the badge, but Duggan passed the plastic ID back to me. "Hang on to that. It'll help with the interviews. Just tell 'em you're an ex night club mind reader or something just as stupid." He ran his window up and drove away.

I laughed. Earlier I'd been thinking about the recent fad in TV cop shows, the traditional partnered cop-with-cop team now reimaged as cop-with-whomever, reporter or scientist or sculptor and maybe next season, ghost shark or zombie. It could work.

As I came back inside, Krazy Kat was standing at the door, meowing piteously and acting forlorn. I'd dared to make the mad dash for the thumb drive without petting or otherwise noticing him, and he was miffed and timorous, thinking that I no longer cared. Cats are like that, fickle. And very manipulative. Manipulative doesn't even begin to describe it. What's the adage? *Dogs have owners, cats have staff.*

I snagged another Ensure from the fridge and headed to my office. The desk still bore telltales of last night's binge, half bottle of Maker's Mark, a now-empty glass, pitcher of melted ice. I told myself that someone else, possibly the Bourbon Fairy, put these sleazy leftovers on my desk. I cleaned away all the evidence and sat down, drank my slightly chalky Ensure and skimmed through Meierhoff's email.

The notes were sketchy, understandably so, as they'd only been a quick run to document the names and IDs of potential witnesses. Meierhoff would fill them in later and give me the revisions.

As I scanned the text I thought about how the stereotypical image of the private eye differs from reality. My imaginary hardcore private eye Bugsy Binton eschews technology, relying on his fists and trusty Smith & Wesson .38 snubbie to find the truth. He'd seize up like an old Dodge if he even saw a PC, let alone be asked to use one.

In truth, a private detective wouldn't stay in business a month without modern technology. Database searches are routine now, as are automatic surveillance cameras and bugs, some illegal as hell. Every PI whom I know has smartphones, laptops, every flavor of electronic device you can buy. And if they didn't know how to work them, they soon learn. Even older operatives have to change. That, or slowly strangle on an increasing dearth of clients.

Cops the same. When the Homicide group was first issued Toshiba notebooks, Duggan invaded my house one Sunday afternoon, computer in one hand, six-pack of St. Arnolds in the other, insisting I show him the basics. He'd gone through the orientation and taken plenty of notes, but computers as handy tools were still an alien concept to him. He'd always regarded them as the enemy. Joe of course knew about my knack for computers and seized upon me as his personal tutor. "Just don't let Meierhoff know," he warned.

"Between us, Joe," I reassured him. "Long as you keep bringing beer, we're good."

So we began. At first, Joe asked lots of low-level questions. Thankfully I'm pretty good with explanations and things moved quickly. One thing I noticed, though. Joe never asked the same question twice. And by the time he left for home, he was fairly comfortable with the basics and could handle all the specialized software that HPD loaded onto his new PC. Joe Duggan was set for the new age of the networked investigator.

But were I to ever worry about the fading of a genuine street cop, I only had to remember that in addition to his tablet, smartphone and laptop, Duggan also carried his Les Baer Custom Concept forty-five. And nothing says tradition like a 1911 pistol.

Chapter 7

With Duggan asking me to hang back from interviewing witnesses, my social calendar was temporarily empty. So I stayed home and stayed away from the booze both, went to bed early. I tried to sleep but found myself staring endlessly at the bloody crime, perfectly burned into my brain, visible regardless of whether I shut my eyes. It was about four when I finally dozed off.

I slept until nine and it felt like five minutes. After a shower I phoned my business partner Andrew at *Fairview Consultants*. "You emailed. I've got a couple contracts to sign?"

"Certainly. I want to talk about Carolyn anyway."

"She okay? Problems at work?"

"Not exactly, Mitchell." Andrew deferring, as he often did. "Better you and I discuss her problem in person."

"Okay," I said. I'd get no more from him on the phone. That was Andrew's way. "Be there in a while." And just so he'd know—we share all the news—I told him about the horrific murder scene I'd witnessed yesterday and rang off.

I've always had a touch for computers and found a niche. I noticed that many small law firms are woefully underpowered in their computer operations. Larger firms have their own IT departments, but other organizations are often foundering.

So I dipped into my trust fund and set up an internet access enterprise. We go into a lawyer shop, design a custom website, install a first rate server system and network them to our home office, where we maintain their software and provide secure offsite backups. Being a shoestring operation, our fees are lower. And via friends-of-friends, I'm able to cajole firms into taking a chance with us. Thus far, we've not let them down. No crashes, no viruses, no problems.

Of course, I wasn't technically up to speed, nor did I have time to run things myself. So I took on Andrew Capshaw, who'd been recommended. Andrew provides the technology and I finance operations. We turned our first profitable quarter a year ago and have already expanded, Andrew hiring an assistant, Carolyn Vinh.

Fairview Consultants is, duh, on Fairview Avenue in the Montrose. I parked in the adjacent lot of a gay biker bar with the sign *Leather Lads Parking Only After 6pm*, strolled to the rear entrance of the house next door and let myself in.

It was cool inside, as they used to say about movie theaters back when home air conditioning was rare. Just by the door, two work desks, each with three flat screens, cables strung everywhere but with precision that only someone obsessed with neatness would ensure. The adjoining room is full of commercial computer racks, rows of servers, disk drives, communications hardware. Everything is aligned and labeled without a single wire out of place. Can you say *anal retentive?*

My friend Andrew, never Andy, always Andrew, as he is wont to remind everyone to the point of exhaustion, was on his bluetooth. Andrew is whippet thin with a widow's peak and Van Dyke, making him look exactly like Ming the Merciless from the old Buck Rogers serial, something I carefully avoid ever mentioning.

Andrew waved, pointed me to a chair, continued talking into the air. "Certainly, Mr. Denton. We can set up training at your office or at ours. I however recommend your place, as your staff will feel more comfortable." Andrew rolled his eyes, showing frustration at the apparent density of the client. "Yes sir, let me check the calendar—we're so busy right now…" Andrew of course looked at nothing, just stared off into space briefly. "Yes, we can do the ninth. Shall we plan for two pm? Excellent. I'll call the day before and ensure that everything is on track. Yes, thank you. Goodbye."

Client dealt with, Andrew turned his attention to me. "Two new contracts, then Carolyn."

"You want my John Hancock?"

"Absolutely, the Han*cock*!" he replied, grinning like a Cheshire cat and emphasizing the syllable *cock*. It was an in-joke for us and I always indulged him. He retrieved folders from a file cabinet, those of two new clients. As I signed the papers, Andrew was celebratory. "More grist for the mill, more bucks in the till."

Andrew Capshaw is extremely gay, way out there and tends to flounce a bit as he talks, but I also know him to be intelligent, sincere and forthright. That, and his being a networking whiz, was why I made him a full partner in the startup. Andrew and I see things pretty much eye to eye and I regard him as an ideal associate. He's smarter than I and he stays out of trouble, too.

"You look tired, Mitchell," he told me.

"That murder. We talked about it. Not something you easily forget. Hard to sleep last night."

"You should visit this glorious masseur I use. Victor simply works wonders!" Andrew grinned mischievously. "And no, he won't put a move on you. He's got plenty of straight clients. And a husband now."

"Maybe after some of this turmoil slows down," I told him. He nodded and we both understood there was no way I'd be hands-on with a gay massage dude.

"Now," I said, changing the subject. "You told me Carolyn?"

Andrew leaned toward me, frowning. "There's a problem."

"Her work fall off? Too many beginner mistakes?"

We'd hired Carolyn Vinh straight out of her senior class at University of Houston. They have a good computer science department and their grads are readily snapped up by Big Oil. We couldn't offer Carolyn the perks of these behemoths, but we tried to make up for it by higher salary, flexible hours, more autonomy and an informal workplace environment.

Andrew shook his head solemnly. "Nothing about her work. She's tops, smart, the clients like her. She's over at Binderson right now, installing a system upgrade."

"What is it then?"

"Had a visitor yesterday, young man named Kurt Slocum. I eventually had to ask him to leave, none too politely." Andrew flicked his fingers dismissively toward the door. "I thought about phoning you, but he left."

"Boyfriend?"

"Ex boyfriend, apparently. And Carolyn wants to keep it that way. Unfortunately, the young Mister Slocum cannot take the hint."

"Oh, boy," I said.

"Oh, yes, and such a big boy he is, too."

I sighed inwardly. Another headache. "Did he threaten you? Anything like that?"

"No. But I got the feeling that he was prone to violence." Andrew leaned back in his chair, glanced at the ceiling. "Thing is, Mitchell, we in the gay community get harassed, most times verbally, but sometimes physically."

"I know."

He looked at me, smiled. "That's why I went to work for you in the first place, Mitchell. I never sensed any of that antagonism coming off you."

I shrugged. "What can I say? My folks raised me to look at individuals and not color my opinions with prejudice. I couldn't care less about your orientation, your personal life."

"And that I've always appreciated. But Mitchell, we do learn to feel the vibes and Slocum gave off waves of it."

"But nothing physical, no threats?"

He shook his head. "I was in the back, switching over a server rack, heard the door buzzer. I thought it was Carolyn so I called out her name. And soon as I said *Carolyn?* this loud voice comes back, 'Carolyn? She here?'"

"And it was this guy you'd never seen."

"Right." Andrew nodded. "I asked him if I could help, he said 'I'm Kurt Slocum, Carolyn's boyfriend. I want to see her.' So I said that she wasn't here and he wanted to know when she'd be back, got very pushy." Andrew frowned. "That was when I started feeling the negative energies. It was as if he was wearing a sign around his neck, *Asshole*."

I grinned. "So you got rid of him?"

"I did, but Mitchell, believe me, your Andrew was a bit frightened. I told him that we were closing early, that Carolyn wouldn't be back until Thursday, she was out of town. A real whopper of a lie!" He smiled slyly, flipped his fingers again. "I suppose he believed me. He told me that he'd be back, and to tell Carolyn in the meantime to return his fucking calls for a fucking change. After he left I locked the door and turned off the ceiling lights."

"And you talked to Carolyn?"

"I did. And Mitchell, that girl is scared of him." Andrew waved his arms in the air theatrically. "She got quiet and had to sit down a while."

"When is Carolyn due back?"

"Any time now. You want to talk with her?"

"Absolutely. I won't tolerate threats or bullying, Andrew. No way, no how."

"I knew I could count on my Mitchell."

Chapter 8

I drank coffee, reviewed the new contracts, and waited for Carolyn. It wasn't long, half hour maybe. She bustled into the room carrying two big tote bags, and was slightly out of breath. Her long brown hair was hanging in her eyes, and she laughed at herself. "That darn traffic!"

She saw me, waved. "Hi, Mr. King. Is Andrew here?"

"He's in the back. And it's Mitch, okay?"

"Sure, er, Mitch." An embarrassed smile. Carolyn Vinh is a shy young woman, gawky tall and nerdy, absolute stereotype of the techie girl and very conscious of such little faults that so many people seize upon and make into mountains. Add to this her socially conservative Roman Catholic family upbringing, her grandparents having emigrated from Vietnam when Saigon fell, and Carolyn was initially a basket case of insecurity despite her sterling collegiate record and strong recommendations from faculty.

But Andrew is a fine supervisor, never commenting on her awkward ways, encouraging and supporting her constantly. So she grew into her new job, became less self-conscious, and is now far more confident and relaxed than she'd been when we hired her five months ago.

"Sit down, Carolyn," I told her. "Take a break."

"Okay, sure." She ran to the back room and I could hear her rummaging in the little fridge we kept, came back with a can of Diet Sprite. She sat in one of the roller chairs, rotated back and forth a couple times, held the frosty can to her forehead. Next she popped the top, took a swig and gave out a big cartoonish *"Whew!"*

Andrew had followed her from the server room. "Installation go well?"

She nodded. "Spot on, Booted up the new servers, clocked them onto the net, *whammo*, mission accomplished!"

"You see, Mitchell?" Andrew said. "Is our Girl Friday the best, or what? And she's fine the other days of the week, too."

I smiled at both of them, sipped my coffee, then put on my serious face.

"Carolyn," I began. "Andrew tells me we had a visitor yesterday afternoon. Kurt Slocum."

She grimaced. "Look, Mr. King... Mitchell... Mitch, I'm sorry. I thought it was over and done with. I promise, it won't happen again."

I shook my head, opening my hands in a welcoming gesture. "You are not in hot water, Carolyn. I want to make that crystal clear. Okay?"

She just sat there, looking at me.

"Let me reiterate, and Andrew agrees. Nothing you've done is wrong in the slightest. All the problems are with this Slocum guy, not you. But I do want to know more about it, all right?"

She nodded. "Sure, if you say."

"As I understand, you told Andrew that this former boyfriend was in the past, that you and he were not an item, that you weren't seeing him anymore. Correct?"

"Yeah. I broke up with him before I started here."

"But he won't take no for an answer?"

Another nod.

"It happens, Carolyn. You're not the first person to have a clingy ex and you won't be the last. But you need to tell me. Has he been harassing you? Does he keep calling? Show up uninvited?"

"Yeah. All of that."

"Anything else? Has he ever hit you, shoved you, anything physical?"

She sipped her Sprite, looked across the room.

"I need to know, Carolyn."

"Er... last week. I already quit seeing him, told him he was too possessive, too demanding, wouldn't let me breathe without his permission. He's jealous of anyone I know, girlfriends, even my family."

"Typical behavior for a bully or dominator, Carolyn," I told her.

"Mitchell is right, Carolyn," Andrew said. "Listen to him."

"So he hit you?" I asked.

She sipped her Sprite again, reticent.

"Look," she said, glancing at Andrew and me. "I don't want problems. If my Uncle Quan found out..."

"Nothing you say to us goes any further, Carolyn."

"Well, okay. Kurt came to my new apartment Friday night. You know, near the Galleria. I'd just moved in, first time I had my own."

Andrew and I both nodded, encouraging her to talk.

"He phoned, wanted to see my place. I said okay." Another sip. "Then when he got there, he wanted us to... well, you know. I told him we were done. Kurt just laughed at me, called me... called me a dirty name. So I told him to leave or I'd phone the cops."

"And he shoved you? Hit you?" I guessed.

"I could tell he was drunk. He jerked my arm real hard, made an awful bruise." Carolyn normally wore long sleeve pullovers. She reached to her left bicep, rubbed it, grimaced.

"Kurt reached his fist back and I thought he was going to punch me! I'd seen him in a fight once before, he really beat up a guy at this bar, real bad. I guess I screamed."

"And he left."

She nodded. "He shoved me against the wall on the way out. It hurt! And he laughed at me, called me that dirty name again. Said I wasn't worth hitting."

Carolyn started to sob. Andrew was right there, arm around her comfortingly, murmuring kind words.

I grabbed a box of tissues, handed it to Carolyn. She ripped out a handful and wiped her eyes, blew her nose, laughed a bit, tears still coming.

"Did you tell anyone else about this?" I asked.

She nodded. "I was at my mom's house Sunday for church. She saw the bruise. His finger marks were still there. I told her it was Kurt but that he was out of my life now, forever. I asked her not to tell Uncle Quan." She shook her head. "I don't know if she did."

I left Carolyn to be comforted by Andrew, told her everything would be okay, that I'd maybe talk with Kurt.

"No fighting," she admonished me. "I don't like violence."

"It won't come to that," I told her. "Promise."

Chapter 9

Out in my 4Runner, I sat and thought. Carolyn said something about her Uncle Quan, not wanting him to know that Slocum had been rough with her. She sounded hesitant, apprehensive when mentioning her uncle, and this was what we private eyes call a clue. I phoned Meierhoff.

"Yeah, Mitch?"

"Got something unrelated to the Slicer thing, thankfully. Can you to run a check, guy named Quan Vinh? Vietnamese ancestry, he'd be middle age, I'm guessing. What's his story?" I had the correct spelling from Carolyn's emergency contact list, gave this to David.

"Name sounds familiar...give me a sec, run his name through R&I." A brief pause, Meierhoff shifting his phone around, griping at his computer. "Okay, here it is. Quan Vinh, age forty-six, known to be the leader of *Sat Nam Tay*. Don't ask me how to pronounce it, but in English, the Iron Fist."

"Sounds like a Nazi fight club."

Meierhoff laughed. "Iron Fist is a sort of old-school protective association, borderline legal, some connections to the rackets, like all these groups. Mostly a way for the Vietnamese to keep their businesses and homes safe from gangs. You know, same as the Irish during their time, turn of the last century, fresh off the boat, vulnerable."

"Not necessarily a bad thing," I ventured.

"I guess not, depending. Most all the immigrants and ethnic minorities are easy prey for the criminal element and they're reluctant to take their problems to the cops. So they often protect themselves, hence the Iron Fist. According to the write-up, it was founded by Quan Vinh's father, Dohn Vinh. He was a colonel in the ARVN. You know, South Viet Army. Worked intelligence."

"It's likely the old colonel was a toughie."

"Probably. He brought the family here in seventy-five, after South Vietnam went, you know, south. Died in oh-seven. That's when Quan Vinh took over running the Fist guys."

"Nasty, are they?"

"Not too much, not enough to notice. They keep pretty much to themselves and if there's a bunch of outright criminal activity on their part, it's not something that's waving a red flag for HPD."

"Hey, thanks," I told him.

"You need any contact with the Viets, I've got a couple pals on the force, solid dudes, Vietnamese cops, the best. They'll be glad to get involved if there's a problem."

"I'll let you know. Right now, nothing worth worrying about."

"Ha!" Meierhoff grunted. "With you, I'm always worrying."

* * *

I thanked David again, rang off, drove home. I fixed a sandwich, cranked up my laptop and searched for Kurt Slocum on the University of Houston website.

Slocum was a grad student, originally from Waco, majoring in *Athletic Concepts*, whatever that is. From glancing at the online student catalog, I got the impression the major existed for jocks who just couldn't make the team. Trainers they used to call them. Now they're experts in *concepts*. A grainy photo of Slocum showed him as broad shouldered, handsome in a rough way, scowling beneath a toss of tightly curled black hair.

I phoned a pal of mine, Gerry Voisin, assistant coach for the track team at UH, asked him about Kurt Slocum.

"Oh," he said. "Curly Kurt, eh?" I could tell from his voice that Kurt was trouble.

"That bad?"

"Aw, not really. He's a jerkoff, yeah. But nobody takes him serious. Spouts off a lot, bragging, loudmouth. Then last month one of the soccer forwards bent him like Uri Geller used to bend spoons. Shut him up but good."

I had to laugh. "Thinks he's a tough guy?"

"Yep. I suppose you could say that he is. You know, big, strong, always copping an attitude. He woulda been a good center or guard but his personality sucked so bad the coaches passed him over."

"So he's a back marker, works in the locker room, like a trainer?"

"Uh huh. At least he can do that without fucking up, most of the time."

"Ah, gee."

"What?" Gerry asked. "He come across the ol' private eye threshold?"

"In a way."

"Need my help, lemme know."

"Where might I find Slocum, off campus?"

"Hmm... ya might try this bar, *Touchdown Ted's*. You know, sports bar. He's there mostly when he's not in school. I think he's a bouncer, works nights."

I said goodbye to Gerry, looked up the number and phoned the bar, asked for Kurt.

"He's in the back. Want me to get him?"

"Naw. I'll call later," I said, hung up.

Chapter 10

Touchdown Ted's is on Scott Street near the UH campus.

It's an okay place, standard issue tavern for the sports-minded college crowd, scruffy on the surface but clean and well kept. There were tall but teeny tables all over, stools to sit, a long bar at the back with two bartenders, a young woman and an older guy whom I guessed as the manager. There were lots of flat screens tuned to sports channels, University of Houston Cougar posters plastered on the wall.

I sat at the end of the bar, ordered a Bud, paid, just surveyed. The place was about half full and more customers coming in, kids whose IDs were scrupulously scanned by the bartenders, a few wizened folks like me dotting the clientele. I was dressed casual, jeans, sneakers, a light tan jacket, looking just the same as anybody else. Except for the pistol on my waist, of course.

I soon spotted Slocum, working what's known as a *bar back*. He lugged a case of Miller Lite from the storeroom, dumped it noisily onto the floor next to a long cooler, started shoving bottles into the recess, none too carefully. He was a big guy, six-four at least, maybe two-thirty, muscular, fit and yes, handsome.

"Hey," the older bartender said, a pleasant voice. "Take it easy, Kurt. Don't bust any bottles like last time. You know what a mess that was to clean up."

"Uh!" was all that Kurt said, but he did rattle the bottles more carefully, nevertheless grimacing and frowning at being admonished. What a guy.

I just sipped my beer, watched in silence a TV show about how the Houston Astros were headed for another surprisingly good season, but mostly kept an eye on Kurt, how he interacted with the other employees and customers. And from his abrupt conversations and tight glances, I'd guess not so well. Handsome maybe, but a handsome jerk.

The bar got busy then, happy hour. Patrons a mix of students and other Millennials, every sort of ethnic category and appearance you could imagine. Everyone was behaving and having a good time, nothing out of line, just kids kicking back.

I did get my private eye hackles up when I spotted a slender young Asian guy who was checking Kurt's every move, same as I. He was pretending to watch the TV, but that was a sham, because Kurt Slocum was the true object of his affection. The kid was sitting at one of the far tables and fiddling with his drink, not into the booze, just marking time. Occasionally he'd glance over to another table where there sat two more Asian men, both older, heavyset, big stocky guys, each dressed like used car salesmen, cheap suits, open neck shirts. He'd say something to them and they'd both nod vigorously, deferential. They seemed uncomfortable and very out of place at a collegiate sports bar.

I kept my focus on the TVs and tried not to let the Asian guys see me watching them. I think I succeeded. A little later and Slocum came over to the bartender near where I sat. "Gonna take a smoke break out back."

"Okay. We're not so busy now. Go ahead."

Not replying, Slocum stalked toward the rear door behind the bar, slammed his way through the narrow passage. Real prince of a fella, he.

I went out the front door and started around the tavern toward the back parking lot to confront Slocum. A brief shower had come through and it was still spattering and misting into the early evening air, rain now picking up a little. I got about thirty feet and was around the side of the building, felt a hand on my shoulder.

"Hey," a voice behind me.

I turned. I'd not seen or heard him coming up on me, but it was the Asian guy, fast and silent. I reached under my jacket, and he said simply, "Don't."

He tilted his head toward the two hefty salesmen-guys standing adjacent, each of whom had a hand beneath his own coat. I let my hand drop, got ready to fight anyway.

I suppose my defensive posture gave me away, because he said, "Not to worry, pal. I ain't gonna give you grief, not gonna fuck with you. Just wanna talk, okay?" He had a pleasant grin, spoke with no accent whatsoever, plain flat American.

"Sure," I replied. What else was I going to do? Disappear? "Talk about?"

"Why you watching Slocum?"

"Was I? Who's Slocum?"

He smiled again. "I got the moves, dude. Been there, done that. Be straight with me."

"Okay, I know a young lady, she got roughed up by Slocum. I want to chat with him about it."

"*Chat*, he says. Maybe more than chat?"

I shrugged, noncommittal.

"What's she to you? Girlfriend?"

I shook my head. "She works for me."

"Ah. You're the King dude, huh?"

"Yep." He had me pegged, totally.

"Starting to rain harder." He nodded toward the parking lot. "Let's talk in the car."

We walked together, the bodyguards behind us, but I didn't have trepidation. They could have shot me or punched me or tossed me into a dumpster if they'd wanted. And the kid now knew who I was, which seemed to lighten the tension. We got into a big Lincoln SUV, the two shadows in front, kid and I in back. The rain came in gusts now, a typical passing front. Sitting inside, rush of water against the windows and roof, I felt separated from the rest of the world and somehow more in companionship to the men whom I was with.

He reached his hand to me. "I'm Bobby Vinh. Carolyn's my cousin."

We shook. "Mitch King. But I guess you know that."

I glanced at his forearm and saw an ornate tattoo, a medieval-style armored hand, clenched. "Iron Fist?" I asked.

"Hey, yeah, however you wanna tag it." A sly grin. "Or maybe I just dig my inks?"

I looked. No other tattoos were visible. "Quan Vinh send you after Slocum?"

He nodded. "Carolyn's a great girl, first in our family to go to college. We look out after our own, not gonna let her get fucked with. Quan Vinh says keep her safe, that's what I do."

"This Kurt Slocum," I said. "Thinks he's a tough guy so I want to take him down a notch or two, tell him to stay away from Carolyn."

"Think you're all five for it?" A frown as he appraised me. "You that bad? He's a big fucker."

"I can deal with him. Big guys think they're unstoppable."

"Sometimes they're tough as they look. Why not let me do the deed?" he asked.

"I don't want the guy killed."

"Not to worry, dude. It's deck. I'll take it easy on him. But click on it, he won't fuck with Carolyn again. And he won't call her a cunt no more, neither."

I gave it thought. I'd promised Carolyn that I wouldn't get violent even though I'd planned on maybe slapping Slocum around. Having a gun helps with those little tasks. But hey, if they wanted to keep it family feud, who was I to complain?

"Sounds good to me," I said. I gave him my card and we shook hands again. All this time the guys in the front said nothing, didn't even move.

Bobby Vinh grinned. "We're down, dude. Down nine yards."

I gave him a little salute of approval, stepped out of the Lincoln, dodged puddles, got into my 4Runner and drove home. Leave Kurt to the Iron Fist and check on him later, await the outcome. But I got the impression that Carolyn wouldn't be hearing from her ex anytime soon.

Chapter 11

Sometimes things just work out on schedule. Soon as I'd finished with Kurt Slocum and decided to let the Vinhs look after their own, I got clearance from Meierhoff to proceed with witness interviews on the Martinez murder. I'd get to that presently, but I first had some other work to catch up on, and then a couple days later, a prior appointment on my calendar, something that would be a fun break from my everyday charter of woe.

So I put the 4Runner through a nice wash and even vacuumed the inside. I cleaned up my personal act as well, dug out a nice off-white silk tie I'd been saving, matched it with a charcoal dress shirt and black sports jacket and slacks. Black dress shoes replaced the Nikes. Mafia approved attire, absolutely.

Which was only fitting, as I was attending the eighteenth birthday of a client whom I privately regard as my own little mob princess in waiting, Cheryl Stern, daughter of local crime boss Julio Cardozo, known in the vernacular as Julie Cards.

I first met Cheryl as the rebellious teenage adopted daughter of millionaire investment banker Walter Albertson. When Cheryl's life was in danger from her crazed stepsister Paula, David Meierhoff and I rescued her, aided by Cardozo's trusted lieutenant Ricky Perdon.

Cheryl hadn't originally known that Cardozo was her father, but she reacted positively to the discovery, and the affection was mutual and genuine. With her eighteenth birthday, she'd be free from the court-ordered guardianship that was requisite after the death of her mother. And although the fact of Cardozo being her father was kept secret, Cheryl now lived in a townhouse where he'd set her up and was working diligently on the move to legitimizing her father's business, taking it straight like Michael Corleone did for his people. Today, reaching legal adulthood, Cheryl could assume a stronger and more visible role in the business. And I was off to help her celebrate.

Just before I left the house, I got a surprise call from Gerry Voisin, my coaching pal at University of Houston. "Hey, Mitch, thought you'd like to know. That dude Slocum?"

"Yeah?"

"Two nights ago he got jumped, coming out of his apartment."

"And?"

"He never got a look at 'em, but he said there musta been five or six. Grabbed him, stuck a plastic bag over his head so he couldn't see and knocked his curly ass clean off."

"Bad hurt?"

"Yeah. They busted both his arms in several places, all up and down. He was in Ben Taub ER of course, then his folks flew him home to Waco to get well. He's done at U of H."

"Couldn't happen to a nicer guy," I said.

"You didn't do the honors, did you?"

"Nope, no way. I don't go with the rough stuff." Lying through my teeth, but truthful this time around.

"Well, anyway, thought you'd wanna know."

Driving off, I thought. *Both arms? Several places?* I sure hope Curly Kurt has some trusty people to manage the cleaning and wiping for a while. But things are tough all over.

* * *

Cardozo Enterprises is located in what had once been a ratty, rundown warehouse that ostensibly sold auto parts and truthfully serves as gang headquarters for the Fifth Ward Apaches.

This squalor hadn't survived Cheryl's revitalization campaign. She had the exterior refinished and the grounds swept clean and set new again. Where there'd been a dusty barn with old tires and radiators gathering dust, there was now a brightly lit office beset with computers, copiers, faxes, all the trappings of a thriving auto parts franchise.

As I drove to the gate, however, I noticed that not everything had gone legal and pure. A couple of big guys chewing toothpicks and wearing matching trench coats were manning the entrance. They recognized me and slid open the heavy reinforced gate, gave me a high-sign and waved me through.

The whole warehouse was emblazoned with confetti and birthday placards, Spanish and English, a big table across the room piled with food, salsa band warming up in the corner. Observing were the Perdon cousins, Ricky and Angel. Ricky is heavyset with dark features and a brooding, rough face, but he also possesses a bright, winning smile that overcomes the image instantly. Angel is taller and thinner and was known to carry two .45 autos, shades of the old pulp hero Lamont Cranston, the Shadow.

The two men were well dressed, as usual. And they both looked exactly like plainclothes cops. Which is a gas, since they are criminals up to their shirt collars. Or former, I suppose, with the revision to legality for the Cardozo business still on track.

"Hey, *ese!*" Ricky came over, smiling, put his hand out. We shook, then he leaned forward and we awkwardly embraced. Ricky had recently slimmed down to the tune of about thirty pounds, but hugging him is still a challenge. "How you been, my friend?"

"Good, I'm good. And you?"

"A proud uncle. Angel, his wife, they have a lovely baby girl." Ricky pronounced his cousin's name *Anhel*. He called to him, still watching the band set up. "Angel! Don' be rude! Here's our pal Mitch."

So I was again embraced, Ricky hugged Angel and we next all hugged each other. I could give lessons now, *How to fake being Hispanic and enjoy hugs from other guys.*

The Perdons were ever in debt to me for my part in having saved the life of their beloved charge, Cheryl. And having them as friends is certainly better than enemies. They could be formidable despite their gentle and easygoing appearance.

A cold bottle of Dos Equis was stuck into my hand and I was happily ushered into the main office adjacent the warehouse. The layout resembles that of a midsize real estate agent, standard office desks, roller chairs, filing cabinets, computers everywhere. All quiet today.

In the receptionist's chair up front sat the eternal watchman, Carlo, personal bodyguard to Julio Cardozo. Carlo is razor thin, handsome in a scary way, perfectly trimmed mustache and nattily dressed in 70s gangster garb, black shirt and white tie. Just like I was, but for him, it fit. I was simply showing off. He meant it.

I'd never seen Carlo smile. Or frown. Or much of anything. He is just *there*, a continuing presence, cobra in the room that everyone pretends not to see. And as always, he was sipping from a can of that oversweet Mexican fruit soda, *Jumex*. Carlo doesn't drink alcohol, or smoke, or talk, or maybe even breathe. I heard that some years back, he shot and killed four men in as many seconds, protecting his boss. Of course that was likely urban legend.

Carlo nodded to me imperceptibly and clicked me off his chart, for which I was grateful.

Ricky called out to the closed door marked *Private*. "Mitch is here, my darling!"

A moment later the door opened and Cheryl Stern bounced out. Bounced because she was hopping as she came, trying with limited success to pull a high heel pump onto her left foot while balancing on the right. Cheryl came unsteadily toward us, somehow smiling and frowning at the same time. She nearly succeeded in getting her foot stuck into the shoe but finally lost her balance and went sprawling in our direction. Both Ricky and I reached for her, but a pair of thin arms beat us to it. Carlo leapt from his chair and caught Cheryl gracefully, even though he'd been several yards away. I never saw anything so quick.

And now I believed the rumor.

"You okay, my dear?" I asked Cheryl.

"Fine now. Gracias, Carlo." She smiled at him and for a flicker, I thought I saw a return grin cross his impassive face. Was Cheryl turning him into an old softie? In a few centuries, perhaps.

Cheryl looked a million bucks. Already a beautiful young woman, petite, dark-haired and slender, she'd maxed out her wardrobe today, a yellow chiffon-thing dress with sequins and bows and all sorts of quaint trappings, a far remove from her usual hip hugger jeans and sloppy pullover. She'd even tempered her normal Goth-inspired makeup, only using hints of eye shadow and lipstick.

Of course, she's growing up fast. When I first met her, she'd been a deliberate rebel in demeanor, lifestyle and dress. Losing her mother to a vicious killer, being nearly murdered herself and abruptly relocated under her crime boss father's wing was traumatic. Thankfully she weathered the storm and was finding herself. But she's still an unrepentant flirt. "Hey, Mitch, welcome to the party!" and she sealed it with a big smoochy kiss on my cheek, bringing embarrassment to me and laughter to the others.

"How's your father, Cheryl?" I asked.

"Terrific!" She gestured toward the inner office from where she'd come. "But nursing a headache today." Cheryl proffered a little *moue* of disappointment. "I want him feeling good, helping me celebrate." She grabbed my arm and dragged me toward the office. "C'mon. You can snap him out of his saggy 'tude."

Propelled by Cheryl's insistent shove, I stepped inside the office where Julio Cardozo sat quietly at his desk, head down, fingers massaging his temples.

"Mister Cardozo?" I offered.

He looked up, smiled broadly, stood and came around to greet me. As always, he was stylishly dressed, upscale British fashion with the higher shirt collar and three-button jacket. A handsome but stark man, resembling the old character actor Victor Jory. "Not Mister, it's Julio, please!"

"Julio," I repeated, correctly pronouncing it *Hoolio*. "Cheryl's ready to party and you're hiding in your office?"

He smiled again, beaming at both Cheryl and me. "My apologies. Work has been very stressful. And I do have a headache." He gathered Cheryl in his arms, embracing her with joy. "But not, as this lovely young woman thinks, from too much tequila." Cardozo stroked her cheek, pushed her gently away and gave her a small twirl. She turned once around and curtsied to both of us, snickering all the time.

"Ah, so lovely," Cardozo said. "And now eighteen!"

* * *

The party was going full blast. After the band began with traditional music, Cheryl intervened and insisted on something more upbeat. So we were treated to the excruciating assault of trumpets and accordions making every attempt to play rock and roll, and falling short with stunning verve.

But they did provide an under beat of rhythm, which was all Cheryl and her school friends needed. They'd quickly taken over the dance floor and were leaping and pumping and twerking away such that nobody else ventured forth. We old folks were therefore relegated to the sidelines and stood safely around the food and drinks where we belonged.

After a while, Cardozo stepped near me. "Mitch, may we speak privately?" And led me back into his office, shut the door.

"Is there a problem?" I asked.

"Please," he said. "Sit. A moment, first." He wearily lowered himself into his chair, opened a desk drawer, retrieved a bottle of aspirin. He shook out two and washed them down with bottled water. He rubbed his temples briskly, sighed. "The joke is that Julio has been sampling the tequila this morning. But I no longer drink. Age is finding its way into my life, Mitch." Cardozo spoke with the measured precision of someone who learned English as a second language and learned it well. I could imagine him lecturing skillfully to a civics class.

I knew he hadn't pulled me into his office to complain about a headache, so I sat quietly and allowed him to gather his thoughts.

"Do you know of *Barrio Colombia*?" he asked.

"Yes. BC for short, gang affiliated with MS-13. Having problems?"

"We are." Cardozo frowned. "As you know, we are taking the family business legitimate. Fifth Ward Apaches are no longer."

I couldn't help grinning briefly, hearing the name of Julie Cards' old gang.

Cardozo joined me in the humor, an embarrassed cough. "My choice, Apaches. I wanted a name that sounded fierce." He shrugged. "I was twelve."

I guessed about his concern. "And BC is trying to take over your old territories?"

"They are. And businesses too. Car repair shops, parts stores, gas stations."

"How do you mean, take over?"

"Some history first, my friend," he said, leaning back in his chair, tenting his fingers. "When we began, we were, ah, fencing stolen tires, rims, radios, selling them to small shops in the neighborhood. The shop owners would use them for the customers, sell at a low price, and everyone would be happy."

"Except for the people who found their cars sitting on the frame."

Cardozo smiled. "As is said, you have to break eggs."

"So you built up your business, more inventory?"

"Yes. And then we invested in the shops. If the owner was behind in his rent or loan, we would take over the financing, allow him to stay in business."

"Loan sharking?"

He grimaced. "No! We charged a lower rate than even the banks. We helped our neighbors, Mitch."

"All right. I understand."

Cardozo continued. "We grew larger. We invested in restaurants, bars, clothing stores, groceries, shops of all types."

"So in truth, much of your business has been legal for a long time anyway."

"Yes. There were, ah, contests for territory and that often brought trouble. But we did not seek it out."

"And you're now restoring these businesses to their original owners?"

"And their families. You understand, Mitch, in the barrio, many places are owned by the same family for generations."

"So how is the other gang causing trouble?"

Cardozo gazed at the ceiling and ticked off a list on his fingertips. "Arson, threats, blackmail, damage to the stores, robbing them every payday. There are many ways."

"Let me see. During this transition, things are upset and difficult, and BC is working against you, taking advantage of the changing times."

"Exactly."

"But how can I help?"

Cardozo smiled cannily. "You are friends with the police."

Chapter 12

So that was it. I was now reduced to being an informant for the mob and I was to pry helpful information from my cop buddies to help Cardozo against his mob opponents. Great.

Despite the grudging respect I had for Cardozo, in that he was loyal to his people and unequivocally loved Cheryl, I really didn't want to be beholden to him or his organization. I also felt this could sully my feelings of genuine fatherly affection for Cheryl. I knew full well that I'd transferred my failed fatherhood for my own daughter onto her, but I also didn't want that to lead me into any sort of permanent obligation toward Cheryl. Or her shady father.

I was stuck.

So I deferred and made a layering of falsely solicitous yes-man offerings to Cardozo, trying not to sound too much like a sycophant in the process. I think he partially believed my promises, too, although it may have been that the headache was interfering with his usually erudite mind, and maybe later he'd have me rubbed out.

I should be so lucky, all my problems solved at a masterstroke.

Tired from the pretense and sham, I made my exit, shook hands with Cardozo, survived yet another dispassionate scrutiny by Carlo, hugged Cheryl, was hugged by Ricky and Angel and got the hell out. Eventually I'd find a way to extricate myself from the expectations that Cardozo placed on my shoulders. And maybe without angering the entire clan?

* * *

About a block from the warehouse I noticed I'd picked up a tail, gold sedan, Impala I thought but was uncertain, as most new cars are lookalike clones. Deep tint on the windows so I couldn't tell how many were inside.

Cops? Thugs from Barrio Colombia? Random gangbangers? No way to know, but I had a brainstorm and needed to buy time. So I played it cool and drove leisurely in the general direction of home, but with a little detour. I cut over to White Oak, meandered west along the scenic twists that overlooked Buffalo Bayou and just past Studewood, turned into the parking lot of *Jimmie's*.

Jimmie's is a Texas tavern of the popular dive bar genre known as an icehouse. Many of these icehouses were once exactly that, places where you'd go to pick up blocks of ice for your home icebox prior to refrigerators, and grab a cold beer too. Nowadays, beer's the requisite calling card for Jimmie's and dozens of places like it all through the Gulf Coast area.

Icehouse taverns are deliberately low-tech, simple downscale wooden structures with big roll-up doors and wide windows, floor fans, a jukebox, eternal TVs tuned to sports only and of course, icy beer. Since it's usually warm in Houston, icehouses beckon year round.

I parked in the gravel lot around back, came in the rear door of the tavern, ordered a Bud. I caught a glimpse of the tagalong car out the front doorway as it drove past. Impala it was, neutral and nondescript. The car continued westward down White Oak a block or so, slowed, pulled to the curb in front of a BBQ. Nobody got out.

I plunked a ten on the bar, sipped the beer, thought about Julio Cardozo, his daughter Cheryl, and the tail behind me. Neither police nor rival gangs could afford to put a car onto everyone leaving the warehouse. They'd be stacked up around the block, waiting. So someone must have recognized me and decided I was worth the effort.

I phoned David Meierhoff and he picked up right away. "Yeah, Mitch."

"David, whom do you know in organized crime division, do me a quick favor?"

"Got several. What's up?"

I told him about the tail from the Cardozo warehouse. David was familiar with the situation, as he'd partnered with me when we rescued Cheryl from crazy Paula last year. I didn't mention Cardozo's new direction or his request, as that was privileged info, embarrassing, and I didn't want to jam up my relations with the cops. So I simply asked David whether HPD was running tabs on the Cardozo warehouse.

"Lemme check. I'll call back."

So I sat at the bar, relaxing, nursing the beer, idly watching an ESPN report on pro golf, about which I cared not a whit. The tavern was mostly empty, lunch crowd gone and happy hour regulars yet to show.

I'd not been to Jimmie's in a while and the bartender was new to me, a short, skinny, much-tattooed guy with about nineteen earrings on each side. He did however smile and made sure I had a fresh beer, so I tipped him a couple bucks and wandered out to the front patio. My Impala pals were still there, one block away and beer-less, so I had the clear advantage.

My phone buzzed, Meierhoff. "Vice hasn't got standard surveillance on the Cardozo place at all. I talked to Juanita Hertza. You know, Hispanic gang task force. She pretty much confirmed what you've told me, the entire business is going straight, with Cardozo essentially liquidating all their illegal stuff. So vice discontinued routine patrols and is pushing elsewhere, MS-13 and Tango Blast gangs mostly."

Tango Blast? Another gang that could be considered a solid rival for Cardozo's businesses. They weren't as large as Barrio Colombia, but they were a factor.

"And therefore the tail I've got isn't cops, but bad guys," I surmised.

"Most likely. Undercover doesn't use Impalas anyway. Want me to call in a traffic stop?"

"I'd appreciate it."

"Where are you now?"

"Jimmie's Icehouse on White Oak, in the Heights. You know the place. Gold Impala is parked on the street just to the west."

"Driving the 4Runner?"

"Uh, huh. Dark green, big antenna out the back."

"Okay. Wait at the corner of the lot till you see the police cruiser. Give 'em a heads up and go west young man on White Oak, nice and easy, pick up the tail. The cruiser will hang and then close the gap, do a bogus stop on the Impala just so we can see who's driving. You head on home, I'll call later."

"Should I circle back around, watch what's going down?"

"Absolutely not. If the Impala guys spot your car again they'll know it's a setup. Just get the hell home, okay?"

"Will do. Thanks, and tell Detective Hertza thanks, too."

"Juanita won't accept thanks from you. She thinks you're a worthless hotshot and in the pocket of Julie Cards."

Yet another cop who had me on the shit list. I was a popular sort of guy. "Thank the beat cops, at least."

"Happy to oblige. I'll check the schedule of the uniforms in the cruiser, we can meet later this week and you'll spring for lunch all round."

"Count on it."

I set my nearly-full second beer on the counter, waved goodbye to the bartender and walked back to my 4Runner. As I eased toward the street, I saw an HPD cruiser idling to my right, one guy driving, no partner. I flashed my headlamps and the cop echoed.

Traffic was light and I pulled out, turned left, headed west. The Impala sat waiting, and as I passed he moved behind me. I tried but still couldn't tell who was inside. The cop was visible to the rear and as I approached Yale, I turned onto a side street to better accommodate the traffic stop. A half block further and the cop gave a little *whoop* on the siren. The Impala pulled over, cop behind, and I merrily trundled toward home, smiling.

* * *

I was chopping some salad fixings when my cell rang. Meierhoff with the info, his name on the display.

"So who was it?" I asked, happy to have inconvenienced some lowlife thug courtesy of Houston's Finest.

"The fuck!" Meierhoff yelled. "Turn on your fucking TV!"

I grabbed my remote and clicked to the little flat screen sitting on the kitchen counter. "What?" I asked Meierhoff. He normally never cursed unless he was angry or excited, then he liberally dropped the f-bomb.

"The cop's been fuckin' shot dead! Get your goddamn gun! He might be headed for you right now!"

Channel 12 had a live copter feed, a huge assembly of cop cars jamming the street where I'd been minutes ago, text crawl beneath: *Houston police officer murdered in Heights traffic stop... Manhunt for killers... Chevrolet Impala, Texas license BX...*

I turned to the center island and snatched my .45 from the holster lying there, flipped off the safety. I took a quick peek outside. No Impala on the street, no movement. I toured the house and checked around back. Nobody.

My cell was beeping again. "You okay, Mitch?" Meierhoff, still agitated.

"I'm fine. All clear here. What the hell happened?"

"Neighbor heard gunfire, looked out her front window, saw the officer lying in the street, fuckin' Impala speeding off."

"Dead you say?"

"Dead, multiples, caught him above his vest, two or three neck, plus head shots, poor fucker." Meierhoff's voice was less strained now.

"What exactly?" I asked. "Cop was at the Impala's window?"

"Looks like it. He was lying on the street about twenty feet in front of his cruiser, driver door open, lights flashing. So it matches that he was shot standing beside the Impala."

"Jesus Christ, David," I said. "I had no idea. You know that."

"This isn't on you, Mitch. The officer knew the driver might be a gangbanger, knew the rules. Fuckin' happens, is all."

"Crap."

"Yeah, crap. You okay for now? I'll stop by later if you want."

"No, I'm good. Keep me updated."

"Thing is, Mitch," he said, "I called the stop as a favor, so there'll be questions. When a cop is killed, it goddamn hits the fan."

"I still feel responsible."

"Don't. We're professionals and we'll get the sonsabitches."

"Whatever I can do."

"Hang close. They'll want to interview you. Just tell 'em the truth."

"What about the Cardozo thing? What do I say?"

David was silent a moment. "Well, you've done work for the daughter before, we both have actually, it's a matter of record from last year. Just go with that and say you were checking on a former client. Play it close to the chest, though."

"What was the cop's name? Did you know him?"

"Bart Deely, and nope, I never met him. He was just in rotation, name came up. An older guy, grown kids and divorced, if that's any consolation."

"Small comfort is no comfort."

"Don't let it get to you, Mitch," David said. "Hey, I gotta go, they're calling for me," and he rang off.

Chapter 13

I'd stuck my stupid face into a situation and my smug satisfaction at getting a gangbanger arrested had turned to tragedy. Another death, courtesy of good old Mitch King. The tally was now up to ten.

And so to celebrate such achievement, I proceeded to get staggering drunk, not pussyfooting around this time, heading straight for the 101-proof bourbon. And as I chugged shot after shot, somewhere in my despair I knew that this childish behavior wouldn't assuage a single thing. It would only draw me deeper into misery. Nevertheless I kept at it until I summarily passed out.

I woke fairly early, about nine am, sprawled on my sofa. I found that despite the volume of whiskey I'd wallowed in, my head was relatively clear and free from pain. Either I'd not drunk that much or what I most feared, I was becoming acclimated to the alcohol. I told myself I'd deal with that later and decided to just go through the motions, whatever those may be.

Joe Duggan phoned not long after, asking me to come into Homicide and talk about what I knew. So next I called Meierhoff for more details on the shooting. The Impala license plate had passed the quick check that Officer Deely ran on his in-car computer before he was shot. The car was owned by an out-of-town sales engineer for a local petroleum firm, stolen from a long-term parking lot up by Bush airport and therefore not yet reported missing. The car later turned up in east Houston, down by the ship channel. HPD was now checking for prints or other evidence.

On the TV news, police were closemouthed about further details, simply asking that anyone with information contact Crime

Stoppers or HPD and yes, to be very careful about approaching suspects. Someone who would murder a cop in broad daylight wouldn't hesitate to kill again.

* * *

The new Houston Homicide is a big step up from the old cop shop on Reisner. HPD leased a modern office building in midtown and remodeled it, with floors for homicide, robbery, vice, other major crime divisions. The offices are spacious, comfy, modern, all the amenities and communication goodies like you'd expect. Cop heaven is also properly adjudicated, there being Starbucks, Krispy Kreme donuts and Mickey Dee franchises on the ground floor.

I parked in the adjacent garage and took the second level skywalk, then elevator to Homicide on four. Every cop I saw was grim-faced with a business-only look. The uniform police had a small black band of mourning stuck across their badges, text in silver on the band, *Nemo Me Impune Lacessit*, or *No One Attacks Me With Impunity*. This Latin slogan an ancient one, derived from the Scots Order of the Thistle, now a universal statement of solidarity within law enforcement worldwide whenever a colleague is sacrificed at the altar of evil.

I had caused yet another death, cost someone else his life. Would I continue to spread my disease even among those I didn't know, had never met? Was there any cure for my infection, the plague that raged inside me? Some way to immunize myself, or at least others? Again, I decided to table the thoughts for now. I'd done that several times previous and never got back to myself for contemplation. But thinking leads to pain. Best to not think at all.

* * *

I was a few minutes early when I stepped into Joe Duggan's office and Joe was already impatient and fuming. "About fuckin' time! Buncha folks waitin' in the conference room. But I got a couple personal questions, so sit your ass down for a sec before we go over."

Last year that would have been impossible, Joe's old office jammed and cluttered with crime folders, murder books, reports, stacked on every available flat surface, chairs included. The revised Captain Joe Duggan Mark II however banished any ancillary disarray along with disreputable clothing, and Joe's new office is impeccable, flat screen computer displaying HPD logo, TV monitor above a filing cabinet, photo of wife Margaret neatly arranged on his desk, plaques and awards in fine array along the wall. Of three orderly visitor chairs, one was occupied by Detective David Meierhoff.

I sat down, looked to Duggan. "What can I do for you?"

"Tell Unka Joe. Why the fuck were you hanging around the Cardozo place?" His grin predatory.

"Cheryl Stern's a client. And the fact that she's Julie Cards' daughter is confidential, don't let's forget."

"Haven't forgotten, pal," Joe said curtly. He was miffed I brought it up. Then, "What about Julie Cards himself? How's he involved?"

I thought it best not to mention anything that Cardozo talked to me about, even among friends like Joe and David. "He's not involved. Julio Cardozo is retired, anyway. He—"

"Retired? Retired from goddamn what?" Joe interjected. "Auto parts distributor or a friggin' gangster? He runs the Fifth Ward Apaches, in case you fuckin' don't know!"

"Whatever," I said wearily. I was becoming defensive now and regardless of the tragic situation, I didn't need Joe Duggan or anyone else impugning my personal affairs.

But Meierhoff spoke on my behalf before I could object further. "Joe, Mitch and I explored this thoroughly. He has Cheryl Stern as a client from last fall. You know how that went down, her being kidnapped, the shooting. Hell, I was the one who got shot!"

"I know that, David," Joe said agreeably.

"Anyway," Meierhoff continued. "I asked Mitch yesterday whether Cardozo himself was a factor, he assured me not, and I'm good to go on that point. It's off the table, far as I'm concerned."

Duggan looked at Meierhoff, to me, back to Meierhoff. He raised his arms in a gesture of acceptance. "Okay. We'll get into that later. Let's head over to the meeting. The others will wonder where the hell we went."

We snagged coffees from a concession station and carried them to the conference room. Joe's cup was a big ugly ceramic mug that identified him as *World's Best Cop*, while Meierhoff's announced *Houston Grand Opera*. And here I was, stuck with a flimsy foam thing that held about a third cup.

Figures.

Chapter 14

First thing I saw when entering the conference room was boots, a pair of hand-tooled beauties decorated with an Alamo theme and propped on the table. The boots were worn by Texas Ranger Arvis Danforth.

He's about six-two, slender and athletic, salt-and-pepper hair cut just long enough to offer a Western take without being gaudy. Danforth is a handsome man with the weathered appearance of someone as used to the saddle as his Ranger issue SUV. His attire was completed by light brown slacks with a law enforcement-style stripe down the leg, a white Western dress shirt, bolo tie, a silver Lone Star badge on his belt and a fine leather holster that matched the boots. In the holster a big 1911 .45 pistol, Kimber I thought.

Ranger Danforth was sitting next to a man who appeared his polar opposite. He's FBI Special Agent Ed Scudder, an older guy, unkempt grey hair, well-used overcoat, rumpled appearance. Agent Danforth bears a striking resemblance to actor William B. Davis, the subversive Cigarette Smoking Man from *X-Files*. And the fact that Danforth is a chain smoker doesn't help dispel the image. He once told us that he would often get stopped by people in airports, asking for his autograph. "What do you do?" I asked. He smiled, shrugged. "I just sign *Bill Davis* and thank them."

To Danforth's right was Detective Juanita Hertza, head of the HPD Hispanic gang unit. I'd never actually met her, just knew her by sight. I figured she was here to gig me on being pals with Julio Cardozo, pick up on the mantra where Joe Duggan left off. Hertza is late forties, a heavyset Latina, face worn and tired, lined with worries concomitant with her difficult job. She looked unhappy and I guessed I was the cause.

The three cops were glancing through copies of the Slicer file, discussing entries, speaking to one another when we came in. We shook hands all round, sat.

Meierhoff took the lead. "You all know about yesterday, the ambush of Officer Deely." David quickly outlined the thread of events to ensure that everyone was up to date. "Now," he said. "I want to focus on exactly what happened with the Impala. Mitch will fill us in from his perspective."

So I repeated what I'd told David, how I spotted the tail a block away from the Cardozo place. That I phoned him and set up an intercept. The intercept that led to murder.

"Was the tail a close one or did he sit back?" Scudder asked. "Pro job, amateur?"

"Made no attempt to drop away, put cars between us, otherwise conceal, like it didn't matter. But he did keep far enough back that I couldn't tell who was in the car, even how many there were." I shrugged. "So it may have been an amateur or a pro who simply didn't give a damn, either way."

"And you figure he knew it was you?" Danforth asked.

"Probably. Why else would he pick me to follow? There are people in and out of the warehouse all the time. But soon as I pulled out, he was behind me."

Detective Hertza had been frowning while I talked and now she opened a folder before her, swung it around for me to see. Photo of Cardozo, shot from a telephoto lens as he was getting into a car. He was younger, the picture from years back. Hertza poked at the image, glared at me. "You know who this is, right?"

"Yes, of course. Julio Cardozo. He's the legal guardian of my client, Cheryl Stern."

Her gaze was dark. "And you know he's a gang leader and overall thug?"

I sighed. *Here we go again.* "Yes," I replied. "I'm a private investigator. We often have clients who are on the other side of the law. Like attorneys do."

"Nothing like attorneys," she snuffed. "I'd like to know exactly what you were—"

"Juanita," Joe Duggan surprised me by interrupting. "Me and David already talked this into the ground with Mitch. He was straight with us and I'll vouch for him. Julie Cards is not involved and I think we oughta focus on the murder, if we can."

Hertza wasn't deterred. "I think it's relevant and I think that Mister King here knows more than he's letting on." She ponked her stubby finger at the photo of Cardozo, glowered. "How are you involved with Julie Cards' criminal enterprise? Are you getting kickbacks for feeding him confidential information? Information such as what might be discussed here?"

With that, she hit the nail on the head. Exactly what Cardozo had asked me to do. And I had no real comeback except to lie again, lie to a group of experienced police professionals. Keen on succeeding with that tactic.

But within seconds, my salvation came and I was rescued by an intrepid Texas Ranger. "Ma'am?" Danforth leaned forward, a placating look on his slender face.

"Don't call me *ma'am*, Ranger Danforth. You're older than me!"

"My apologies, Detective." He turned on his best smile. "I realize you've got plenty of issues here and want to explore them. But maybe it'd be better you take them offline, chat with Mitch later, 'cause we need to focus on the shooting right now."

There was momentary silence. Hertza squinted at Danforth, Duggan and me in turn, harrumphed to indicate her displeasure. "Okay. For now, okay. But I'm not through with King here. Not if half the LEOs in Texas try to stop me. Not by a goddamn Oklahoma mile!"

Duggan sucked in his breath, let the tension dissipate a bit, glanced around the table, eyebrows raised inquisitively. "Any further comments?"

Meierhoff looked at me. "Mitch, think back carefully, because this is important. Are you absolutely certain he didn't follow you to the warehouse first? That you might've been tailed from your house?"

I thought about this. "Good point. How would he know I was going to see Ms. Stern otherwise? He'd have no clue. She called me and I drove right over, never planned it or told anyone." I was lying about the visit, but hey, didn't everyone massage the truth, especially when talking to cops?

"Ya see?" Joe said. "No way the tail's gonna just sit at the warehouse, hoping you'll stop by."

"But you didn't see the Impala until after you left the warehouse, right?" Danforth scribbled in his notebook as he talked.

"Sorry, guys." I shook my head. "I really can't say. I was preoccupied, thinking about what my client wanted. I might have been tailed on the way over, yeah."

We talked a while longer but nothing was resolved. Duggan stood up, signaling that the meet was concluded. "Okay, Mitch, I think we're done for now, unless anybody can think of anything."

And predictably, Detective Hertza had her say. She shook the folder and gave me a tweaky smile. "Mr. King, I want you in my office immediately. It's five-oh-seven, one floor up. We've still got things to talk about."

I smiled sheepishly. I was stuck and would likely be grilled forever if she wanted to string things out. There went my afternoon. "Do I need to consult my attorney?"

Hertza frowned. "Not unless you plan on confessing your involvement with the Fifth Ward Apaches."

I sighed inwardly. More bullshit, more denials. And more headaches. Hertza left the room, striding quickly away, but not without staring at me again, pointing upward to her office.

Everyone else was gathering notes, downing the final dregs of coffee, shuffling around the room. Ranger Danforth reached over to an adjacent shelf and retrieved his spotless and perfectly blocked white hat. It was of course Western style, but not the deep-range cowboy cut, more of the wealthy cattleman style. On anybody else it would look foolish. On Danforth, it was perfect.

Joe tugged my sleeve. "We'll be waiting for lab work on the Impala, keep searching for leads. Give me or David a call if something comes up. In the meantime, Mitch, stay safe from this trophy-hunting asshole."

"Trophy?" I asked. That word again, and thinking of the Martinez murder made me shudder.

Meierhoff grimaced. "Yeah. Stole the cop's badge after he shot him."

"You mean…" I said.

Duggan finished my thought. "Poor sonsabitch layin' on the ground, bleeding out, and the killer gets outta his car and rips off the badge. Uniform torn, the stickpins busted, not part of the gunshots. So we know he took it."

"Any idea why?" I asked.

"Nope," Meierhoff said. "Trophy is all we can figure. And don't tell this to anybody. We're keeping that point confidential."

I got ready to trudge up to five, nothing to add to this meeting that made sense.

Then Agent Scudder glanced at me. "Regarding the guy picking you to tail, what's the chance there's a bug on your car?"

"A bug? Tracer? I never considered…"

"Shit! Hang on," Duggan said, picking up the desk phone on the conference table, punching a number. "This is Captain Duggan. Yeah, Homicide. Is Bobby Pinter there? Yeah, I'll hold…" Duggan looked at us. "CSI's down on three, Pinter's their best bug planter and finder."

I shrugged. "Never crossed my mind."

"Jesus, Mitch," Meierhoff griped. "You're the goddamn private eye. Stuff like that should be second nature to your business."

"Don't use 'em much, too many lawsuits. Besides, any evidence I obtain using a car tracker is likely inadmissible in civil court, my case blown before I even—"

Duggan waved me to silence. "Bobby? Joe Duggan here. Yeah, I'm fine… Look, you got a few minutes? Yeah. Bring your car bug detector thingy, all your gear, come up to the Homicide conference room, you know where it is… Yeah… There's a car in the…" Duggan looked at me, I pointed west. "…the parking garage, we want you to give it a quick scan. Naw, no warrant, don't need it. Owner's here, gives permission. Sure, see you in a couple."

I knew Bobby Pinter casually, although not from his being CSI. Pinter is close with my business partner, Andrew Capshaw, but I was unsure whether Pinter's still in the closet. So when he came into the room and we were introduced, we shook and I simply said to the others, "We've met."

Pinter is a stocky, muscular Anglo guy in his thirties, brushy dark beard and long hair done up in a biker-style pony tail. In fact he looks just like a surly biker forced to wear casual business attire because he lost a bet. Pinter's one of those men whom gays call *bears* for their chunky and hirsute appearance. From chatting with him on occasion, I'd found him an intelligent, educated criminologist, albeit prone to occasional displays of arrogance. *As are we all.*

We strolled over to the garage where I'd parked the 4Runner, stood there while Bobby Pinter opened his carry bag. Other than Pinter, who was unarmed, there was enough firepower among us to furnish a small uprising, especially considering Ranger Danforth's pistol.

"That's the biggest damn forty-five I've ever seen," I told him.

"You think?" He unsnapped the keeper strap and hefted the 1911 from its holster. "Kimber custom long slide, longer barrel, y'know. Have a look, but be careful, it's cocked and locked." I knew he meant there was a round in the chamber, the hammer back, safety on and all that was needed to fire was to swipe the safety down and pull the custom trigger. He handed the Kimber to me first and I passed it around. Everyone was cautious not to put his finger into the trigger guard and keep the pistol pointed upward. Thankfully we were all cognizant of basic firearm safety.

Familiarity with weapons however didn't prevent us from admiring Ranger Danforth's 1911, emitting juvenile *ooohs* and *ahhhs* typical when a handsome firearm is shared. It's a gun lover thing.

The Kimber was engraved with a Texas Ranger logo, and other Western-oriented decorations, beautifully worked. We all had a look, then Danforth returned the 1911 to its holster. "Daughter and son-in-law gave it to me, celebratin' my 20th with the Rangers. First off I thought it was too, ah, *fotched on*, as grandma used to say. But it kinda grew on me, and now I like it."

Joe clapped Danforth on the back. "Arvis' daughter works for the Feebs, FBI field agent outta Memphis, her hubbie the same." Danforth grinned, happy for his LEO family.

We broke up the little gun delights confab, turned our attention to my 4Runner. Bobby Pinter took a gadget from his shoulder bag that unfolded to look like the metal detector you'd use at the beach to hopefully find pirate treasure but instead just locate old beer cans.

"If you find something," Meierhoff cautioned, "don't touch it. We might need DNA and prints."

Bobby sniffed, laughed. "Hey, Detective, this ain't my first fish fry, y'know." *Yes, a slice of arrogance, to be sure.*

It took Pinter less than ten seconds. His finder's handset beeped. "Got one here, under the back bumper."

My stomach twisted and my face reddened. I was the private detective and I'd been tricked by a simple amateurish ploy.

Pinter rummaged in his pack, retrieved a mirror with long handle and flashlight attached, knelt and glanced. "Survey Tech model five-sixty. Buy 'em online. Short battery life, limited range, but otherwise okay for everyday stuff."

The rest of us looked at each other, smiled. CSIs don't carry guns, don't go around arresting crooks like on TV and aren't even cops, but they're damn good at their job.

Pinter stood up, dusting his slacks. "I take it this is prime evidence?"

"Bet your ass it is," Joe said. "Everything points to it coming from the fucker who shot Officer Deely yesterday."

"Jesus. Lemme get some pics before I touch it." Pinter took his digital evidence camera, clicked views of my car, the rear, bumper, underneath. He dictated everything into a recorder, waved it at us.

"Logging the info, keeping the evidentiary trail clean. That way it's unimpeachable in court."

Pinter checked the rest of the SUV, but found nothing. He gloved up, knelt behind my car again, took a thin pry bar and jiggled the tracker off my bumper, letting it fall gently into a plastic zip bag. He glanced up at Duggan. "I'll get the DNA started and check for prints right now. And we'll run the serial number, see who bought it, where."

"This is a priority case, Bobby, no delays," Duggan said. "Have your boss call me if there's a problem."

"Will do. I'll jump on it asap. DNA will take time but I can get you the rest of the stuff quick, this afternoon."

Pinter verified my car registration and contact info, scooted away to his lab. We all uneasily shook hands and I went straight home. Detective Hertza could take a flying leap.

On the way I kept an eye peeled for any suspicious cars tailing me, saw none. I parked under my carport and headed up the walkway.

A small padded postal envelope was propped against the screen door. No stamps, no label, nothing written. I picked it up carefully by the edges. Something inside, heavy and metallic. I cautiously pried the flap open with my Kershaw pocketknife, let the contents slide onto the concrete.

A Houston Police Officer's badge, splattered with blood. Wrapped around it, a note, printed neatly, *For Mitch*, and the phrase *Nemo Me Impune Lacessit*.

Chapter 15

The neighbors were apparently used to seeing police cars and CSI vans parked on my lawn and driveway because they no longer stood and stared, instead just went inside and drafted email complaints to the homeowners' association. My attorney would be busy next week and so would my Amex card.

There was a teeny digital surveillance camera over my front door, but I only used it previously to check on whoever rang my doorbell. Now I'd get a DVR attached. Unfortunately, they don't make the type that can record the past.

I had to take it with a grain of salt and see warped reality in the situation, however, because the alternative involved lots of late-night whiskey. So I simply leaned against my 4Runner under the sunshade and watched the CSI techs at work.

Meierhoff was there beside me, on the phone to downtown. He hung up, frowned. "It's just as we thought. Prints on the bug from your Toyota came back as George Burgess. No smears, no attempt to wipe them. He simply doesn't care. We know it's him and he knows we know."

"You figure the same on the badge and envelope?"

"No doubt."

"What about the bug, where was it purchased?"

"That's a dead end, I think. Two of them bought online with a prepaid card, delivered to one of those fly-by-night postal drops. No video, no hard evidence. We know it's Burgess but he left no extra clues. He knows the tricks, how to avoid the gotchas."

I slumped, weary of the emotional burden. "This isn't going to end well, is it?"

"Ending well isn't the issue. It's already a can of worms and can only get worse."

"I know he blames me for his brother's death, but all I did was walk in on the situation. Ray Burgess was just a casualty of war. Collateral damage."

"Try not to let it get to you, Mitch."

"It has, it certainly has." I tried to shake it off but I kept thinking about that new fifth of bourbon in the cabinet, calling for me. Like Hamlet, I was sick at heart. Unlike him, I couldn't speak anguished soliloquies about it, had to bear it silently instead.

At least I didn't need to procrastinate. And keeping busy was the recommended alternative. "How did the interviews go?" I asked David.

He extended his hand, wiggled it back and forth to indicate a mixed result. "Talked to the people at the apartment, all of them cooperative, but like they say, *nobody ain't seen 'nuttin.*"

"How the hell did Burgess get into the girl's apartment, do all those… those things to her and not alert the neighbors?"

David shrugged. "Most apartments buildings are flimsy, paper-thin walls. But wouldn't you know, this one is built to last, solid. You could throw a bar mitzvah next door and nobody would hear the music."

"Should I go talk with the neighbors now? See if I can come up with anything they might have forgotten?"

"Sure. You've got their names, contact info, right?"

"Yeah. Your emails, thumb drive you loaded, I have it all." I pushed away from my 4Runner, dusted myself. "I think I'll head down there, see if I can do something useful."

Meierhoff retrieved his tablet, scrolled. "You might start with the neighbor in apartment five. Name of Eddie Macintyre, student at St. Vincent. He was visiting his folks in Amarillo when it went down. We haven't interviewed him yet, but he'll be back in town now. Of course he'd be innocent of the crime itself but he may be able to give us some insight into Martinez' friends, her social habits."

I called up Macintyre on my screen, checked that I had his phone number. "Will do."

"Just tell him you're working in conjunction with Homicide. Should grease the skids." Meierhoff glanced over to where the CSIs were packing their gear. "They're pretty much finished. I'll let you know if they turn up anything new."

Before he left, David gave me a scanner that he'd borrowed from the crime lab, urged me to make it a habit and check my car frequently, since there was one more bug yet to surface. Good idea, that.

* * *

I said goodbye to David and the CSI crew, ran the scanner to verify that Burgess hadn't psychically materialized a second bug onto my 4Runner in the presence of cops, headed south toward Montrose and with purposeful illegality, called Eddie Macintyre while driving.

"This is Mac," his voice high pitched and rushed. Breathy.

"This is Mitchell King, calling on behalf of the Houston Police Department. I'd like to chat with you about the murder of your neighbor, Renata Martinez. Hopefully you can provide us some information? Can we have about an hour?"

Sound of a door slamming, chatter in the background. "Look," he said. "I'm just in lecture and I'm stuck. I'll be home later. Maybe about five?"

"Sure. Five it is."

"Thing is, I got back in Houston yesterday. I was at my parents, my dad had heart surgery. I wasn't even here when it happened."

"Your father okay?"

"Yeah. They put in a stent. Otherwise he's fine."

"Good to hear. And we realize that you weren't a witness to the crime *per se*. We just want background info on Ms. Martinez. Hopefully it might lead us to find the killer."

"I don't know what I can say, but I'm—hey, the professor's starting the lecture, I got to quit talkin'. Five, okay?"

"Five it is. See you at your apartment," I told him, and clicked off.

I checked the time, after two. I could get some other things done in the interim, so I phoned Sister Mary Frances, driving as I spoke, to hell with the law. She was teaching but could see me at three, in her office. I got directions and said goodbye.

Incoming call, Andrew Capshaw.

"Mitchell, are you all right? I saw the news about that policeman. Terrible, terrible. The poor man."

"It was terrible, my friend, and it was a shock, but yeah, I'll be okay."

"I worry about you, Mitchell."

"Don't."

"Hard not to, the life you lead. And yesterday, Carolyn told me about her boyfriend—former boyfriend, that is. He got beat up, beat up awfully, friends at school told her."

"Heard the same thing myself."

"Now, Mitchell, you didn't have anything to do with it, did you? Tell your Andrew the truth."

"I had no involvement. I swear."

A slightly chiding voice. "Well... if you say so..."

"Cross my heart, Andrew."

"All right, if you promise. Carolyn says hello anyway."

"Oh," I said, eager to change the subject. "Met a pal of yours this morning. Robert Pinter, the CSI tech?"

I could hear Andrew gush, even over the phone, and imagined him quivering. "Bobby Pinter? He's such a hunk! But *shhh* on Bobby. He's still not comfortable with his sexuality. Covert, if you know what I mean."

"Not to worry. Nothing was said."

"Some folks take a while, I guess. But in time…"

I said goodbye, left Andrew to his hairy bear fantasies.

Chapter 16

St. Vincent College offers a gracious campus, with verdant, sculpted lawns and placid walkways, comfy places to sit and chat along your way. Students who were certainly older than the thirteen they appeared, teachers and staff also younger than I, occasional old timers in their forties creeping along. Was it only a few years ago that I was immersed in a similar student life? UT Austin is mammoth by comparison but all colleges look the same, I think. A mixture of intellect, learning and youth. Plus lots of fun, hopefully. I envied the kids, their lives ahead of them.

But how many might squander their opportunities as had I? How many would emulate me in that most vital of studies, life itself, and resolve themselves into abject failures? Only time and blind chance would tell.

I followed the directions that Sister Mary Frances gave me, strolled halfway across campus to the Liberal Arts building. Like most structures on a college campus, it was conventional, educational, somewhat unimaginative, but friendly nonetheless.

Photos of George Burgess were everywhere, of course, his handsome yet austere face, suitable visage for a retired Marine colonel, not a brutish and clever murderer. People were warned not to approach him but to contact HPD immediately, as if you'd eagerly strike up acquaintance with a serial killer unless cautioned otherwise.

Mary Frances' office was on the second floor, 212. Just like Andrew, she was on the phone when I stuck my head in the door and just like Andrew, she waved me to sit. As with many faculty provisions, the room was small, scarcely space for a desk and a couple of chairs. Not to mention the heavily laden metal shelves all around the room, crammed with books and folders.

"Yes, yes," she said into the phone. "I'm okay. Still a little shaken up, but I'll be fine, really. No, I'm certain. But thanks." She hung up. "Dean of the department, checking on me. Third time he's called." She shrugged. "Means well."

We shook hands, then she stepped over to the door and closed it. "Privacy," she told me, sat back down. Today she was wearing another Dana Scully suit, this one a darker blue, but with a longer hemline than TV would ever approve.

"Honest," I asked. "How are you feeling?"

"Not too bad, considering. But whenever I think about Rennie, I get all queasy, just want to lie down somewhere dark, pull a sheet over my head. Right now I'm crashing in the campus dorm, can't bring myself to sleep in my apartment." She frowned. "Does it get better?"

"Sometimes. You never forget what you've seen, ever. But it grows tolerable."

"I'm thinking that if it ever becomes okay, becomes something very ordinary, it's… well, wrong."

"Not necessarily for those in the business. Police, medics, pathologists, others. They have to persevere and force a sense of detachment to do their job. Familiarity breeds distance."

"Still," she said. "Becoming accustomed to… to what happened?"

"You're right on that, agreed. Horror such as what occurred isn't likely every day." I thought a bit. "If I may offer a suggestion?"

Mary Frances raised her eyebrows and smiled, inviting. "Of course."

"Counseling," I said. "I know a therapist, psychoanalyst, Doctor Carol Chen. She's terrific. I can give you her name, number."

She pursed her lips. "Maybe, maybe. Couldn't hurt." She smiled again. "Of course, we faculty have access to our own counseling. Nuns and clergy, some of it mandatory, you know."

"Of course." And I next broached the subject. "I'm therefore sorry, having to ask you to recall things that you may find difficult."

"Go ahead. I'm tougher than one might imagine."

"Okay. As you know, we're certain as to who the murderer is—"

"Called the Slicer, right?"

"Yes. George Burgess. A former cop for Travis City. And a serial killer." At which Sister Mary Frances crossed herself. No other reply was needed.

I went on. "But the primary question is whether the victim was chosen at random or if there's some link, some way that Burgess was drawn to Ms. Martinez. If we find out, either way, it should help our search for him."

"And you want what?"

"Anything. Any sort of information, who Ms. Martinez was dating, friends, students or otherwise. Every lead we gain will be thoroughly checked out."

She nodded. "I gave Detective Meierberg—Meierhoff—all the names I could come up with. You've got those, right?"

"Yes. But after a while, a new name, added info might pop up in your recollection."

"So far, nothing. If it does, should I call you or the police?"

"Either of us. But I'm putting the bulk of my time on this, whereas Detective Meierhoff has other cases on his docket. So feel free to call me whenever." I gave her my card.

She examined the card, turned it over to the blank side, handed it back. "Your shrink's name?"

* * *

I still had time to talk with Renata Martinez' faculty advisor, Father Daniel Gibson. Sister Mary Frances called him to check that he was available, gave me directions.

Gibson's office was adjacent a beautiful new chapel where he also served as priest, according to Mary Frances. He's one of several Dominican Fathers on campus, providing both spiritual and educational help for the student body. His name sounded familiar to me somehow, but not in connection with the school. Maybe a news story?

The moment I laid eyes on him, though, I knew. He was Danny Gibson, a congenial, intelligent, and very much in the closet gay man in his late twenties. I'd met him at Andrew Capshaw's birthday party two months ago. And of course he was in street clothes then, not the grey slacks, black liturgical shirt and clerical collar he now wore. But he was the same person, mid-size, dark eyes, short brown hair, handsome.

There was very little I might say that could rationalize his behavior, either. At the party I'd seen him flirting with, later passionately making out with another young man. No doubt, Gibson is firmly a member of the gay community and extremely vulnerable because of it. One word to a bishop or cardinal and he'd be out of a job and done with his career, defrocked and discarded.

When we shook hands I immediately saw that Gibson recognized me too, his grip hesitant, eyes averted. Being an experienced priest and counselor, he must have realized that he was broadcasting despair and reluctance.

So I bailed him out by being direct. "We met at Andrew's party," I said. "Not that it makes any difference. As a private investigator, keeping my mouth shut is paramount."

"I was undergoing some stressful times," he said. "Things are different now."

"Stressful or not, different or no, it's all the same to me, confidential. Okay?"

"Okay," he agreed. Gibson seemed a bit relieved, sat behind his desk, leaned forward. "About Renata, Captain Duggan said you'd be contacting me. What can I do?"

"Fill me in on her social life. Active or not? Was she seeing anyone special?"

He thought for a minute. "There's this one fella, Oswaldo Lopez—Ozzie. I think he's a senior, I can check. I saw them around campus this past semester, coming to student movies together, that sort of thing."

"This Lopez boy okay?" I remembered the name from Meierhoff's initial notes.

"Yeah, a good kid. Out of town when Renata was killed, student retreat up in the Hill Country. He's here on one of the special scholarships, grants to barrio kids who wouldn't otherwise have much of a chance at school. We talked once..." Gibson broke off. "Just talking, you realize, not confession. That would be privileged."

"Understood. So what did you talk about?"

"How he'd had it tough, his older brother in a gang and always getting into trouble, cops coming to his house all the time. Brother tried to recruit Ozzie, he refused, major tension between them. Fighting, some of it physical."

"Happen to remember the gang name?"

Frowning, "Yes… something like *Columbine*, maybe?"

"Barrio Colombia?"

"Yes, that's it. Barrio Colombia."

Echoes of the ghetto, resonance into my own dilemma, reminder of Julie Cards' admonition, his imperious assignment to me, task I would in no way honor.

"I'll want to talk to Ozzie, very casual. Not in the confessional, however," I added.

That got a chuckle from Gibson. Good, he needed to relax. "Sure, meeting it is," he said. Then he waved a finger, cautioning. "This can't be an official police-type interview, understand. Informal or I really can't be permitting this."

"Agreed, and thanks, I appreciate it. So will HPD."

We chatted a little longer, Father Gibson unable to think of any further leads or remember close friends of the Martinez girl. He promised he'd check with her teachers to see if they had any ideas, that he'd get back to me.

I stood up to leave, shook his hand, gave him my card, thanked him.

"And thank you," Gibson replied. "About the other thing, you know."

I passed my fingertips across my lips, zipper style. His secret was safe with me. But I wondered how long he'd be able to stay aloof from reality. Some day it would come smashing through the ceiling and down upon his neck, ripping away that collar he wore. This I knew because it always happens, fantasy transformed to reality, facts overriding sham construction, always, try as we may to deny the truth, eventually it will rise up to slap us in the face.

Chapter 17

I snagged a Coke from a row of vending machines in the student union, sat at a small table apart from the general bustle, and mulled over what little I'd learned. Apparently, Renata Martinez had been a fairly conventional young woman, good student, modestly devout Roman Catholic, but nothing evident pointed to why she'd been chosen as victim by George Burgess. Maybe I'd pick up something when I spoke with her friends?

An electronic bulletin board on the wall above the snack bar caught my eye. It was a message that tomorrow night, Friday, on the central campus mall at eight pm, a student candlelight rally and prayer vigil would be held to memorialize their lost friend Renata Martinez.

I rang up Meierhoff, told him about the event.

"We should be there, hey?" he asked.

"For sure," I said. "Never know who might pop up."

"I'll organize things, bring some other officers with me, meet you there about seven."

"Try to pick younger cops," I told him "You and I stand out like yeti."

"You think?"

* * *

Four thirty, so I drove the short blocks to the apartments to interview Martinez' neighbor, Eddie Macintyre.

I parked nearby, walked to the small complex. All the crime scene tape and other barriers had been removed, except that the door to apartment four was completely boarded up, windows shrouded with plywood, HPD signs cautioning to keep away.

Otherwise the surrounding area was scrubbed completely clean, no leftover coffee cups, cigarette butts, fast food wrappers, or other signs that police had been here.

I let myself through the wrought iron pedestrian gate that led toward Macintyre's apartment, number five. I'd been extra vigilant since the Impala incident and noticed a tall, skinny young man coming down the sidewalk just behind me. I casually put my hand inside my jacket. He frowned, smiled crookedly, stopped at the gate. "You the private guy, the detective?" No indication that he perceived I was armed, an open look.

"Yep. Mitch King, call me Mitch. I take it you're Eddie Macintyre?" I put out my hand to shake.

He took my hand tentatively, unused to the gesture, as are many young people. "Yeah, I'm Mac."

I handed him my card and we stood there, Macintyre nervously shuffling his feet, awkward. He was easily six five, but not basketball material, way too thin to be genuinely athletic. His narrow face was nearly clean shaven, a shadowy and faint mustache trying, failing to gain much notice. Macintyre was carrying a shoulder bag which he slipped off, held down to his side, then put back over his shoulder again, pulling nervously on the strap. Streaks of sweat dampened his shirt, even though today it was mild, mid-eighties, low humidity, scarcely warm by Houston standards. Maybe he'd been running?

Macintyre stood there without speaking, just looking at me. Then he suddenly glanced behind me, which made me pivot rapidly, my hand reaching for the grip of the pistol under my jacket. Nobody there. *Was he seeing things or was I just imagining he was?* True, I'd been extremely jumpy since the Deely murder.

"Look," I told him. "Okay if we sit down and chat a while?"

He nodded rapidly. "Sure. Place is a mess, though."

"Don't give it second thought. I went to college, too." So Macintyre led the way to his apartment, ushered me inside.

Mess didn't come close to describing it. Empty microwave pizza boxes were stacked in a shaky mound on the kitchen counter, crumpled beer cans all over the place, shirts and jeans and ratty underwear scattered about the efficiency. I could smell body odor, rotted food, plus a distant chemical underlay I couldn't identify. Even I had maintained a cleaner residence when in school. Even I.

Macintyre yanked at some discarded clothes, clearing the two barstools next to the filthy kitchen. I sat hesitantly on the edge of one stool, gave him my card. "Your father okay?" I asked.

"Yeah, they sent him home already. Thanks for asking."

"Fine," I said. "Now, why I'm here. I need to see whether you can provide us—the police—I'm helping them interview, provide us with any information regarding Ms. Martinez' friends, anyone at all whom you may have recently seen coming into her apartment. Students, whomever."

Macintyre perched on the other stool, stood up, sat again. His face was sweaty and he was extremely nervous, why I couldn't put my finger on. "Er, nobody really. She kinda kept to herself, y'know. Quiet."

"Anyone at all?"

"Lemme think." Macintyre stood up once more, went to the fridge, retrieved a can of Dr. Pepper that was already open, chugged the leftover. "That was my last soda. I can give you some water."

"No. I'm fine, thanks. But did Ms. Martinez have visitors at all? Try to think back."

Macintyre flattened the now empty can, looked to the trash bin that was already overflowing, instead put the can precariously on the edge of the small stove, wiped his face with his hands. I looked carefully at him, dilated pupils, more sweat breaking out, his continued nervousness.

Then I knew the chemical odor, what it was. Eddie Macintyre was a tweeker, a meth head. And my showing up early prevented him from getting a fix. Tough shit. Deep down I didn't think I'd learn anything reliable, but I still needed to persevere. "Anyone?"

"Uh," he said. "I think Renata was dating this one Mex—er, Hispanic guy from school, ah, name's Ozzie I think."

"Anything else, anyone?"

"Mmm, no, sorry." Macintyre glanced around his apartment nervously. "Look, Mister…"

"King. Call me Mitch."

"Ah, Mitch, I got a test tomorrow, need to study. Can we finish this, like, another day, Saturday maybe?"

I stood up. I'd get nothing further. "Sure. I'll phone you soon and in the meantime, if you think of anything, please call me. You've got my card."

"Uh, sure. Yeah."

I headed for the door. "Good luck on your test."

"What?"

Chapter 18

I called Meierhoff, told him I thought Martinez' neighbor to be a tweeker.

"Crystal meth, eh?"

"Likely. He's already half in the tank." I described his appearance.

"Sounds like," Meierhoff said. "Think he needs a bust?"

"Naw. Leave the kid be. He'll self-destruct soon enough anyway."

"That's Mitch, Mister Compassionate."

"Fuck Eddie Macintyre's drug addled brain," I said, clicked off.

Okay, I'll admit. I was tense and unruly and needed a break. So I phoned my friend Kathryn Morley to see if she was free.

Kate and I have been dating about a year, off and on. I met her in conjunction with the Albertson case, she having been a pal of the tragically murdered Valerie Albertson, mother of Cheryl Stern. Kate wasn't involved, innocent and unaware of the whole sordid mess. She therefore became my friend, a go-to gal when I needed to vent. And I was the same for her.

It's customary that fictional private eyes have sex with any woman they meet who's between fifteen and fifty. Okay, sixty. My imaginary Bugsy Binton would immediately bed Kate, then dump her because a shamus, well, just has to go it alone, y'know.

So it may be amusing to some that Kate and I hadn't made the beast with two backs and likely never would. But this is real life, not a hardboiled private eye novel. And in this modern society, men and women often become friends, not lovers, and maintain this status despite—no, *because* of the genuine semi-sibling affection they feel for one another. This bond is as solid and authentic as a physical relationship might be, perhaps stronger.

Yes, Kate and I contemplated the sexual connection, flirted and smooched occasionally when first dating, but it never gelled, never led to sex. And so we remain close friends, each of us greatly benefitting, having one another to gripe and complain to, knowing that someone special is listening intently, someone who cares.

Kate picked up on the first ring. "Morley speaking. And if you run across that two-bit bum Mitch King, stay clear. He's no damn good." She'd seen my ID on her phone. Or so I hoped.

"Busy tonight?" I asked.

"Depends. I've been busting my butt all day, not in the mood for a lot of folderol. What you got in mind?" Kate's a commercial artist, a good one, and toils in the gardens of advertising, often to excess. She knows her trade, enjoys a top reputation and lucrative career, has garnered two Houston *Addie* awards, but at the cost of long hours.

"Say I grab some barbecue, you come by and we sit out by the pool, maybe swim, kick back, drink ourselves silly, gobble the food?"

"Keen. Just what I need. Seven, seven-thirty?"

"Be there or be round," I joked, lamely.

* * *

Three years ago I helped an insurance firm uncover the vice president who was embezzling their accounts, took their very generous bonus check, put in a small pool and Jacuzzi out back. Not long after I inaugurated the pool, the whirlpool and much of the surrounding lawn with the help of one of the female attorneys at the firm. It was monumental and if not for the fairly high fence around my back yard, we'd have had our fifteen minutes of fame with the cops. But she later took a new job in Dallas and we rarely talked these days. It comes, it goes.

I swung by Goode Company, great Houston BBQ, picked up brisket and ribs, splurged on one of their amazing pecan pies, more than enough food to suffice for a squad of hungry Marines. Next to Spec's liquors, a couple six packs of St. Arnold Elissa Pale Ale, a fave of Kate's to go with food.

It was just after seven, still light. I was by the pool, sitting in a bent-up lawn chair, sipping a Bud. I wore my intensely awful swim trunks, the ones with garish pink flamingos, an old faded NRA pullover, flip-flops.

My neighbor across, Ernie Banks, walked over to drink beer with me, and his son Malcolm soon joined us, a pleasant surprise.

Ernie came through the Vietnam Tet Offensive without so much as a bruise. Promoted twice in the field, Ernie won several decorations but always deferred, saying he'd just been doing his duty to the country he loved.

Ernie Banks loved baseball, too, and amassed a decent collection of memorabilia of his more famous namesake, the great Cubs shortstop. That, he bragged about eternally. Ernie and I made it to quite a few Astros games together, enjoying as true fans. What seemed to frustrate Ernie wasn't the Astros losing games particularly, but their switch to the American League. He rarely got a chance to see his favored Cubs anymore.

Ernie's son Malcolm is a huge, strong young man, highly intelligent. Like many, he joined the Army principally for the tech training and college tuition toward what he expected to be an engineering career. Posted to Afghanistan but assigned to a brigade maintenance facility, back marker to the action, Malcolm's luck inexplicably ran out. His second week in country, an insurgent mortar struck the building where he was and rendered him a paraplegic, paralyzed from the mid-thighs down.

For a long time after, Malcolm rode a path of hatred and vindictiveness. He blamed his father, his country, all whites, the world in general. He drank himself into a daily stupor, crashed his wheelchair several times and it was only by the good graces of the police who picked him up that he was escorted home or to the ER instead of jail. Nevertheless Malcolm lashed out incessantly at everything, himself especially.

I knew some Gulf War disabled vets and got them visiting Malcolm regularly, hoping they might help. If Malcolm thought he had it tough, he'd never met these guys, Wounded Warriors all. One of them, another black guy who operated his mechanized wheelchair by puffing into a tube, befriended Malcolm and refused to let go.

Persistence came to fruition, and gradually Malcolm became less angry and withdrawn. He broke off the excessive boozing, began to treat his father Ernie better and the veil of hatred finally began to dissipate. Recently Malcolm was playing wheelchair basketball and training for the *Paralympics*. He would come home in his van almost too tired to work the lift gate, let alone lash out at his father. He even began to say hello to whitey, me.

So when Malcolm rolled across the street to my house and pulled around back to poolside, I said nothing, not wanting to break the moment. I just reached into my cooler and handed him a beer.

"Thanks," a low reluctant sound from him but a big move forward. He popped the top and drank a gulp, smiled. I still didn't say anything, we simply clinked cans, three of us, and sat quietly, sunset and a gentle breeze making the beer taste especially good.

Malcolm looked at me, gestured to the flamingos. "Those swim trunks you got?"

"Yeah?"

"They suck shit, dude."

That got us all laughing and we were still sounding like goofballs when Kate drove up in her vintage Mustang convertible, custom pipes rumbling, briefly setting off my next door neighbor's car alarm.

She got out, carrying a tote bag, habitual Marlboro dangling from her other hand. She was dressed casually, cutoffs with a kind of paisley pattern, a bulky Texans sweatshirt, sandals. Kate had recently changed her hairstyle, a cute short bob or whatever they call it, my knowledge of women's fashion totally clueless.

Kate Morley is fairly tall, decidedly not thin, and some might say hippy but not in my presence. She has a pixie face with curved up nose, blue eyes, honey hair. She's a lovely woman, a treasure.

I got up, flipped open another lawn chair, handed her a Coors Light, her regular kick-back brand. She leaned over and planted a big smooch on my cheek and I said "Mmm."

"Me and Malcolm could go," Ernie joked. "Don't wanna cramp your style, y'know."

At that, Kate stepped over to Ernie, kissed him on the cheek, turned and did the same for Malcolm. "Nobody cramps my style, Ernie," she laughed. "How you been, Malcolm?"

"Fine, ma'am."

"Kate. It's Kate. Don't you *ma'am* me." Another laugh all round. And I picked up a hint, to never call a woman under sixty ma'am.

"Since we're stayin'," Ernie said, "You got another of those?" Gesturing to her cigarette. "Left mine at the house. Mitch here don't smoke, totally rude of him."

Kate reached in her carryall and retrieved a small chrome case. She flipped it open to disclose about a half dozen joints, nicely rolled. "Maybe this instead?" She handed a joint to Ernie, then her lighter.

"Girl, you bad!" Ernie laughed. He took the doobie and lit it, a long drag, passed it back to Kate. After a moment he let out the smoke, grinned widely. "Good weed!"

"Only the best for my friends," Kate replied, taking a toke and handing the joint to Malcolm. He took a hit, passed it to me. We sat quietly, sipped beer, finished the joint.

"So tell me," Kate asked. "What were you all laughing about when I got here?"

Ernie pointed at my trunks. "Malcolm says that Mitch here is wearin' the most sucky and most honky swimmin' suit ever made. You think?"

Kate sipped her beer, studied the flamingos carefully, nodded. "Malcolm's got a point. But you gotta cut Mitch some slack. After all, he is a honky and it's expected that he dress like one."

"And you're not a honky?" I complained. "Or at least honky-ette?"

Malcolm's voice was faux angry. "Mitch doesn't get to say who's honky or not. A honky can't tell the difference between honky and real, and anyway, only us black folks get to say who's honky. Besides, no way Kate here is honky. She's the most un-honky gal ever." Then added, "For a white chick, that is."

We all just sat there staring, Ernie and I particularly, as Kate was newly acquainted with the Banks men and didn't realize what a big event this was, the longest and most cogent speech I'd ever heard from Malcolm, funny too.

I giggled, breaking the silence and opening the floodgates. Kate snickered loudly, making a sort of cow sound and a second later we were all howling, coughing, red-faced, even the two black guys showing a rosy glow.

Somehow I remembered the barbecue. I got Ernie to help me retrieve it, warm it up, more beer, too. Meanwhile Kate and Malcolm struck up a deep conversation, subject of which I never thought to ask. Another joint and we ate up all the food, pecan pie included, and it disappeared faster than a box of spiked brownies at a Deadhead reunion.

It had been a while since I'd cut loose, consumed alcohol for the pleasure in it and not for its anesthetic feature. Hadn't been stoned in a long time, either. And somehow drinking only enough beer to become generously happy, topped off with the pot and most important, being among friends, was just what I needed. I was at peace with the world and all was in order. At least for tonight.

* * *

It was past midnight when our little foursome broke up. Kate insisted on cleaning poolside, dumping cans and other trash into the recycling bin at the side of the house. We three guys helped. At least I *think* we helped, all of us wobbly. That was okay, however, no driving and just a little happy but erratic stumbling (and rolling) for Ernie and Malcolm to make it home. I stood there with Kate at the front of my house, called out into the dark, "Watch out for cars!"

To which Ernie's voice came back, "Damn honky, we already been across the street a hour!"

And of course this set off yet another laughing fit, a loud one, prompting all my neighbors to flick on their authentic Edwardian LED yard lamps, a mute protest that made me laugh even harder before I tapered off into low chuckles, finally quiet.

"Still wanna go for a swim?" Kate asked.

"Yeah, I guess. If I don't drown."

Kate laughed. "In five feet of water? Even you'd have to work at that."

We went inside. Kate took her bag into the utility room and came back wearing a red one-piece suit, looking wonderful. I'd already shucked off my top and flip-flops.

I fed Krazy Kat and was in the kitchen when she came toward me. "Last one in the water's a klutz!" She pushed me away and scooted out to the pool, making a shallow and somewhat unsure dive into the deep end, such as it was.

We splashed around a while, moved to the whirlpool, which I'd amazingly found the presence of mind to switch on. It bubbled around us as we sat on the submerged bench, warm and cozy and I'd swear that both of us drifted off briefly. No chance of drowning, though, since we'd certainly wake up if we dipped our heads into the water. Okay, almost certainly.

An hour later and we were exhausted, sapped but satisfied, the raucous and dangerous world remote, inconsequential and quickly fading.

Kate and I managed to crawl upstairs. We took turns in the bathroom, drying off and shucking our swimsuits. Kate emerged wearing droopy harem pants and top, myself in baggy gym shorts. We plunked into bed. She gave me a nice hug and kiss, turned away. I put my arm around her waist and we spooned a while, drifted off to sleep, in bed together but just good friends.

Yes, it does happen. And should.

Chapter 19

Kate and I slept well but she'd set her cellphone alarm early, as she had a noon conference with a client. We both chugged orange juice, then I walked her to her 'Tang and she darted toward home, rumbling all the way.

When I got back inside, Krazy Kat was playing his new hide-and-seek game with me. A few weeks ago I'd spilled some coffee on the kitchen floor and the spill ran behind my big upright Seth Thomas dish cabinet, that piece of furniture totally out of phase with my own lifestyle, having inherited it from my parents' estate. The thing is heavy and ornate and ancient, suitable for Victorian bankers. But it's perfect to store a set of fancy dishes that I never use, plus pots and pans galore that eager friends, mostly female, bestowed upon me in a completely failed campaign to nudge me into gourmet cooking. I realize that private eyes are supposed to be experts in the kitchen and can put together a feast from the odd leftovers, shallots and oddly shaped mushrooms and quail that just happened to be in the fridge. Myself, I learned to make coffee without setting the house afire, considered that a victory and ceased further culinary endeavors.

Five minutes after I'd shoved the cabinet away from the wall and mopped up the spill, Kraze discovered the small gap between furniture and wall and squeezed his fuzzy body into what quickly became a hiding place when he felt mischievous. He'd lurk in the slot, then run out joyfully to bat at my bare feet on mornings as I ventured into the kitchen.

Kraze was nowhere to be found, but onto his game, I peeked behind the cabinet and saw a teeny black white-tipped tail sticking out, twitching, betraying the secret. The game of course didn't last more than two seconds after I retrieved a food packet and rattled it. Krazy Kat immediately relented and ran toward his dish, emitting mews and circling me with joy. And his simple animal pleasure transferred a small sense of happiness to me. Such is the greatness of energy that we share with our pets, willing partners in a sacred symbiosis.

* * *

Even though I'd downed a few last night I was committed to not drinking to excess. Those beers were recreational anyway, not binge-worthy and therefore didn't count. So I figured that if I could make it through one twenty-four hour cycle sober or at minimum a social beer or two, I would be on track for combating the dark habit I'd led myself into.

After Krazy was set for breakfast, I went out to the remodeled garage-into-rec-room and uncovered my Brunswick-Balke nine foot pool table for the first time in about a month.

Besides getting into trouble, I can do one other thing well, play pool. I took up the game as a teen and went at it hard, developing both tournament and barroom techniques. There's a shelf next to the pool table where I have two rows of trophies in an admittedly vain display. What most people don't know was that there are several more boxes full of trophies stored away. I do shoot a good stick, as Minnesota Fats might say.

So I played for three solid hours. I don't set up shots or practice breaks at first. I simply dump all the balls onto the table and randomly try to clear them off without a miss. First rack I missed twice, then I got my custom Richard Black cue limbered up and ran about sixty balls straight.

After a while I racked the balls in various ways and practiced my opening shots. I racked all fifteen and tried the gentle kiss needed for 14.1 competition, driving two object balls to the rail but not leaving the opponent a good lie afterward. I next tried my hard breaks, racking for eight ball, nine ball and the quickie tavern gambling game of three ball, which I happily refer to as *three ball fuck-your-buddy*.

Regardless, I bore down and concentrated, trying to put George Burgess and the murders out of my mind. At first it was difficult but I persevered and was finally able to immerse myself into shot making. I've always found pool relaxing, which is probably why I'm good at the game. And by noon I was having fun and all the worry had, at least for the time being, flown. Maybe there was hope for me yet.

Sticking to my new healthier regimen, I went for a brief run and worked out on my Bowflex, cranking up the stereo and enjoying classics from Dylan and Bob Seger. Life was good. Well, at least not bad.

I showered and shaved, cleaned up, called Meierhoff. We set up a meeting at six with the St. Vincent dean of students and their director of campus security. Before I headed out I rechecked my pistol, .45 hollow point round in the chamber and a full magazine, two spare mags on the right side of my shoulder rig. I also remembered to scan the 4Runner, found zip.

* * *

Five-thirty and I was in an anteroom of the administration building, chatting with Meierhoff and the four plainclothes cops he'd brought with him, all male and fairly athletic, should they encounter George Burgess. True to our plan, they were also young enough to maybe blend with the students at the upcoming candlelight vigil. If you figure young and blending being under thirty and wearing what appeared to be castoff yuppie era garb. Better than nothing, I surmised. Each officer was nevertheless handpicked for his skill at identifying suspects in a crowd and each had worked similar scenarios.

We could of course have easily rallied not four but four hundred cops to work the vigil, had we but asked. This was evaluated by HPD brass and the Slicer task force, and they knew that a larger police presence would scare Burgess off. He'd been a cop and knew how to spot his own. It was finally decided that a smaller group would more easily merge and perhaps lure Burgess into attending, his ego being that bold.

"Okay," Meierhoff said to his officers. "You've got a map of the campus layout and a photo of Burgess. We've also got his wanted poster all over campus and they'll be handing out fliers at the vigil. I've already marked where you need to be, primary access points for the student commons where they're holding the memorial. We'll be getting some help from campus security, but they're unarmed and not really able to deal with rough stuff, compared to you guys. So I'll post them at secondary zones." Meierhoff scanned the group. "Questions?" There were none.

So we walked down the hall to meet with the head of campus security, a man named Al Wrightman. "I know him," Meierhoff told me. "A good guy, smart, just lacks experience. He goes to Temple Beth El where I do."

I had to laugh. "A Roman Catholic college has a Jewish guy run their security?"

"You ain't seen nuttin' yet," Meierhoff replied, smiling, as we entered the conference room. And so I was introduced to Al Wrightman, director of campus security at St. Vincent, a slender, handsome and observant Jewish African-American. Only in America.

About a dozen of us were crammed into a small conference room. Besides myself, there was Meierhoff, his undercover cops,

Father Dick Ashmoor, dean of students, he being an older, round, cheerful man, Wrightman and his six security staff, men and women, three each. None of these were much more than amplified hall monitors, principally engaged in such mundane tasks as enforcing parking and wagging a finger at kids who insisted upon smoking on campus. Regardless, they seemed bright enough and since all they had to do was watch for older males at the vigil, particularly anyone resembling George Burgess, they'd be fine. I hoped.

Meierhoff passed out fliers with Burgess' photo. "I want to caution you St. Vincent staff, and I must emphasize this in the strongest way possible." He glanced around the room. "If you see this man, you are not to make any attempt to apprehend him. He's clever and vicious and will not hesitate to kill you in a second. Am I perfectly understood on this?"

Grunts of assent, then one of the campus security women raised her hand. "So what if we spot him?"

"As agreed, hit the group button on your pager and we'll all be alerted, call out loudly if need be, but under no circumstances engage him. Follow if you must, but keep your distance." Meierhoff pointed at a sheet with the campus map, circles drawn. "Each of you has a specific zone at the rally. Stay within that area if you can and should you call, others here will know where you are. Myself, Mitch and my officers will get to you immediately. We're armed and also trained in apprehension. So let us do the heavy lifting, okay?"

* * *

Candlelight vigil was held on the commons just outside the student union. I pegged the crowd at two hundred, two-fifty. Weather was high seventies and calm. As with any assemblage of kids there was the usual laughing and joking around, but they quieted immediately when the chancellor tapped the mike, typical *thunking* noise, precisely at eight. "Okay, are we live here?" he said, an unwitting gaffe that nobody else seemed to catch.

Volunteers had already passed candles among the students. These were standard issue for such memorials, small white candles with a little conical paper cone to catch drippings. The candles began to sputter and flare as the flames were shared from those with lighters.

Ashmoor took the microphone. "In the name of the Father, the Son…" He gave the Sign of the Cross and throughout the crowd, students crossed themselves. So did I, my wayward Episcopal high church liturgy coming to front. Ashmoor next proffered a short prayer of hope and assurance for the soul of Renata Martinez, afterward led the assemblage in the Lord's Prayer.

I kept scanning the crowd, starting at the periphery and working my way in, short arcs across the rows of faces. I was especially watchful for older men or for any movement that seemed out of phase with the rest of the people standing there. Kids all through the crowd were crying and I nearly joined them. The lighting was good, as there were big yellowish area lamps. But I saw nothing exceptional.

The security team was posted at the perimeters of the plaza, standing at each principal entryway. I spotted most of them as we watched, looking for Burgess. Of course there was no great expectation he'd show, but we nevertheless had to be at this vigil, just in case.

A brief message about the Burgess flier, plus warnings to call the cops and stay away if he were spotted. Several friends and faculty who knew Renata Martinez personally came forward to speak. It was predictable but moving, simple and faithful messages from the heart. About an hour and the chancellor spoke again, thanking everyone who came. And finally, Ashmoor gave a benediction, blessed the assembly and the vigil was concluded. But without Burgess' appearance.

Candles were snuffed and the students began to wander away. I saw Meierhoff across the plaza. He looked at me, shrugged. *At least we tried.*

* * *

Meierhoff and I stood together, his team assembled. It was nearly ten. "You guys want to grab a beer at Rudyard's Pub up the street?" I suggested. "I'm buying." There was general and eager assent, a reason to take a break and end of an uneventful evening.

There was a sudden commotion across the way, alongside the union building. A young man shouted, "Help! Please help! Somebody's hurt here!" More shouting, a few screams as we all ran toward the noise.

Students were circled around a prone figure just within the grassy verge of a walkway. "Get back, get back!" Meierhoff ordered. "This is the police, get back!" The kids parted the way and we all then saw the blood.

Lying limp, life's former energy darkly pooling the ground around him, throat slit deeply and completely across, was one of the young campus security guys.

There was no note or message that bragged of the murder, but I knew it was George Burgess' handiwork.

* * *

The dead security guard was a kid named Bill Carter. He was twenty-three, served one tour in Afghanistan, and had aspirations to become a Texas Ranger when he finished college.

The homicide investigation was thorough but led nowhere. No witnesses, the murder evidently occurring while the ceremony was still in progress and nobody saw a thing.

It was also senseless. No signs of a struggle, no indication that Carter had recognized or attempted to apprehend Burgess. Carter's pager was still in his pocket, his dead hand on the key, a final effort to signal trouble, but already too late.

Forensics found that he'd been ambushed from behind, his jaw and mouth clamped shut, the single lethal cut made quickly and forcibly from the left, Burgess being a lefty. So Burgess had not been content to simply attend the vigil. Instead he had to strike out with hatred, and leave yet another gruesome trophy on my behalf.

Eleven now dead on my ticket. Eleven innocents.

Chapter 20

I'd reached a saturation point with the whole Burgess affair and needed a break. I begged off any subsequent interviews, at least for the time being. Thankfully, everyone understood and luckily I had another project ongoing, a relatively easy one, a sort of working vacation. I needed to engage in something else or I'd go nuts and this would do fine. So I headed down to Mid City.

Like any metropolis, Houston has a multitude of surrounding satellite communities, some good, some less so. To the southeast is Pasadena, known affectionately as *Pasa-git-down-deena*, a sprawling center for refineries, chemical plants and enterprises that serve the oil and gas industry. Pasadena is itself a solid, traditional city with conservative values and plenty of country-western music. Mickey Gilley's club, famous from *Urban Cowboy*, had been in Pasadena.

Spencer Highway is a major east-west thoroughfare that serves Pasadena then extends east toward Deer Park, another chemical and petroleum matrix. The highway also bisects the very shabby burg of Mid City that's stuck square between the two larger and more respectable municipalities.

Mid City has been a canker on the rear of Houston forever. Protected by a corrupt city administration, rows of biker bars, topless clubs and counterfeit massage parlors (read: whorehouses) sat proudly along Spencer Highway, essentially a money source for the Satan's Slaves biker gang. But no longer.

Last year the Texas Attorney General indicted most of the Mid City council, and threw them out, with new elections closely monitored. The honest people living in Mid City quickly elected a reform-minded government and closed all the shady businesses.

Of course, there were repercussions. Mid City's crime enforcers were bikers from the Satan's Slaves, and the Slaves kept up efforts to reverse the trend of reform. Several businesses were firebombed, staff jumped and badly beaten.

The Governor was not amused, and she sent two Texas Rangers to fix the problem. This led to a showdown in which four bikers were shot, three of whom died. The Rangers were unscathed, which is normally how Texas Rangers do their job.

Things settled down afterward and new money finally began to revive the Mid City economy.

I'd taken a contract from a group of investors who were opening several bars and restaurants, generally along Spencer Highway and mostly in Mid City. They wanted to vet their new hires and ensure that they weren't bringing thugs back into the startup enterprise. They also wanted a bit of old fashioned security.

Private detectives perform this sort of investigatory and security service as bread-and-butter assignments. It's how they pay the rent and keep their gas or water from being cut off. Most PIs work on retainer for insurance companies and law firms, and an attorney friend of mine, Karen Morales, was ironing out property leases and deeds for the investment group, and she recommended me.

First I subcontracted to Jensen Security, a firm with which I often partnered. They were staffed exclusively with off-duty and newly retired Houston-area cops, mall ninjas need not apply. Having armed and authentically experienced guards on your property deters occasional and random troublemakers, even those sponsored by a one-percenter biker gang.

I'd also finished my interviews of new employees and prepared a comprehensive report and evaluation for the group. We were meeting tomorrow at one of the new enterprises, *Mid City Crab Shack* on Spencer.

Things looked just fine, but you know what Matthew cautioned about wars and rumors of wars. Satan's Slaves were still hanging around, and there'd been phone call threats and vandalism at the new places, so I thought it best to take out insurance for the meet. A special policy named Tony Vee.

Antonio Villarreal is a longtime pal. He's a huge guy, part Samoan, part Salvadoran, all Bigfoot. Tony played tackle for the old Houston Oilers till he blew out his knee. He did a turn with pro wrestling, then opened his own bodyguard and security service. It was mostly legal, too, at least the part that I let Tony help me with. His other contracts I had no business knowing about. And didn't want to.

Last time I spent any quality sojourning in Mid City was memorable for brawls and general gunfire, when I'd gotten my butt generously kicked. Tony extracted me with considerable aplomb, using a sawn-off shotgun to enhance the mood. So I phoned him to see whether he'd be available to join me for some free seafood tomorrow afternoon, and I'd pay a couple hundred bucks for his trouble.

"Mid City again?" he laughed. "You got a thing about fightin' with the bad boys, or what?"

"Or what," I said, outlining the meeting, promising him all the crab he could eat, knowing full well that would be impossible without the restaurant arranging for a semi full of crustaceans to drop off cargo at the kitchen door.

"Suppose I got to dress up for the meet. I should charge you three small instead of two."

"Clean clothes are recommended and you must wear shoes. Otherwise, no biggie. So two bills is tops, take it or starve."

"Okay," Tony agreed, laughing. "You drive the 4Runner. I can't fit in that little blue Limey toy you have."

"You dare disparage my classic MGB? I'll have you know the parts that fall off my elegant sports machine are evidence of the finest in British craftsmanship."

"The damn steering wheel ain't even on the right side—*correct* side, that is."

"It's a special import, pal. I paid extra for it and they all drive on the wrong side of the road there anyway. That's how they made the car."

"It's the Toyota or nuttin', pal."

"If you insist, big guy. Come by about noon, okay?"

No sooner than Tony clicked off, my phone rang. The ID said *JCar*, short for Julio Cardozo.

I'd deferred checking back with him, irritated that he'd imposed upon our friendship to work me as a snitch, asking for police information regarding rival gang activity. So I was supposed to betray the trust placed on me by my law enforcement buddies? *No way.*

I regarded Cardozo as a casual friend, but held him absolutely at arm's length. I did have a close bond with his daughter Cheryl, but I wasn't about to allow Cardozo to ride that wagon to his own objectives.

"This is Mitch."

"Mister King." Cardozo's quiet and measured voice. "I thought it important to call you, warn you."

"Warn me?"

"Yes. I've been told on good authority that your name has come up with Barrio Colombia."

This was the rival gang encroaching upon Cardozo's businesses, whether dishonest or not. The gang Cardozo wanted me to gain insider cop info about. "In what regard?" I asked.

"Regarding their plan to kill you, Mister King."

Great. I'd not done a single turn against this gang and yet they had me tagged. "How did they get my name? I've had zero contact with them."

Silence. Then, "I'm afraid it came from our people."

"What? How exactly?"

"I asked some of my, ah, assistants to see whether there was any news on the street. Apparently one of them gave your name as our ally, and a vendetta was put out."

"Thanks. Goddamn thanks," I said, and pushed the *off* button.

Chapter 21

Tony called me a little after twelve the next day, said he was running late, so I was already sitting in my 4Runner, air conditioning cooling, Chopin on the stereo when Tony appeared, piloting his shiny Eldorado. He got out, lugged a heavy canvas tote bag, pushed his bulk into the 4Runner.

We bumped fists and I handed him the two Franklins. He stowed them away in his jeans and glanced at me, smiling. "You look positively ravishing today, my dear."

"Sorry to disappoint. I'm already spoken for."

Tony's remark was predicated on my upscale attire, very preppie and showy, neat rep tie and polished loafers, pressed slacks, white-collar dress shirt, nice sport jacket, the works, costumed for mainstream success. I'd learned long ago that looking the part could get you ten, fifteen percent more in fees, no questions asked. *Who am I to refuse?*

Tony on the other hand was in his signature black, knit turtleneck, black dress jeans and some sort of exotic custom boots, also dyed black. I pointed down to his boots. "Lizard? Crocodile?"

"T-Rex," he replied, a wide bright smile erupting across his big pockmarked face.

Tony Vee's grooming is eclectic at best, presenting a thicket of going-to-grey hair and shaggy beard to match. His hair got any whiter, he'd resemble a huge demonic Santa Claus with whom to frighten the kids.

We picked up I-10, east till we hit I-45, south toward Mid City. Tony had already taken charge of the radio, cutting off my Chopin and finding a classic rock station, catching Steppenwolf's *Magic Carpet Ride* from the outset. Fine with me.

Not a lot of conversation, just digging the music, heads bobbing along, two pals.

"What's in the bag?" I finally asked.

"Tactical nuclear device."

"Okay," I agreed, not wanting to query Tony Vee too carefully. It's best to leave a sleeping Bigfoot lie.

* * *

The meeting went well. Everybody was introduced all round, the small conglomerate's principals outlining their progress on either purchasing or leasing property, and everyone got a little flier that showed photos of the acquisitions, each in various states of remodeling. And if the place where we sat was any example of the level of commitment, I knew the group would succeed. The newly tricked out restaurant was fresh, modern and spotless, yet the décor held true to the traditional crab and seafood house, keeping a quaint if modestly commercialized overview. The crab were also fresh, tasty and perfectly cooked. Somebody was doing things right.

Small to midsize business is the backbone of the US economy. And these folks were so very typical of the genuine enterprising investors we see today. There were twelve in all, maybe a third Hispanic, one black, four women. Nobody was wealthy, all were simply people who'd climbed up from virtually nothing, maybe managing a little bar or restaurant after college or the service, working their butts off, scrimping to keep their investment capital growing.

Hollywood views corporate America as only one notch up from ax murderers, always greedy, venal, devoid of the slightest capacity for humanity. When in fact the reverse is usually true.

Small business owners are essentially regular people who've worked hard for their success and try to share their good fortune. During my interview and vetting process, I was continually urged by the group to be patient and not form any quick judgments, to be amenable to those who'd had some run-ins with cops in their past, just so they were clearly on the right path now. I was admonished to be fair, always. And I was exactly that, presented my personnel report with only a few caveats.

We'd all sampled the excellent crab before the formal meeting, so afterward we chowed down with considerable vigor. I kept an eye on Tony because I didn't want him eating the new restaurant into bankruptcy before they had a chance to get started, but he was a shining example of decorum, knocking back only a dozen or so crab and maybe a hundred shrimp. Pristine behavior for Tony.

* * *

Most of the folks had already left, but I got into a long discussion with their attorney Karen Morales and two of the investment group's leadership. We talked taxes and both Karen and I extolled the benefits of spending money in Texas. Karen outlined the low overhead and favorable climate, both weather-wise and legal.

Colin White was an investor from Atlanta, a short, pudgy black guy of about fifty. He'd started business from a little barbershop owned by his uncle. Now he had two dozen unisex salons, plus about twenty 7-11s.

The other investor was Jack Hanover from Mobile. He owned a chain of car repair and lube spots that were scattered all across the South and Southwest. A hands-on kind of guy, he and his wife spent much of the year touring the country in their motor home, seeing the sights and visiting his shops. As this was their first restaurant venture, the couple had been here nearly a week, familiarizing themselves with the new venue.

Hanover is an interesting man, teaching high school chemistry for years after a hitch in the Army, now retired from teaching and relying on his knack for car repair to maintain a staff of top employees for his shops. He's pushing seventy, but fit for his age. He has grey hair, a bushy mustache and resembles former UN ambassador John Bolton.

Tony Vee found his own niche. He's an amateur chef and was busy trading recipes and cooking tips with Hanover's wife, Cherie. I had to smile. Here's this huge, looming and reasonably dangerous almost-thug, laughing about how he managed to overcook a brace of pheasant. And across the table, Cherie was looking like everyone's grandmother, taking it all in.

A fun time.

Chapter 22

It was about six. We were headed to our cars in the front lot and that was when the real fun started.

I was unlocking the 4Runner, Tony lagging behind, still chatting with Cherie Hanover about some sort of Texas-style *crème brûlée*. The other folks were standing at the restaurant door, some grabbing an outdoor smoke, just relaxing.

A pop sounded from somewhere over my shoulder, too loud for anything but gunfire!

I crouched instinctively and several sharp reports sounded, smacking into the Toyota's door, cracking the side glass just above my head.

I drew my .45 and flicked off the safety, searching for the source of the gunfire. It came from a van parked near the highway, blocking the exit. The van's rear doors were open, several men crouched inside and firing handguns. All were dressed in biker garb.

I was about thirty yards distant, too far for accuracy from my compact pistol, but I let off several rounds anyway, just to get the shooters to break fire. They ducked but kept shooting and it was clear that I was their primary target, being the closest. Put me down and they could go for the unarmed group behind me.

The slide of my .45 locked back, so I ejected the spent magazine, grabbed another from my rig and shoved it into the pistol, and racked the slide. I got on one knee and leaned carefully around the rear bumper, trying to hide as much as possible. I braced the pistol on the car and aimed, fired, caught one of the gunmen in the chest. He grabbed at himself and plunged out the van door onto the gravel lot, unmoving. One down.

A hot burning sensation ripping at my side, just under the right armpit!

I looked down, saw blood, felt strangely energized and dizzy at the same time, tried to ignore the wound.

"Fuckers!" a shout to my right, Tony Vee, his .357 Mag out, firing, all the time tugging at the zipper of his shoulder bag between shots. "Coming our way, Mitch!" he yelled.

I turned to see another van, this one crossways in the parking lot. The driver was shooting out his window with a small pistol, maybe a nine mil. I was exposed to this gunman, returned shots and either Tony or I hit the man, his arm and shoulder flipping up. He disappeared from view, and there were two down.

Splatters now all around me. Three men jumped from the second van, each holding a pump shotgun, firing toward Tony and me as they advanced. We were both caught in the open, crossfire from each van. A grunt and Tony went down, wounded but not out, sprawling in the lot while still grabbing at his carryall bag.

I tried for the shotgunners, working cover for Tony, but they scooted behind their van, regrouped and I could see them reloading under cover. They started forward again.

A moment later and two shots from behind me, loud. I quickly glanced to see Jack Hanover standing by the restaurant door. He was holding a pistol two-handed and taking aim at the nearest shotgunner. A long shot, but a good one! The man jerked to the side, the back of his head flying away in a spray of blood. Three gone.

I looked to the first van. Two men had stepped out and were advancing on us, firing now from pump shotguns like their pals. The driver joined them and there were three, spread out and headed our way fast. The other group was also shooting, bracketing us with crossfire.

I aimed and was ready to fire again when Jack Hanover was beside me, leaning over the hood of my 4Runner, pistol jumping in his hand. Two shots and a scream from one of the attackers. The man dropped onto the gravel lot, grabbing at his stomach. Four out.

We were doing our best, but were outnumbered and outgunned, and they were advancing from two zones. We had nowhere to run and they'd soon kill us all.

Then an angry yell, "Fuck you, assholes! Say hello to my little frien'!" and the quickstep *tac-tac-tac* of automatic fire. Tony was holding a wicked looking AR, long curved magazine beneath. He let loose a spray of bullets at the men to our right. All fell. Tony jerked out his empty magazine, slapped another into the weapon, swung to the second van and raked it with more rounds. He finally returned to the first and emptied his magazine into the bodies, some of whom were still moving. But not for long.

It was over in two minutes. Tony limped to where Jack and I stood, rifle dangling from one hand, looked out over the carnage, gleefully remarked, "Fuck 'em all and the fuckin' horse they rode in on!"

* * *

Tony was okay. He caught two ricochet pellets in his left thigh, and the surprise and shock knocked him off his feet, but the wounds were only topical. The medics plucked out the shot and patched him up after he refused a trip to the ER.

I'd been very lucky, bullet grazing my right side, breaking skin, but apparently not too deeply, maybe cracking a rib. They checked me out and wrapped a tight bandage around my body that hurt worse than the original bullet.

Both Tony and I were urged to seek further care and to absolutely get X-rays and tetanus shots. Otherwise the EMTs let us alone.

Jack Hanover had come through clean and everyone else was fine. Everyone, that is, on our side of the fence. The Satan's Slaves motorcycle club was now, however, short eight members. There was another shooter in the second van whom I'd never seen—he apparently hunkered down—but Tony's AR was indiscriminate, rounds punching through the van's body like... well, like a military grade rifle bullet through sheet metal.

Two of the shooters somehow survived and were hauled away to the ER, one via Life Flight copter, a caring professional attitude that treats the just and unjust alike. The attackers had taken the helpful step of wearing their Satan's Slave colors, most of their vests embroidered with nicknames, which made them easier to identify. Both vans were stolen from a used car lot the night before, no surprise that.

* * *

The Mid City police teamed with Texas State cops and we were all debriefed. We sat around a table in the restaurant, writing our first person accounts while the state CSI team cleaned up outside. The cops let Jack Hanover's wife go to their motor home, play hostess to other investors who'd been at the shooting.

Most of the bystanders had wisely scrambled for cover and kept low, witnessing nothing, and so were allowed to go their way. But Tony, Jack and I were still being questioned, as we were all shooters.

Lead investigator for the State cops was a gal named Beverly Simms, whom you'd think wouldn't know how to tie her own shoe, she being stereotypically gorgeous and young and affecting an east-Texas twang. She was however a smart cookie and knew exactly how to work a crime scene. The State could use more Beverleys.

Everything was surprisingly cordial and it was immediately made clear to us that we'd been accorded good guy status and our interrogation was therefore perfunctory. Turned out that the Mid City mayor's brother-in-law was one of the investors, and he stood for us with a staunchness that bordered on patriotism. You'd think we were defending the Alamo.

One of the cops brought in our guns. We were asked to ID them and given receipts, our weapons held until the grand jury met and no billed us. Probably.

The cop laid Tony's AR on the table. The weapon was formidable, a quick-aim daylight sight, combo tactical laser pointer and LED flashlight, custom grips and stock, flash suppressor and a snap mount to hold two more 20-round magazines alongside the frame. All legal in Texas, thank you. "You don't mess around," the cop said. "Heckler and Koch 416."

Tony smiled. "It's actually an H&K 417, .308 caliber." Then he looked to officer Beverly Simms. "Civilian semi-auto version, of course."

"Of course," Simms replied, a neutral pose, grin not showing. "Most folks would stick with the .223. That .308 must kick like a mule, climb all to hell and gone."

Tony advanced his patented wide grin. "What can I say? I can handle it. I'm a big boy. I play with big boy toys."

Simms just nodded, not wanting to take this further. She was apparently under instructions to keep it simple and let us off whatever hook we'd put ourselves onto. She also seemed to agree with that approach. "If you acknowledge that the firearm is yours, Mister Villarreal, just sign the receipt. We'll take good care of it for you." And that was it. Another case of us versus them, with the fix being in.

They'd already impounded my compact Springfield, Tony's revolver and now were getting the serial number off Jack Hanover's pistol, a full size Colt 1911 that had undergone some customization, now sporting adjustable sights, special grips and a Crimson Trace laser.

"Nice pistol," I told Jack.

"Thanks," he said. "I fiddle around with gunsmithing, mostly as a hobby. Spent lots of time on the old gal, tweaking her accuracy." He looked at us, shrugged. "Guess it worked."

Jack Hanover earlier produced his Alabama concealed carry permit, reciprocal in Texas. Jack had proven himself a lifesaver for both Tony and me, and I was quietly applauding how law-abiding people could exercise their Second Amendment rights. And that at least one of them could step in and rescue two supposed tough guys.

All of us kept our traps shut regarding how Tony's very legal and very civilian-seeming H&K had amazingly erupted into full auto. I took a quick glance at the selector on the frame and it had two positions, safe and fire, as it should. But no auto, which would make it illegal for civilians without a special Class Three license.

I had to know. After we were finally cut loose and were pulling out from the restaurant, I asked him. "How the hell did you get full auto from your AR? Not that I'm complaining."

"Special job a pal did for me, little gimmick I thought up. Push in on the selector, turn it another notch. 'Course, it ain't marked."

Of course it ain't marked. Ah, Tony, you and your gimmicks. Nobody games the system like you.

Chapter 23

So my easy day and laid back job hadn't exactly worked out as planned. I should have known that any attempt by me to do something halfway sensible would morph into disaster.

Barrio Colombia was still gunning for me and George Burgess was bearing down onto my spirit. Plus my poor faithful 4Runner had been shot up like the baddie in a Bruce Willis *Die Hard* movie.

One step at a time was the only way to make this work. I ran the shootout through my insurance agency, learned surprisingly that I was covered, and so arranged for a rental at Apollo Paint and Body, left my Toyota to be fixed. The estimator thought that maybe the electric window motor on the passenger side would need replacing but otherwise, purely cosmetic except for new glass, plus fourteen souvenirs of buckshot and bullet holes. I thought briefly about simply highlighting them with red bullseyes but decided to take the more decorous route instead and had them patched. I even sprung for a total repaint.

The little KIA I rented was nice, serviceable enough, well made and all, but it was severely underpowered for Houston freeways. Truthfully, it was underpowered for a golf cart. But it would do fine until the Toyota was ready. And then serendipity came calling.

Private eye Bugsy Binton leads a life of exhaustive depravation. He squats in a candlelit hovel and conducts business from a vermin-infested walkup just above a bowling alley operated by the Mafia and beneath an illicit slaughterhouse run by Iranian terrorists. Noise from downstairs and blood draining from the third floor is only a slight hindrance, however, as Bugsy still manages to bed the quivering but determined heiress, redhead of course.

It's just my bad luck that I've got cash in the bank and were it common knowledge, would get my membership in the Shady Shamus guild revoked. My father was a successful civil attorney and when he and my mother were lost in a private plane crash a decade ago, the firm became wholly mine, his only offspring and prodigal but loving son.

With no interest in becoming an attorney nor managing a law firm as suzerain, I liquidated the assets and sold off the client list to Vinson and Elkins, Houston's top drawer attorneys. That, plus the life insurance I split with my ex-wife, and we were both pretty solvent. I bought my two-story brick colonial outright and spent some of the rest on my very expensive vintage pool table and rec room surroundings, a shrine to vainglory, as Meierhoff tauntingly labels it.

I also inherited a decent trust fund, supremely conservative and administered by a very honest and tedious firm. And this year, the disbursement letter made me sit down and zone out for a few minutes. Over seventy thousand dollars.

* * *

Texas is a community property state. Meaning, no alimony. Of course I regularly pay child support to my ex-wife Sandra for our daughter Chrissie, but again, no cause for complaint. Sandra and I simply found that although we didn't exactly hate one another, we were as incompatible as James Carville and Mary Matalin. Oh, wait, they've been happily married for ages. Bad example.

I called the bank, verified the direct deposit of my disbursement, asked my banker to transfer half the windfall to Chrissie's savings account in Scottsdale. It took about five seconds. I realize it would have been more dramatic and exciting for an intrepid private eye like me to get the money in cash, drive nonstop to Arizona and fight off Road Warrior rejects enroute, but hey.

Familial obligations concluded, I sent money to *Wounded Warriors* and Houston's *100 Club*, a charity that aids families of cops and firefighters who die in the line of duty. Also to my church and yeah, the NRA political action fund. But taxes notwithstanding, I still had a chunk of money that had essentially fallen into my lap.

So I went car shopping, after I called Kate Morley and invited her along.

It was a mild spring day, lower eighties, nice breeze, so I took the ancient and tottering right-hand drive MGB, top down. With the Springfield under lock and key courtesy of the Mid City cops, I switched to my Glock 30, a reliable and accurate compact .45 auto. Pistol neatly tucked beneath my windbreaker, I was set.

Kate's home setup is similar to mine, office in the front of her house, living in the rear, a cozy restored bungalow in a pleasant residential neighborhood of the Montrose district. She was waiting outside, smoking her Marlboro and chatting with a neighbor when I drove up. Kate was nicely dressed as always, a frilly gold top and black dress jeans. She got in, leaned across, gave me a kiss.

"So what kind of car you gonna buy me?" Kate of course knew the car was to be mine, but she enjoyed teasing me.

"Got my eye on this Ford Falcon or maybe a Corvair. Perfect retro junk for a hippie chick artist."

"You always know how to please, Dear."

We stopped at a light and I turned to her. "Seriously, Kate, I really did come into a fair piece of change. I've got no problem buying you a car. Be happy to."

"No way. Dinner, yes. The opera, sure. But I'm too independent, way too much my own boss to accept a car as a gift. Besides, you're not old enough to play sugar daddy." She patted my cheek. "And the light's green, idiot."

I'd checked various websites before picking Kate up so I had an idea of what to look for. The 4Runner had been a faithful workhorse and although still in good shape, it was retirement age and would make a good vehicle for Fairview Consultants. Let Carolyn have it.

I also checked with my accountant and she recommended I lease any new car back to my own firm, *King Investigative Services*, a better tax break than buying outright. I therefore persuaded myself that with leasing, I actually wouldn't be paying for the car at all. *Right.*

This is another page in my fictional versus real private eye exegesis. We PIs are a business like any other and we have to run a careful, above board and savvy enterprise. The law demands it. So we watch our expenses, have an accountant do the books and reluctantly suck up tax wise to Uncle Sam as would any small business. Shamus Bugsy can't be bothered with such trivia as income tax and he somehow avoids an audit. But in the real world, you pays your dues or you goes directly to jail without passing Go.

Surfing the net for ideas, I checked Toyota first. But the new 4Runners look like guided missile cruisers and so do most of the SUVs and crossovers, so I found myself lingering over a tempting automotive brand more and more, and eventually my mouse somehow got locked onto *Bayerische Motoren Werke AG* and wouldn't be dissuaded. And I'd therefore made up my mind before I got into my car that it was Bimmer all the way. Hey, I was entitled, and *entitled* is the magic gimme-word of the Millennials.

* * *

It took us about an hour, maybe two, at Houston BMW to decide. We were cordially assisted by the salesperson—correction—expensive cars aren't sold by lowly *salespeople*. This sort of vehicle isn't even sold *per se*. It's simply *acquired*. And instead of a salesperson, we were *represented* by an impeccably dressed, cordial and judiciously helpful *Customer Associate* named Jane Camp, whom I thought resembled a somewhat less scary version of Tilda Swinton. But despite the duplicitous job title, Jane was indeed well informed, knew all the model details, and as Kate and I agreed, earned her commission. Nevertheless we jawed until a less than exorbitant price could be negotiated.

I need an SUV-style car because of luggage space for hauling bulky items like a camera rig. Size however isn't a factor so long as I have a reasonable interior. My ego drew me toward the X5 but I settled on a jet black tricked-out X3, all-wheel drive, the big engine. I checked every single electronic goodie box for interactive touchscreen, full internet capability and the extra-cost cloaked configuration and transwarp drive (cleverly concealed as a sport handling package). Kate approved, but only if she got to drive it too.

Papers signed, my Amex tapped for the starter fee and car promised sometime next week, we were done. We bade our farewells to our now handsomely commissioned Customer Associate Tilda Swinton doppelganger and drove away, smoke cheerily piping from my 1965 Morris Garage hunkajunk.

Chapter 24

Joe Duggan of course knew of the big shootout in Mid City and he wisely put me on hold for any more interviews regarding the Burgess case. "Something like that sticks in your craw and holds onto you a while, Mitch. Can't have you working at half staff, making mistakes, blowing leads. We can handle the investigation fine. Take some time off and don't get shot. Think you can handle that okay?"

I realized how right he was when I tried to get regular sleep, found myself replaying the Mid City incident in my mind, working through all the scenarios, finding flaws, getting myself killed rather than just grazed. It didn't help that my side ached each time I breathed. My doc checked me out, found one cracked rib, prescribed some awesome pain killers. Problem was, they made me want to go base jumping without a parachute while singing *We are the Knights of Camelot*, so I flushed them and stuck with Tylenol. After a couple days I took off the bandages and winged it.

I was puttering around the kitchen Wednesday afternoon when I got another call from the Cardozos, this time Julio's daughter, Cheryl.

"Mitch, you need to come over now. It's important." Her voice was severe and absent the usual freshness.

I'd deferred any further contact with her father, sending his repeated calls to voicemail and not responding, but would move mountains for Cheryl Stern. "Half hour," I told her. I fed Kraze some dinner and scooted east in the rental KIA, thought about Cheryl as I drove. Cheryl didn't say why she wanted to see me, nor did I ask. I consider her my friend. We'd have lunch occasionally, usually joined by her bodyguards, cousins Ricky and Angel Perdon, still technically mob henchmen, I suppose, despite the recent move of the Cardozo business to legitimacy. Or maybe I was just being charitable because of their commitment to keeping Cheryl safe. Both men did carry guns and were adept and unrelenting in their use.

I turned off Fulton, drove a few blocks further and pulled up to the gated entrance of Cardozo Enterprises. The two rough-case guards whom I knew from previous immediately appeared, one on each side of the KIA, peering harshly into the interior. They'd been looking for my green 4Runner and didn't recognize me at first, but the guy on my side smiled, gave me a little halfhearted salute and clicked the gate open. I drove in, parked and was immediately forgotten by the sentries. I let myself into the office.

Unlike other times, people were at desks, working, making phone calls and tapping on their computers. They glanced up and went back to their job. Before Cheryl set the company onto its new legal path, the office was always deserted. Now there are real auto parts orders to be filled from real distributors and real paying stores to be stocked. Hence real people making that happen.

Cardozo's personal bodyguard Carlo was also there, looking much the same as always, slender, contained, custom snakeskin boots resting on the desktop nearest Cardozo's private office. Carlo was sipping his habitual Jumex fruit punch and not smiling. Carlo is very good at not smiling or doing anything else that displays emotion. I caught the flicker of his reptilian eyes and that was all he gave me, for which I was grateful. Having Carlo stare full on makes my heart slow down and blood pressure plummet.

"Mitch?" Cheryl said, opening the door to her father's office, a frown on her normally smiling face. "Come on in."

Julio Cardozo sat erect behind the desk, impeccable in his tailored jacket and silk shirt, tie perfectly knotted, hands in his lap. He always sat this way, but this time he didn't get up and shake my hand. Instead, he kept sitting there, staring straight ahead, not looking at me or anything else in the room.

I glanced at Cheryl as she moved protectively behind her father. Ricky Perdon and his cousin Angel sat quietly on the wide leather sofa, both men nervous and embarrassed, unspeaking.

After a moment I realized that Julio Cardozo wasn't going to be shaking hands with me or with anyone else. His eyes blinked but otherwise didn't change. A small drizzle of saliva exited the corner of his mouth. Cheryl reached quickly with a Kleenex and wiped. Cardozo still didn't move.

"Stroke?" I guessed.

"Three of them," Cheryl replied. "Two small ones a month ago, a big one last week. He came home from the hospital Friday."

"What do the doctors say?"

"We brought in specialists, one from Mayo, the other from some fancy neuro place in San Francisco. Plus the doctors here, they all agree, say the same thing, that..." Her voice trailed off.

"That?"

"That he's gone, Mitch. The scans show permanent damage, doctors say there's no chance he'll get better. Instead he'll get... get worse." And that last word came out with pain from the daughter who loved her father dearly.

Ricky Perdon stood up, placed a comforting arm around Cheryl's shoulder. She sagged into his bearlike carcass and started to cry. I simply stood there, impotent and ineffectual.

I waited until Cheryl's sobs abated, then asked, "How can I help?"

She glanced around the room as if searching for an answer, her eyes finally resting on her placidly seated father. "I don't guess you can do anything, really. Nobody can. I just wanted you to come here, see for yourself. He can eat, but it's hard to get him to take anything but liquids. It's only a matter of time, his kidneys and all, they say, shutting down."

I looked at Ricky. "Who knows?"

"Not many, only those who are very close."

"Try to keep it that way," I advised. "This gets out, there are plenty of greedy competitors."

"You might check with your cop pals, see if they heard anything," Cheryl said.

"I'll make some discreet inquiries."

I hugged Cheryl and looked down into Julio Cardozo's eyes. They were blank. I patted him on the shoulder, but he gave no indication that he'd felt it.

An intelligent, powerful man, now enervated and drained of all humanity, a husk. I knew that Cardozo lived a life of crime and violence, that he'd participated in the death of some, created turmoil for many others. Yet I still felt some sympathy, if only because of his deep love and concern for his daughter, she for him.

As I leaned toward him his eyes seemed to turn toward me. I grabbed a chair, sat down as close as possible. "Mr. Cardozo? Julio?"

His lips moved, mouth a smallish gap. He was attempting to speak. "What is it?" I asked him. "Tell me." Cardozo's right hand moved, his arm lifted as if he was trying to give me something. "Anyone know what he's doing?" I asked the others.

"No," Cheryl said. "He's never done this before."

Cardozo kept moving his arm and trying to speak, an aimless little *ahh, ahh.* It was a sad parody of the scene in the original

Frankenstein film, the monster reaching for light beams and moaning. After a while, he ceased any movement and again sat stone-like.

"I haven't seen him do that to anybody else," Angel said. "Like he had something to give you."

I stood, shook my head. "No way to know." I got up, embraced Cheryl. "I'll keep in touch. Take care of him best you can." I shook hands all round, waved to Carlo on the way out, and left for home.

Chapter 25

Homicide Detective David Meierhoff and I were hanging out and drinking beer, sitting at a picnic table on the front patio of the West Alabama Icehouse. I had my regular Budweiser longneck but David was experimenting with one of those trendy new brews that came in a slender faux-metallic bottle and featured pushy TV commercials with lots of CGI and boldly energetic young people parasailing or mountain climbing, all in slow motion. I speculated silently whether both beers were filled from the same vat, his bottle simply costing a half buck more.

It was a normal spring afternoon in Houston, about ninety-two degrees. But we had a good breeze, humidity was thankfully low and our beers were frosty cold. The Icehouse owner had also recently installed a big aluminum sunshade over the picnic table area, so we weren't glared upon directly by Our Mister Sun. An engaging setup on a non-busy afternoon, the Houston version of a German Biergarten.

Meierhoff and I were concentrating intently on being unproductive, idly watching traffic rumble along the street in front of the tavern and less idly observing the newest barmaid, Annie. She had curly blonde hair, eager blue eyes, a voluptuous figure and looked about sixteen, although I knew she already had a BA and was working toward her master's in marketing.

The two of us had been here a while and had thus far spoken not one meaningful word between us. This is often a good thing, saying nothing. You simply relax and let the world circumscribe its insane spiral past your field of view and for a while, you're immune. Or pretend to be.

I sipped my beer. "Called you Saturday, went straight to voicemail. Thought you might want to head down to the range, shoot those new pistols."

"I was at Beth El. You know, the Sabbath and all."

Temple Beth El is a midsize Reform Synagogue down near the Med Center. "You getting back into that? For a long time you were the archetypal apostate. What do they call it, nonobservant?"

He snorted. "Nonobservant Jews are like Libertarians, neither for nor against anything of particular importance."

"Aren't we being the snarky one today."

He shrugged. "I'm a believer. Not dyed in the wool, but…" He held his hand out flat, wiggled it back and forth as he often did. "Kind of."

"Isn't there only one sense of the word believer?" I asked, showing off my James Joyce.

"You're not gonna go all *Ulysses* on me, are you?" He instantly picked up on my reference, as trying to upstage David Meierhoff on literature is a mistake. "Anyway, to quote another philosopher, *I yam what I yam*. So sue me."

Rather than file a lawsuit I got up, took both our now-empty bottles, exchanged for two more full ones from the impossibly pert but very smart Annie.

"I thought all you cops were Catholic," I said, sitting across from David again.

"Only TV cops. They all have Glock nine mils, too. The kind that make this weird snapping noise whenever they pull them out of the holster, nonexistent safety being let off."

"Yeah, the expected stereotype. Like all of us private eyes carry vintage Smith and Wesson thirty-eight snubbies?"

He laughed. "Guess my forty cal and your forty-five just don't cut the muster. We should read the rule book more often."

We clinked bottles at that. Or rather, *clicked* them, as his titanium beer was in some type of extreme polymer container that would likely survive a terrorist EM pulse.

"You should talk," Meierhoff said, smiling. "You go to, what is it, Saint Michael's?"

"Hey, three generations of snooty Episcopalians, family tradition, what can I say? Church of the Good Cadillac." We both laughed. "I get there, like, Easter, Christmas Eve mostly. Or when my conscience is acting up."

Meierhoff grunted. "I know all about your conscience."

"Speaking of which…"

"Mmm?"

"Speaking of my conscience, I'd like to resume the Burgess thing, maybe talk to the witnesses some more, help fill in on the interviews."

"You think?"

"I think."

"I'm okay with that, actually believe it'll help you in the long run anyway, getting back to work. Let me clear it with Duggan. I'll call you later."

"I'm good to go," I told him.

Meierhoff nodded, a look in his eyes. I knew he had something on his mind but wasn't ready to talk about it. Instead he glanced toward where we'd double-parked, his unmarked cruiser and my new toy. "How's the X3?"

"Terrific. Lots of power but smooth and quiet, all sorts of electronic goodies for me to screw up. BMW makes my old 4Runner seem like a Flintstones pedalcar."

"Using that wand I loaned you, checking for bugs on your new ride?"

"Haven't turned up anything, but yeah, I scan it every day."

A monster Houston firetruck thundered by, no siren, headed back to station. The driver tooted the huge air horn a couple times, like a friendly wave. Their station was just down the street and many of the firefighters came to the Icehouse after shift.

"Know what they say about Episcopalians?" I quipped. "Whenever three or four are gathered together, there's always a fifth."

That only earned me a wan smile. "Don't get me started on the Jewish jokes," David said.

I didn't. Instead we both went quiet again and looked at Annie, drank beer.

We started our third and last beer when David finally got down to it. "Some of the guys at the cop shop tell me you're spending a lot of time with the Cardozo people. And that you somehow got on the Barrio Colombia shit list."

I didn't reply, instead looked out at the traffic, took another sip.

"Not that you have to tell me, your best friend." Meierhoff pursed his lips, a half smile.

"You already know about Cardozo, how I've been keeping an eye open for Cheryl. And the gang? Part of the job, my name gets around, one thing led to another. Very sidebar."

"It's a rough crowd," he said. "Those drug gangs are nasty, kill you or me in a flash."

"I'm careful."

"Bullshit. That'll be the day." David shook his bottle, frowned at the label, set it aside, taking out his frustration with me on the brew. "This beer is crap."

"Want something different? I'm buying."

"Naw, had enough." Meierhoff hunched over toward me, spoke in a low voice. "I just don't want you go and get killed. You're my friend. Got any idea what those gangs are like? I don't like wasting my time attending funerals, even yours."

"David, I can take care of myself."

Meierhoff stood up, irritated, started for his car. "Yeah, right. And I'm the Pope."

"Didn't recognize you without the hat," I told him, but he was already out of earshot.

Another fine icehouse afternoon blown. Maybe I'd someday learn to keep my mouth shut and not irritate my friends so readily.

Chapter 26

True to his word, Meierhoff phoned the next day, gave me the go ahead on chatting with acquaintances of Renata Martinez again. And true to his friendship, made no mention of our little spat. "We've pretty well run the gamut on people to interview, but you may want to talk with Oswaldo Lopez, her sort-of boyfriend."

"You already interviewed him, right?"

"Yeah. Good kid, broken up about Renata. He came across as straight arrow with me, but you may still find something. Not with him personally, but some sort of clue as to why Burgess picked her. Anything."

"Will do."

I already had Lopez' number so I called him, set up a meeting at the student union in about an hour. I drove to St. Vincent, took a brief stroll around campus. Its placid elegance was jarred by the many wanted posters of George Burgess and a similar number of memorial photos of both Renata Martinez and the murdered security guard Bill Carter. Somber reminder of how strident realities of the world come rolling in whenever we let our attention wander.

I entered the student union, grabbed a coffee, and since I had a photo and description of Oswaldo Lopez and had seen him speak at the ceremony, I spotted him immediately. He was a fairly big guy, over six feet and hefty, a round face, small intense black eyes and a short thatch of stringy dark hair which made him resemble an Hispanic Oliver Hardy.

Lopez was red-faced and out of breath. "Sorry. Class ran late, I had to run, too." He smiled, a little chuckle. "Everybody calls me

Ozzie." We shook, he grabbed a Pepsi, we found a table away from the busy area.

I identified myself, assured him that anything he said was not binding nor did it expose him to liability. "I'm a private citizen and don't have the rule of law behind me. So please feel free to speak as you wish, and realize that everything you tell me is off the record. It's simply a conversation."

"I understand," he said. "But I really don't think I've got anything to tell you. Rennie and me, well, we were just friends. We weren't that close, really. We didn't, hadn't, ah…"

Ozzie was a self-conscious kid, as most overweight folks can be. He kept tugging at his shirt and jeans, sipping quickly at his soda, glancing nervously at passersby. In truth he wasn't that large, bulky more than anything. Still, the mindset was there, slight undercurrent to an otherwise affable young man.

"Be that as it may, Ozzie, I'm not as concerned about your relationship with Renata as with what random details you may have subsequently been able to dredge up. Whom else she knew, people she may have known but didn't seem comfortable with. Maybe some guy who kept hitting on her, that sort of scenario."

"I can't think… I've tried to. The homicide guy, er, curly hair…"

"Sergeant Meierhoff. He's a friend of mine."

"Yeah, Meierhoff, that was him. Anyway, he asked me the same questions. But I'm sorry, nobody. Rennie was friendly to just about everybody. She never said anything negative to people. I even kidded her about it. You know, friendly teasing." Ozzie frowned, pain at the loss.

"When you kidded her, was there anyone in particular?"

"You know, yeah, now that you mention it. That guy, hmm… Mac I think, her next door neighbor."

"Eddie Macintyre?"

"Yeah, him," Ozzie looked off, remembering, sipped his drink. "I guess he asked her out or whatever, two, three times. More than that. She told him she was already seeing somebody."

"Somebody meaning you?"

A nervous smile, embarrassed. "Uh, yeah, me."

"And what did Mac tell her?"

"That she shouldn't be wasting time with, uh, you know, a fat guy." Ozzie's face red again, reluctant to refer to himself that way, even in the second hand.

"That's pretty rude, if you want my opinion," I told him. "But what did she say to that?"

"That I was, um, a thousand times nicer than anybody she'd known in ages so what did he know, huh?"

"Did Mac quit pestering her?"

"Mostly. He kept…" Ozzie glanced around, ensuring we weren't overheard. "I don't know if I should be saying this…"

"Look, Ozzie, I'm here for one thing and one thing only. I want to find the man who murdered Renata. Anything you tell me is for that purpose and nothing else. I don't have a secondary agenda, okay?"

"Okay, so Mac kept asking Rennie if she wanted some blow. But she'd never touch drugs, ever."

"Blow as in speed, coke?"

"I think meth, but you know, it's just a guess. He's kind of a weird dude, scary sometimes."

"I interviewed him, and I'd agree. Someone to avoid spending time with."

Ozzie nodded. "Friend of mine has the same history class as Mac, said he's flunking out big time."

"You're right to be circumspect, though," I told him. "Talking about a fellow student doing hard drugs isn't smart, especially at a conservative school like Saint Vincent. But what you tell me is confidential and nobody here on campus will ever know of it. Only the cops and only those cops in charge of the murder investigation, rest assured."

"That's good," Ozzie said, with more confidence. It was difficult for a shy kid to come out with things about other students. He'd likely been teased unmercifully about his weight when he was younger and signs were evident that he still felt the stings. And though he'd obviously be proud to date a girl as pretty as Renata Martinez, he'd also be out of tune as well, thinking in his deepest of hearts that he was unworthy of her attention. Now she was gone, lost from him in the worst way possible. No doubt he was still somewhat askew about her, uncomfortable even in remembrance.

I privately hoped Lopez the best, and that someone else would come along in time. "Let's change the subject, Ozzie. Okay?"

"Sure. Finished with classes today. Plenty of time. Go ahead."

"I understand you had it rough as a kid, Fifth Ward, gangs and all."

He sat back a bit, blinked. He hadn't felt that one coming. Still, he seemed to take it in stride. "Yeah. My mom did her best with us. I got an older brother, a kid sister. My dad…" He paused. "I don't know where my dad is. We think he's gone back to Mexico."

I reached out, patted him on the arm. "That's okay, Ozzie. Lots of people have a tough start in life. But look at yourself now. College degree this June."

"Yeah. Wasn't for my mom, I don't know where I'd be."

"Your mom? She good?"

He smiled, feeling better. "Yeah. She's got this great job now, bakery manager. And my sister got married last year, a nice guy, never been in trouble, ever. All okay there, y'know."

"Your brother. What about him?"

Ozzie shrugged, regretful. "Huntsville, ten to twenty. Armed robbery."

"Sorry."

"Hey, Manolo had his chance. He's smart, got good grades in high school, graduated even."

"But the gangs grabbed him."

"Yeah. Those fu… those…" and then quiet, avoiding curses in such a sedate environment.

I took it forward. "Sergeant Meierhoff told me Barrio Colombia," not wanting to reveal that it was actually the faculty priest Dan Gibson who'd given me that little item.

"Yeah, BC, those…"

"They bother you much any more?"

"Naw. Mom moved to a better part of town when she got her new job, more money, y'know. After Manolo got sentenced, they never came around again." He gathered himself. "Don't believe what other people say, Mr. King. Not all us Mexicans are crooks and lazy bums. Most aren't, in fact."

I smiled. "I know. I just wish more people knew that." I patted his arm again. "I don't have anything more to chat with you about, Ozzie. I really appreciate your spending time. You've got my card, call me if anything comes up." I paused, looked him in the eye. "And I know it's not pleasant, Renata being gone."

We stood up, shook. Ozzie Lopez breathed deeply, sighed. "I still dream about her, I hoped we… well, you know."

"My advice to you is this, Ozzie. Never forget her, but still, someday, move on. Another will come."

He thought a bit, smiled. "I hope you're right, Mr. King. But right now I can only think about Rennie."

Chapter 27

Tony Vee and I were playing in a golf tourney at *The Ship*. This was ironic because I've never actually played a round of golf in my life. Not that it matters, as we weren't playing golf as much as we were bashing a golf ball at random around the inside of a bunch of interconnected wooden buildings.

The Ship is a bar, sort of, keeping irregular hours and even more irregular clientele. The beer is cold and cheap and patrons are a fun mix of Houston oddballs—musicians, painters, newspaper reporters, attorneys, an occasional cop and random private detective scum. The Ship is also a real life boat storage and repair shop that performs excellent work. The fact that the place is miles from navigable water seems of little concern. Owners trailer their precious cargoes up the freeway just to let the shipwrights perform their magic.

The property is cobbled together from several old frame storehouses and such, indiscriminate size and purpose, connected via hallways and open gardens, a business that seems to have grown much of its own accord. The owner, Dalton Envers, is an old time jazz pianist whose family left him a lucrative boating facility. Dalton retains a small staff of loyal workers and the place's boat repair reputation prevails.

Dalton also hosts jazz concerts and opened a bar in the front building mainly to support the music. He tolerates rock groups too, their louder music subjugated to another building to the rear of the property, but hardcore jazz musicians and buffs from all over the Southwest come to The Ship for sessions. And occasionally, to partake in impromptu and insane indoor golf tournaments that the place hosts. Nobody knows why.

How the tournament works is that you each toss a ten, maybe a twenty into the kitty and pick a club from a basket of old nine-irons. Play starts alongside the main bar, golfers teeing off from one of those rubber putting practice things, hopefully driving the ball out the back door into a small courtyard, then into the larger concert area, across to the warehouse, which marks the course turn and where everyone stops for a fresh beer. Next, down a hallway through the stoner room where jazz musicians gather to jam, play poker and where late night smoke is green and intense, out to the courtyard again, finishing back at the bar with a putt into the cup.

Par for the one-hole course is twelve. Or ten maybe. Nobody knows that either. Nor cares. Windows are sometimes broken, but there's a fund. Players also get hit a lot, but no compensation is provided for that misfortune. The winner keeps half the pot (the money, not the weed), buys the losers a round and the rest goes into the waitress tip jar. It makes little sense, but the real game of golf doesn't make sense either and that hasn't prevented vast sums from being spent on it annually.

"Fore!" I called out. I was in the warehouse and aiming at a ball that I assumed to be mine although nobody really kept score or paid much attention to whose ball was being hit. The ball was stuck against a wooden joist and I had to stand crossways to swing. A difficult lie, made even more tricky because everyone else was hovering, drinking beer and giving rude advice.

"You don't have to fucking say *fore* here," Tony Vee told me, just as I was stabbing at the ball.

I ineptly hit the ball sideways and the damn thing only bounced a couple feet. But I caught a lucky tilt in the concrete floor and the ball rolled right out of the warehouse and headed merrily down the hall toward the stoner zone. Perfect. I looked up at Tony and smiled. "Five, then."

"Beginner's fucking luck," he declared, talking around his cigar. Tony strode over to where his ball lay. Watching Tony hold a too-short club in his meaty fists and stoop over the ball like Godzilla perusing an army tank was amusing. But Tony actually plays genuine golf, and quite well. He swung briskly and drove his ball straight down the hallway with terrific velocity, where it rattled around and apparently bounced off the smokers sitting in their specially reserved room.

"Hey, the fuck!" A cry of pain from an invisible target. "You guys watch it! We're tryin' ta chill here!"

We all laughed.

Bill Tebaldi, a petroleum engineer and real life scratch golfer was next. His stroke was less vicious than Tony's and precise, the ball nicely chipped.

There were only four players tonight and we all made it through the combination jazz session and smoking room without much hazard. Tony ordered a round of beer for any who claimed devastating injury from his ball, which of course turned out to be everyone sitting there, listening to an old *Cream* album. Their smokes had magically disappeared but just playing through got me a contact high anyway.

A *Houston Chronicle* sports writer named Jarvis Hinton won. At least we think he won. We all congratulated Hinton as though he'd just been victorious in the British Open at Old St. Andrew's. Hinton is a tall, thin black guy and he bowed gracefully to us. "Yet another indication of my superior African heritage."

"Shit," Tebaldi laughed. "Cheated three times."

"Just taking my mulligans. Check the scorecard if you don't believe me."

Scorecards for a golf game at The Ship? *Yeah, right.*

Chapter 28

It was a little after ten and the weather had chilled to about eighty. Tony and I sat on an old fashioned wooden swing on the front porch of The Ship. We were side by side but had placed ourselves as far apart as possible, like a teenage couple being surveilled by the girl's father just inside the house, peering out the front widow.

Tony and I both laid off the beer, he drinking Ozarka spring water, myself a Coke. "Fun game tonight," I said.

"Least nobody got killed."

"There is that."

We lazily swung back and forth, more from random body movement than deliberate intent. A local rock band had started their gig in the barn area behind us and we could hear the bass rhythm. We earlier watched them set up and they looked about twelve years old. Like most clubs, patrons at The Ship become younger as the evening proceeds, the 30ish golf crazies gradually replaced by kids whom I knew had been carefully ID'd as at least twenty-one, but didn't seem much older than the band.

"Wanna go back and listen?" Tony asked.

"Naw."

"Mind if I smoke?"

"Naw."

Tony retrieved a leather case from his jacket, took out a small cigar, considered it a while, put it back. "Too much work."

"Golf wears you out."

"A considerable challenge," Tony remarked. "The course at The Ship, not quite Pebble Beach, though."

Tony and I sat quietly a while, then he said, "Street talk is you've been hangin' with the Perdon cousins, Ricardo and Angel." He pronounced the name correctly, *Anhel*.

"Christ. I went through this crap with Meierhoff. Now you?"

"Perdons work for Julie Cards. Of course you know that."

I sipped my Coke, stayed quiet.

"Julie Cards' real name is Julio Cardozo," he said.

"I know that too."

"Julie Cards is into all sorts of crap."

"And you're not?" I countered.

"Point taken."

Tony half turned toward me, spoke just above a whisper. "Rumor that the girl, Cheryl, Cherie, whoever she is? Went through all that shit with her crazy stepsister? You were down with that. Rumor she's mixed up with Julie Cards."

I sighed. It was inevitable that Cheryl's name would eventually surface as connected with Julio Cardozo. "Do me a favor," I asked. "Don't pass it on about Cheryl Stern. She's had enough bad mojo come her way."

"Won't say a word, dude. But way I heard, Cardozo's her real father."

I looked out across the skyline. "You know what that would mean, it becomes general knowledge?"

"A'course. Cardozo's made enemies. Most gangs won't touch a family member, but some don't give a shit."

"Which is why nobody needs to speculate further on that," I said.

"Nobody'll ever hear it from me, dude. You and I are tight. You know that, Mitch."

"I know."

"Maybe you wanna tell me how you're connected?"

"You ask a lot of questions for a guy who's so large."

"I'm just a big curious kid, wants to know stuff."

"I happened to be there when Cheryl needed somebody last year. Meierhoff was with me, too. You know all that. She phoned me last week, asked for help again."

"What about?"

"Nobody," I said. "Nobody knows this except the Perdon cousins, other insiders."

"Lips sealed, dude."

"Cardozo had a stroke, a bad one. He's essentially paralyzed, can't speak, nobody knows for certain whether he's still there inside, or just an empty shell."

"Jesus," Tony said. "If word got out…"

I nodded. "A takeover war. Lots of blood."

"So the Perdon boys are running things now?"

I shook my head. "Cheryl is. With their help, of course."

"Christ. She's what, twenty?"

"Eighteen actually. But she's a natural leader. How and why I have zero idea. Of course, the Perdons are the organization and give orders to others. Cheryl's stepped in, learned the ropes, making more and more decisions. She's also taking the business legit."

Tony chuckled. "Gangsta gal. Who woulda thunk it. And you're what?"

"I'm nothing. Cheryl trusts me, so we talk occasionally."

"And Julie Cards?"

"He just sits in a wheelchair next to her," I said. "Sometimes he cries."

Chapter 29

It was well into July and things had quieted down. No more problems with Barrio Colombia, nothing heard from George Burgess.

The new BMW X3 was running beautifully and I even managed to operate the GPS and touchscreen computer sufficiently well to totally foul myself up when driving, necessitating several quick curbside stops and refresher tutorials before I dared venture forth again.

Such is our life now, enslaved to the computer as we were once bound in serfdom to the TV. I was as much hooked as any other person living in the modern era. Of course my job requires that I be proficient with all the modes of communication these days, internet and email and smartphone. Everything is interdependent and networked out the wazoo. Price we pay for entrance to the business community of the twenty-first century.

Part of this price being that I'd ordered two biometric safes to install in the X3, same as I had for the old Toyota, except the new safes had all the goodies, opened with a fingerprint or touch pattern or combination, whichever. The 4Runner, bless her soul, was now happily ensconced as the support vehicle for my computer business, Carolyn darting all over town on rescue missions for our clients. I'd used the safes for firearms and private data, and now Carolyn was storing backup modules and similar junk.

Which left my Bimmer prey to mischief, so the new safes were needed. One was fairly small and I'd position it just behind the passenger seat where I could reach back and open it while driving. That safe would hold a spare pistol and ammo, extra magazines.

The second safe was larger and accessible from the tailgate, and there I'd store cameras and other pricey gear.

FedEx delivered the two safes so I called Apollo Paint and Body, and set up the installation. Both safes would be anchored into the frame with heavy bolts.

Next I phoned Kate. "May I buy you dinner tonight, Miz Morley?"

"Delighted. Where did you have in mind?"

"Pizza Pete is running a special and I've got the coupon. Right now that's all I can afford."

"Changed my mind. I'm tied up tonight. All week. All month."

"Okay, got me," I said. "How about *La Mora*?"

"Sounds good. And the occasion?"

"Well, I kind of need a shuttle ride, switch of cars and so on."

"It'll cost you big time. I may even order dessert. What's the plan?"

"I'm having new storage safes put into the X3. Nice night, got the MG's top down. Can you come here, take the MG and follow me to the car shop? I'll leave the Bimmer and we'll take the MG for our fine Houston dining experience."

"So I have to use a British left-hand shift? I may grind the gears."

"Don't worry," I told her. "MG gears grind all the time anyway. They're designed to do that."

* * *

Kathryn came by the house. She was dressed business casual as I was, pressed jeans and a pullover. "We look okay for La Mora?" she asked.

"Yeah. But if they object, I've got my gun."

Kate rolled her eyes. "Always with the guns."

"Sorry."

"That's okay," she said. "I was just kidding. Somewhat."

We played car tag along US-59 freeway during rush hour, always a thrill in itself, but we did manage to get to the shop before they closed. We took the cranky old MG back into the city, stopped off at the semi-underground bar *Marfreless* for a drink, and then headed over to the restaurant.

La Mora is a cozy Tuscan spot located in an old house in the Montrose, not far from Kate's place. I called ahead to verify a reservation and we drove there, happy, Kate alternately messing with the radio and mussing with my hair.

It was early and a Tuesday night, so we got a nice table in a converted breakfast nook.

We deferred a cocktail, but I did peruse the wine list as if I were a seasoned oenophile. It's a ritual every man performs when in a decent restaurant, especially if endeavoring to impress the lady. We picked a vintage California Calcareous Vineyard red and the sommelier presented me the bottle as though it were a relic from the Crusades.

I nodded, he popped the cork, gave it to me to examine. I took it, smiled, laid the cork on the table. I knew you could sniff it to see if the wine was corked, but I skipped this procedure. There's only so far I'll take a thing for the sake of good manners. I had this silly fleeting notion that were I to actually sniff the cork, everyone in the restaurant would stand up, point and laugh at me for falling for the famous "smell the cork" ruse, like a *Saturday Night Live* skit.

But I lucked out. Nobody erupted in guffaws. The sommelier simply poured me a dollop and I tasted it, smiling all the time like the greeter at a Vegas casino. Approval noted, Kate and I were rewarded half a glass each and were finally left to ourselves, having passed the tricky taste test ritual to the satisfaction of the house, and having declared the bottling very drinkable indeed.

"Wine's good," Kate told me, confirming the decision.

We were soon given a basket of fresh bread and a small plate of spiced olive oil. Kate dipped a small chunk of bread in the garlicky oil and nibbled, sipped the wine again.

I poured us more.

"Not too much," she said. "You get me plastered and I won't enjoy dessert. And you're driving, so you need to keep it to a low roar yourself."

"Agreed."

"What is this?" she laughed. "Mister Agreeable night?"

"Hey, I shelled out big time for the new Bimmer. I'm celebrating before the next payment comes due."

Then the delicious Tuscan feast arrived and we even quit agreeing. Instead we silently inhaled the food as though we were at the Oakland Raiders training table. Kate had some sort of trout almondine and I had the veal piccata. We shared our entrees and shared a wonderful evening as well.

Afterward we were sitting back and relaxing when the waiter brought me the dessert menu. I waved him off, remembered and handed the menu to Kate. "Sorry. You mentioned dessert? Said you'd leave room."

She shook her head. "Just coffee."

I looked at the waiter. "Two espressos, if you please."

We sipped the delicious steamy brew while I paid the tab, left a nice tip.

We squeezed ourselves into the MG and I drove as carefully as possible, considering there was half a bottle of wine inside me and a lovely woman sitting beside. Kate had brought her swimsuit so we planned for another round of poolside relaxation at my place, a snooze.

It was a glorious evening and still balmy for the hour. We took Montrose Boulevard straight north and picked our way through traffic, on the way to the Heights where I lived.

I stopped for the red light at Washington, a busy intersection. An old pickup was riding my bumper so I waved him around when the light changed. I was really in no hurry because Kate and I had all the time in the world and our friendship was there between us, always.

The gunfire was over before I knew it had begun.

Chapter 30

Throughout the next few days, fragments of it came back to me in disconnected segments like quickly cut scenes in a horror movie illuminated by lightning flashes.

Pickup truck beside us.

Rattle of rusty muffler, stink of fumes.

Ski mask.

Shotgun barrel.

Burst of flame.

Blood.

And more blood.

Chapter 31

I was in and out of it for more than three weeks. They saved my left arm but I'd need two or three refits, stainless implants, plus more surgeries to make everything whole. Even then they said I might never regain full use and would perhaps require more work in the future. My left eardrum was damaged from the blast as well, but they felt I'd regain most of my hearing there. If only there were procedures for repairing the soul.

Meierhoff and Duggan were constant visitors. One of the ICU nurses told me that Meierhoff had sat holding my uninjured hand for hours at a time, talking quietly to me, assuring me I'd be fine. Of that, I remembered nothing.

Apparently a priest from my church came by twice, as well as Tony Vee, Cheryl Stern, a few other visitors, all of these appearances foggy and nebulous, dreamlike.

My ex-wife and daughter were in the middle of a vacation to Japan. She offered to fly back but was persuaded otherwise by Joe Duggan, who promised her that I'd be okay soon and that he'd look after me.

My attorney Donna Boudreaux was awesome, taking care of everything. She arranged to board Krazy Kat at Fat Cat Flats, had my neighbor Ernie Banks keep an eye on the house and collect the mail, and Donna even picked up the X3 from the shop and put it safely into my carport at home. But the MG? I told her to have it junked as soon as it was released from the cop garage. I never wanted to see the thing again.

Eventually my major injuries cleared and I was taken off the critical list, but they kept me in ICU. Pain was still digging deep into my left shoulder and I went from a fast rehab to a second surgery and back to the intense pain with more rehab to follow. Their intent was to get all the operations completed as quickly as possible, before my bones and tissues healed wrongly, and they had the best for me in mind, but it was still hell on wheels. Sometimes even morphine wouldn't be enough and I'd just lie there, hooked up to monitors and drains and drips, seething in pain despite maxing out on the good stuff.

All the surgery and painful rehab and the drugs they pumped into my body prevented me from thinking straight, a regrettable byproduct of trauma care. But through it all, one thing still remained in my rat-infested brain, one thought preeminent. That my beloved Kathryn Morley was dead, and that she was dead on my watch.

* * *

A month later I finally got through all the surgeries and they moved me to an urgent care ward near the ER. I was at a point where my pain rating on that annoying little *How Do You Feel?* smiley face poster on the wall would show a *seven*, meaning I'd live but not especially relish that fact for the next few weeks.

Of course Meierhoff and Duggan updated me on the investigation, but I also kept forgetting they'd even been in my room and therefore asked them the same questions over and over. It was only later that I stopped asking about Kate Morley. Her death was the locus of my emotional despair and I suppose my brain was withholding that truth from its inner core until I was able to withstand it. If ever I could.

That, and nights were the worst. I kept reliving the shooting and dreaming that we'd escaped, were driving happily and sedately on an endless street named Montrose Boulevard, no stopping the glory road, no pain, no death, just carelessly meandering along a quiet and magical avenue with no other cars and no annoying traffic signals to even slow us down. Then I'd wake up crying, reaching out for Kate, pulling at my surgical tape and drains, and it would start all over again.

* * *

Eventually they transferred me to a private room and left me pretty much alone. I still had the physical therapist torturing me twice a day, but I actually began to look forward to her stern and unflinching style. This was of course intentional, as she wanted her patients to fear her as much as Nurse Ratched and therefore work hard enough that she'd maybe never come back. Still, I was getting better. I regained all the feeling except for some oddly numb areas just under the bicep and over my shoulder blade. And I worked my way toward sixty percent mobility.

One afternoon Joe Duggan and David Meierhoff came into my room, and pulled up chairs instead of just hovering. I knew it was time for our heart to heart.

"How you feeling, big guy?" Joe asked.

"Hanging."

"Ready to talk?" Meierhoff smiled.

"Yeah. I'm not forgetting stuff any longer. Sure. Let's do it."

"Some of what we got to tell you, not gonna be good to hear," Joe warned.

"Go ahead. Now or never."

Joe was his usual abrupt self. "We're guessing it was the right-hand drive on your MG that made them aim for her. She had short hair. Yours was kinda long, and it was dark. They focused on who they thought would be the driver and hit her instead. You just got the leftovers."

Damn vanity trap, that idiotic British monstrosity! I just had to have it, had to make believe I was Jackie Stewart, pretend I was someone better than my own rotten self. Nevertheless, I absorbed what Joe told me, wanted more. "Got any leads?" I asked.

"None. Truck a'course was stolen, no prints. All the bad guys wear gloves now."

"How did they find me? How did they know where to look for the car? I was off my normal routes."

Duggan paused, uncomfortable, and I knew he was holding something back, something he didn't want me to know. He glanced at Meierhoff, and David took up the remainder. "Mitch, we found another bug on the MG. Same model as the one on your old 4Runner."

God in heaven, I thought. *When would it end?* I'd been immersed in a vat of self-importance and hadn't given it a flash of consideration. Taking ten seconds to scan the MG would have been the smart thing, but I was too involved in being trippy and sporty. So Kate's death was doubly on my head. Mine alone. I lay there, nobody spoke, routine hospital noise around us.

"You gonna be okay?" Joe asked.

"Eventually, I guess. I'm not so sure now."

Meierhoff reached out, rubbed my good shoulder. "We love you, don't ever forget that."

"In the platonic way of course," Joe added, which made us all laugh.

Afterward, "So it was Burgess in the truck?" I asked.

Joe shrugged. "Don't know. Had to be at least two people, one to drive, one to, ah…"

Another uncomfortable silence. Then, "Maybe he paid somebody, wasn't in the truck at all," Meierhoff said. "No prints on the bug. Wiped clean. Still, it was ordered from the same place as the earlier one, sent to the same post office drop."

"What next?" I asked.

"We don't know," David replied. "We've got a twenty-four seven guard on you, only uniform people Joe and I know personally. There are bolos out on Burgess, of course, FBI and everyone else looking. We've done what we can for now. In the meantime, dude, you get well, okay?"

"Yeah," Joe added. "Stop chasing nurses and tend to that arm. That's an order. And Burgess will turn up eventually. He'll fuck up and we'll grab him."

Maybe, I thought. *Maybe*. But it would still be too late for Kathryn Morley.

Chapter 32

My physical wounds were healing, but the scars on my mind and spirit remained fresh and acidic as I sought to blame myself for Kate's death.

The therapist and doctor ganged up on me a couple days prior, helped me stand a few minutes at the side of my bed. It was a small and notable achievement, but the pain in my left shoulder was still blasting me and I was dizzy continually, too weak to do much other than wobble between the two muscular physical therapists they sent to help. I was pretty sick and felt like total crap.

So I reacted in the most inane way possible, a spoiled rotten brat, taking out my vehemence upon the hospital crew. I knew it was rude and nasty and wrong, but I kept it up nonetheless. I felt worthless and wanted everyone around me to feel the same. The fact that I was still too shaky to stand on my own meant bland diet and IVs and catheters and bedpans, all of which made me even more incensed and cranky.

I used all the tactics available to become the worst patient in hospital history, venting upon the helpful and concerned staff. I lashed out at doctors and nurses, their aides, orderlies, and even the quiet and efficient folks who came through the room and cleaned up twice a day. The cop sitting protective guard outside my door stayed beyond earshot and my friends mostly quit visiting. Even Meierhoff and Duggan were scarce. But they had a choice and the people working here did not.

As my energy gradually returned, I ramped up the cursing and complaints until someone finally called in an air strike that would do justice to the Vietnam era bombings known as *Arc Light*.

The squadron of B-52s that soared into my room that afternoon was cleverly disguised as a woman wearing a white lab coat. She had surgical greens beneath, a green hairnet cap that sat askew, stretch green booties over her shoes. There was a stethoscope slung over her shoulder, a badge *A. Colhoun, MD* pinned to her coat and teeny splatters of blood on her surgical togs.

She said nothing, just stuck a business card in my hand. It read *Alice Colhoun, MD, MBBS, FACS, PhD*, with lots more alphabet soup strung afterward and that she was Associate Director of Trauma Surgery for Memorial Hermann Hospital. She had more titles than the Queen and she was pissed at me.

"Mr. King, my people tell me that you're a real jackass. Are you naturally a prick or is this some sort of weird drug reaction? I want to know because I need to fix it and fix it now."

Words failed and I just looked at her. She was short, quite small in fact, pretty, my age or older, trim red hair crammed beneath the cap, green eyes, a linear face, high sharp cheekbones. She spoke with a clear, accented voice, Australian maybe?

Doctor Colhoun pulled the stethoscope off her shoulder and for a second I thought she was going to smack me with it. Instead she began to briskly twirl the long plastic tube around her outstretched forefinger, letting it wrap and unwrap, back and forth. Her glare was intense.

"Well—" I began, but she cut me off.

"Don't! I worked on you when you came into hospital and we got you out of danger, serious shotgun wounds but survivable, vital organs somehow missed. At six each morning, before you're even awake, I go through the charts of every patient and consult with staff, and you appear to be progressing nicely. Doctor al-Najeer is tops and he'll let me know if you need anything medically." She stopped the twirling briefly to wipe her brow with a sleeve.

The stethoscope spun again and I kept my eye on the swinging bell. It could hurt. She went on. "I just finished a five hour surgery, trying to put a woman back together who was run over by a big lorry, a semi as you Yanks call it. She's not going to make it, but we did our best." Colhoun looked straight at me. "Regarding your case, I spoke with Detective Meierhoff a few minutes ago, so I know what happened. Your friend was murdered and you blame yourself. Correct?"

"Maybe. I—"

"Fuck it!" she said, her accent making it sound like *fook*. "I'm bone tired and I don't give a fuck whether you're carrying the sins of ten fucking generations of sons and daughters on your fucking shoulders! You will not fucking take it out on my staff and the other professionals on this ward! You will shut your fucking mouth and heal and let these people do their job! How you waste your miserable fucking life after you're discharged is your own goddamn business. But while you're here you will act like a responsible human being! Do I make myself absolutely fucking clear?"

"Perfectly."

"Good." She stopped twirling, for which I was extremely grateful. Then she flipped the stethoscope back over her shoulder and extended her hand. "I'm Alice Colhoun and I run this little fiefdom. You behave and I might let you out of here and send you home someday."

We shook. "Sorry," was the most I could offer.

"That's all right, so long as we understand things."

A cheeping from Colhoun's lapel pocket, pager blinking its red eye in time with the sound. "Shit," Colhoun said, pushing a button to silence the thing. "I'm overdue to scrub in, assist on a stabbing. And I have another surgery scheduled later. But I had to forego my half hour coffee break to come up here and ream out your bloody ass." She offered me a faint smile. "Get yourself well, Mr. King. Okay?"

"Okay, promise." I tried to say more and ask her to call me Mitch, but she was already gone. I thought about her, liking the way she said *fook* and *sheduled*.

Chapter 33

Home never looked better.

David Meierhoff and my lawyer Donna Boudreaux got me there without much red tape, as I'm guessing that the hospital was glad to see me go. I was walking okay now, a little weak, still had my left arm in a sling. There was a strict food and drink regimen plus lots of medication ahead.

We rolled up in Donna's big Dodge pickup and damned if there weren't yellow ribbons and a small mob waiting. "Who did this?" I asked, amazed and at the same time secretly happy.

"Your neighbor Ernie is mostly to blame," Donna told me. "He insisted on the party. David and I just wanted to slow down, dump you out by the curb."

Ernie was there, Malcolm too, both Andrew and Carolyn from the computer shop. Joe Duggan also stopped by but he got a call and had to return to HPD. "Take care, dude," he said, driving away.

I didn't look for Tony Vee because I knew he was golfing in Florida. And my ex-wife Sandra had returned from her Japanese vacation then promptly fell getting out of the taxi, dislocating her shoulder. But everyone else who counted was there. As I eased myself down from the truck's cab, I was pummeled so much that I nearly fell over, not yet having my legs. Everybody was drinking beer, but they stuck a bottle of spring water in my hand instead. I tried to conceal the disappointment.

"Welcome home, Mitch!" Ernie said, toasting me by raising his beer.

Malcolm did the same, added, "Good to see ya, honky."

After some general hoopla and more beer (none of which I was allowed), the party moved inside, where Krazy Kat was sporting a little yellow bow on his collar. He ran to me and I slowly bent down, managed to reach his head, petted him in joy at the reunion.

The kitchen counter was laden with rows of nutritious, healthy and exquisitely boring packaged foods. "More in the fridge and freezer," Donna told me. "We want to make sure you get the right stuff and don't have to work too hard to fix your meals, either."

"I really don't deserve this," I said, partly believing it. "But I'm happy to have friends such as you. Thanks!"

"Don't mention it," Meierhoff told me. "Especially when you get the bill."

After everyone left, I thought about what had just occurred, how I saw things of late. I'd undergone a harrowing event, loss of a dear friend, near death on my part, slow recuperation. But I was done with the self hatred for now, hopefully forever. A change long overdue.

Lying there in the hospital bed, sometimes in considerable physical pain, always in dark emotional turmoil, I'd plunged into the depths and somehow risen from the ashes of my despair. And no, I bore little resemblance to that mythical bird, but I still played the Phoenix inside, where it counted.

I think it was in some portion due to my ongoing conversations with the trauma surgeon from hell, Doctor Alice Colhoun. I'd asked doctor al-Najeer about her, found she wasn't actually from hell, but in fact New Zealand. Why I enjoyed her company I really didn't know, but when I'd first met her, the Kiwi accent made me smile for the first time in weeks. As to how close New Zealand is to heaven or hell, I can't say.

* * *

There was that afternoon I was sitting in a decidedly uncomfortable chair next to my hospital bed, managing to not tangle my IV too much and absorbing mindless TV in the persona of Judge Judy. There was a knock on my door and not waiting for permission to enter, in came Doctor Colhoun. "Am I bothering you, Mr. King?"

"No, come on in," I said, clicking the judge into electron oblivion. "What's up?"

"If you say *What's up, Doc?* I'm leaving forthwith."

"Never crossed my mind." And of course it had, but I thought better of it. I certainly didn't want to be smacked by her stethoscope.

She perched on the edge of my bed, seemed to relax a bit. She was wearing standard issue surgical greens, no cap today, no green booties, no blood. Just short-cropped reddish hair on top and white-soled sneakers at the bottom. I took a moment, realized how pretty she was despite the lines of fatigue in her face. I also noted her petite and slender figure, decided this was certain indication that I was indeed recovering. Since that awful night I'd not thought about beauty in any form until just now.

"I think I was somewhat rough on you, t'other day. I read you the absolute riot act."

"No, don't give it a second's thought. You were spot on and I deserved it all."

"Perhaps. But I talked to your friend David again, the homicide detective? Talked more than once. He told me things about you, that you've had it bad, not necessarily of your own making."

I shrugged, and that gesture sent a spiral of pain through my left shoulder. *Don't try that again for a while, Mitch.*

"Raw deals have seem to come my way of late, I'll admit. But as to whether I'm responsible? I'm not one to judge."

"How are you really feeling, Mr. King? Are you about ready to head home?"

I shook my head. "Some bad nights still, drainage. Maybe a couple weeks. But again, I'm not the one to make that decision. And please call me Mitch."

"Deal, if you call me Alice."

And so, strange bedfellows (just one bed, mine), the beginning of a friendship. Alice Colhoun would come by, chat. We'd talk about our childhood, school, life in general.

Turned out her upbringing was fascinating, a true world citizen. "Family emigrated to New Zealand in the nineteenth century," she told me. "Sheep farmers from Scotland. And don't laugh! Sheep farming is good business."

"No laughing here," I said, trying not to. She herself suppressed a chuckle.

"Go on," I said. "About the sheep." And we both laughed.

"To hell with the sheep," she came back. "Can't stand 'em, want to know the truth. But it did get us pretty toasty well off, financially. Big ranch on the South Island, near Dunedin and Otago Harbour. Granddad was offered a mint for the farm, sold it and moved to the city, never looked back."

"And your parents?"

"City folk. Dad's a pediatrician, Mum's an attorney. I've got an older brother, he's flight instructor in the Royal New Zealand Air Force."

"And you? Always the doctor route?"

She nodded. "Yes. Never wanted to be anything else. Had my sights set on pediatrics like Dad, but during my internship I got hooked on cuttin' and stichin'."

"Med school where? New Zealand?"

"Uh, huh. Both Otago university then Otago med school, the same. After that, house surgeon in Auckland—house surgeon is what you call a *resident* here in the States. Next spent three years in England, big hospital in Bristol, a fellowship. Learned a lot, read for my doctorate."

"Relationships on the way?"

"Sure. Boyfriends here and there, nothing special. Then along came a neurologist in Bristol, nice guy from Dublin. Whirlwind marriage, whirlwind divorce." She spun her fingertip in the air. "A redhead gal with Scots heritage succeeding with a redhead Irishman? Not going to happen in this lifetime."

"I understand that side of the coin. I was married, too."

"Saw on your chart you were single now."

I thought about this, her taking time to look up my marital status. Anyway. "Yeah. My ex lives in Arizona—Scottsdale—and she's remarried. My daughter's fourteen. Good kid."

"Next time you talk with them, tell them we're getting you well, okay?"

"Will do."

I changed the subject. "So what brought you to Houston?"

"Houston's among the top trauma centers worldwide, you already know that. There was an opening, I applied, they offered to move me here, lots more money. So I jumped at it." She shrugged. "How could I not? Started out fast, last year they kicked me up to associate director." She tossed it off as if it meant no never-mind, her being so esteemed. But I knew what it meant, her career, and respected her for it, someone so young.

"Nestled in with the Yanks, eh?"

"Haw!" she laughed. "Not the bloody hell in Texas! Took me about three minutes to learn that Yankee meant something different to you folks!"

"You like it here? Aside from troublesome patients, that is."

"I do. People in Texas are like those at home, independent. We Kiwis do tend to be a tad more progressive, though."

"Yeah. Texas is pretty red."

"Red, like Red Russians? Communists?" She smiled crookedly, confused.

"The opposite. A few years ago, the famous political commentator Tim Russert charted the political leanings of each state on a map of the US. He used a color scheme where the more conservative and mostly Republican states were red, the liberal and Democrat-leaning were blue, and the colors stuck. So now it's red for conservative, blue for liberal."

"I learn something new about this insane but delightful nation every day," she admitted.

"So now that you're firmly implanted in this crazy country, what do you do when you're not cuttin' and slicin' and demeaning us poor defenseless patients?"

Another smile. "I bought myself a new sailboat last fall. Love to sail."

"I know nothing whatsoever about boats. Don't entertain any distrust or fear of them, simply have zero experience. I'm a full bore landlubber."

"Landlubbers are my speciality," she told me, laughing.

I noted how she gave it the extra syllable, *speciality*. I liked that too, for some reason. "Big boat?" I asked.

"Too big and a single person can't handle it easily. I got a *Beneteau First 20*, small, fast, lots of fun."

"You'll have to show me a photo."

"Photo? Get your ass healed and I'll give you a ride."

After she left, I wondered what sort of ride she meant. Maybe I was getting well after all.

191

Chapter 34

I'd been home about a month and things were moving along. My insurance company had a physical therapist come by each week to check on me, and I really minded the p's and q's. Thankful for my Bowflex, I could set out a series of careful exercises on the left arm, gradually healing, gaining strength. And good news from the orthopedic surgeon. She thought that if I continued to improve, no further surgeries would be warranted. That's always a good thing to hear from a surgeon, even if she wasn't the surgeon from hell.

Speaking of Alice Colhoun, we talked on the phone more and more until I, like Lady Macbeth, screwed my courage to the sticking place and invited her to lunch.

"Where did you have in mind?"

"Enjoy Mexican food?"

"Yes. But do you mean authentic or what you Yanks call Tex-Mex?"

Well, I thought. If she'd moved that far along the Texas food chain, I was in luck. "Either, same restaurant, they have both, *El Tiempo*."

"Huh. I've heard of it, good reviews. Certainly."

"Shall I pick you up at the hospital?"

"God no. Traffic is hideous around the Med Center. I'll meet you there, at the bar. Say, four?"

"Four is good." I verified that we were both headed to the same restaurant, the one on Richmond, as they had several Houston outlets. "Dress is casual," I reminded her.

* * *

Alice was early, her drink half empty when I walked in. "Hi," I said, and she swung around on her barstool, smiled. Today she was in mufti, a plain but clingy sea-green blouse that complemented her red hair, black slacks. The clothes fit her slender figure perfectly.

We shook hands, I sat next to her, glanced at her drink. "Piña colada?"

"Yes. The frozen variety. Cooling off on a warm day."

I nodded to the bartender. "What she's having, please, make mine virgin."

"Still riding the wagon?" she asked.

"Best for my gizzard. I want to avoid more surgery if possible."

She chuckled. "Avoid surgeons as well as surgery?"

"Only most of them. I however seem to have a penchant for the Kiwi variety."

"Haw!" she coughed, swallowing her drink hard against the urge to laugh out loud.

"I hope *Kiwi* isn't an insult. I didn't mean to—"

"It isn't. We call ourselves Kiwis all the time. You Yanks don't need to be so soft tempered. We're pretty rowdy birds, y'know."

We both laughed at that, myself partly subdued in the presence of a fair bit of intelligence and good humor combined. My drink arrived and I paid for both, tipped the bartender and we had the hostess show us a table.

El Tiempo is a regional chain of superb and somewhat upscale Mexican restaurants run by two brothers, sons of the iconic Ninfa Laurenzo, who essentially invented Tex-Mex and created an empire. The restaurant where we sat was airy and bright, plate glass windows overlooking the patio where smokers were banished in accordance with the Houston restaurant code.

There are two general slants to Mexican-theme restaurants. Some have reasonably authentic food, some favor the more popular tacos and nachos, staple for Tex-Mex. Our menu had either in considerable variety. Alice ordered crab enchiladas, I the grilled chicken breast with salsa verde.

"Tell me about your boat. I remember you said it was, what, a twenty-something?"

"Um," Alice replied, munching a big chunk of crab. "Beneteau First 20. Beneteau, French company, makes more sailboats than anybody. They have a class of small sailers, Twenty, Thirty, and so on. The bigger the number, the larger the boat."

"So your is kinda small?"

"Compared with others, I suppose. But big boats require a crew. I want to sail by myself, forget the surgeries, forget the hospital."

"As I said, I'm clueless about sailboats. How big is yours, actually?"

"You Yanks are all about size, aren't you? Texans in particular."

I blushed. "Size isn't the issue. Quality is preferable over quantity. At least that's how I'd personally choose to see it."

That got a laugh. "Accepted, but back to sailing, my boat is somewhat more than six meters, bow to stern."

I just looked at her, blank.

"Forgot. Yanks are still in the stone age about the metric system. Twenty feet, give or take."

"Hey, they call it the English system of measurement. Don't blame us Yanks!"

"English? We don't need those damn pommys sticking their noses in, do we?"

That stopped me cold a moment, then I remembered. "Pommy?" I said. "That's Aussie and Kiwi slang for Brits, right?"

"Correct. Acronym from *Prisoner of Her Majesty*, or pohm. Of course the official and more technical name is *bloody pommy*."

I smiled. "As I remember from an old Aussie pal, it's when British businessmen get sent to Australia or New Zealand, spend all their time complaining about how it's better back home."

"Exactly," she grinned. "They're always loitering in the pub, braying about *Back in England we…* or *Back home we…* and it drives us crazy."

"Got a few of the same here," I told her. "People from New York and such, everything's better back home."

"World is different, people never change."

And to that we toasted ourselves, continued to nibble at the food, then satiated, ordered coffee, chatted.

"How did you get into sailing?"

"When I was at school in Otago, had a boyfriend, introduced me to sailing, fell in love with it. The boyfriend, not so much."

"That happens."

"For certain," she smiled, went on. "Later, when I was at Auckland I joined the Royal Yacht Squadron. Auckland is famous for boating, nicknamed the *City of Sails*."

"Royal Yachts, eh?" I wiggled my eyebrows, Groucho style.

She shook her head. "Not as fancy as you might think, not so's you'd notice. There are all types and levels of sailing, millionaire yachts down to little weekend excursion sailers. I bought into a small boat with some other students. Great fun."

"I love to swim, enjoy the water myself," I told her. "I just don't know boats."

"It grows on you. At sea, even if it's only a klick offshore, fresh air, no worries, sail for hours, drop anchor and jump into the water."

"I understand that part of the world, lots of sharks. Don't you have to watch for them?"

Alice made a dismissive noise, waved. "Sharks you say? They're just big stupid fish. Overrated completely. Not dangerous at all. You're more likely to get bitten by the neighbor's dog."

"I always thought you had to be cautious, that—"

"No problem. We'd even ride 'em."

"Ride them?" I was incredulous.

"Certainly. We'd be swimming around, wait till a medium size shark, say a hammerhead would cruise by, we'd grab that dorsal fin and jump on 'em like a cowboy on a bronco."

"But…"

"Of course, the damn things dive, you have to let go. And their skin is so rough it can scrape you something awful."

"My God," I said. "Riding sharks? I would never—"

Alice Colhoun laughed out loud, rocking back and forth in her chair. "You bloody Yanks will believe anything!"

Chapter 35

I was working on my pool game today, but still had problems getting the left hand to move properly. I'd command my finger to curl and it would rudely ignore the message and stick out straight. So I was affecting an open vee-type grab on the cue shaft instead of the requisite "okay sign" that's formed by arching the forefinger around the cue. And no, my thumbs weren't broken like Fast Eddie Felson in *The Hustler*, either. At least I could get around okay now, all the bandages gone, finally weaned off pain killers. I managed to stay away from bourbon and beer as well. Progress on all fronts.

There was a particularly tough lie, cue ball near the rail and six ball toward the far end of the table. To shoot with the cue ball adjacent a rail, you've got to elevate the butt of the cue and hit the ball at an unnatural angle, and at the same time not accidentally create what's known as a *masse* shot. Normally I had this sort of thing dead on, but muscle memory hadn't yet come into line and everything I did involving my left hand or arm was still clumsy.

I was ready to shoot (and probably miss) when my cellphone beeped, saving me from certain personal embarrassment. I checked, Meierhoff.

"Yeah, David, what's up?"

"Got a lead on your case. Want to hear it now or should I slide by your house later?"

"Lemme sit down." I laid my cue on the pool table, grabbed a nearby chair. "Okay."

"We've got a wit to the original planning and setup for Kate Morley's murder."

"Witness? To the shooting?"

"Not exactly," David replied. "Only the planning. But we're pretty sure it's a good lead and can bring in the shooters with this info."

"Tell me."

"Vice raided a meth lab, dragged in three cookers. One of 'em, Francisco Perez, is a three time loser and he's facing forty to life. Longtime gang member, want to guess which?"

"Barrio Colombia?" I said.

"Yep, BC. And he's plea bargaining for a lighter sentence, no trial, guilty plea for twenty plus. Offered info on the killing in payback."

"And he told you guys what?"

"That he was originally recruited to drive the pickup and knows the shooter, another gangbanger named Castillo Aguilar."

"But he didn't actually do the deed?"

"Nope. Thing is, he was in jail on a misdemeanor warrant when it went down. So he's clear of that charge, but to skip out on the life sentence, he's burning his own brother, Juan. Says Juan drove instead."

"Great! So you've got two gang members to grab."

"Yeah, we've put a warrant on them. If they're still in the area, they'll turn up."

"There has to be more, David."

"There is. The shooter and driver were both recruited by another BC member, Montalvo Santiago. He set up the whole deal, gave them the bug tracker, orders to kill you."

"So there's a pickup for him as well?" I asked.

"Sure is. I'll keep you updated, email you their names and photos soon as we ring off so you have the spelling and all."

"But we know who's actually behind it," I said.

"Yep. George Burgess, of course. Else his prints wouldn't be on the first bug. It all leads straight back to him."

"Thanks, pal. I owe you. Dinner at least."

"No biggie, Mitch. Glad to help. But how you been? I'm so busy lately, no chance to see you. Healing, inside and out?"

"Inside and out, body and spirit both."

Which was true. I was well enough to get back into it. And I now had a mission, a job. Time to hit back. Time to find George Burgess and deal with him.

* * *

I called Tony Vee first. "Want to go make trouble?"

"Sure, I'm game. You got anybody picked out or do we just drive up and down the street, beat on people at random?"

"What say we rout some Barrio Colombia dudes?"

A pause. "Jesus, Mitch. You serious?"

"Serious as Kate Morley's murder."

"Fuck. What d'you know? What happened?"

I filled Tony in on what I'd learned from Meierhoff. "I want to hit them, see if we can ferret out where Burgess might be hiding."

"Get the jump on the cops, eh? They track him down, he goes to jail. You find him, it's Western justice?"

"If you say so."

"Okay. I'm good for this, you know I'll stand by you anytime. But just the two of us?"

"I'm gonna call the Perdon cousins, Ricky and Angel."

"I'd rather have Seal Team Six, but they'll do in a pinch."

"Thanks, Tony."

"I got to ask, you planning to shoot anybody, kill someone, or just do some bashing this time out?"

"Bashing only, unless it goes bad. Still, take the fight to them. They can't do what they did and not expect payback."

"Whatever goes down, I'm with you, pal."

"One, two days, let's meet at my house. Okay?"

"Sure. Let me know when, I'll be there with bells on. And guns."

I next phoned Ricky Perdon, told him I needed help from him and his cousin.

"Barrio Colombia?" Ricky chuckled. "Hell, Angel and me, we jump on them anytime just for fun. We be there when you say, Mitch."

"I need some info, where a couple of them might hang out." I gave him the names. "Santiago in particular."

"Sure. I check, call you."

"How's Julio?" I asked. "Still the same?"

"Same, *ese*. But not the same for long. Doctor said his kidneys, other things, they are going bad."

"I'm sorry for him and sorry especially for Cheryl. Please tell her I care and that I asked."

"I will. And you need us, *ese*, we be there."

* * *

In an old spoof thriller I'd seen on TV years ago, Dean Martin—I think it was Deano—had a safe concealed behind a swing-out pool cue rack. Unable to resist, I'd done the same. I went there now, opened the gun safe, thought about what to bring on my little fact-finding expedition.

Since I didn't hunt nor was into long range shooting, I own mostly handguns. I decided on my new Springfield XD .45, the Tactical model with an extended length barrel. The magazine holds thirteen rounds and if you count one extra in the chamber, it should be plenty. Hell, if I needed more than fourteen shots with .45 plus-P ammo, I should maybe stay home.

I'd been to Marksman range a few times before Kate's murder and the pistol had proven reliable and accurate. I took the loaded gun, two spare magazines, my old familiar Uncle Mike's Kydex belt holster to hold them. A shoulder holster was too painful for me as yet and retrieving the gun would be awkward. Better on the waist, as I wasn't interested in concealment this time anyway. I wore the holster and gun a while, practiced drawing, found I could manage okay.

Nighttime and no word from the Perdons. Tony phoned, I told him we were still on, but didn't have a destination as yet. Soon, I hoped.

* * *

But *soon* was three agonizing days. I ate sparingly, exercised a bit, played pool terribly, tried unsuccessfully to watch TV. I also cleared the pistol and lubed it, reloaded. This I did twice, just to be doing something. And each time I took Tony Vee's gimmicky advice and alcohol-wiped the ammo carefully to erase all fingerprints and DNA, in case I had to shoot someone.

Finally, late Thursday afternoon the call came. "*Ese*," Ricky Perdon's heavy voice. "We got the place. After hour club by Liberty Road, Fifth Ward. Santiago and Aguilar, they members, go there a lot."

After hours clubs are popular among the Hispanic community, other people as well. They operate on a shaky foundation, not permitted to sell booze after 2am in Texas, but byob was technically allowed. Members would therefore have their own bottles to drink from. Legally okay, but many clubs skirt the law, simply selling drinks. With little oversight, gambling, prostitution and fights were common. Shootings. The places could be real crap holes. But if we needed to go there, go there we would.

"When you want to do this?" I asked.

"Tonight okay? We be at your place, mmm, midnight?"

"I'll be ready."

Chapter 36

We held war council around my kitchen table. If you could call it that, four rough and tumble guys, drinking coffee and eating donuts, taking turns to pet Kraze as he circled our legs, trolling for treats.

The after-hours club where we were headed was *La Casa Soledad*. I brought up the address on my laptop, turned the screen so everyone could see. "It's a block off Liberty. Here's the Google Earth photo." The club occupied much of a small strip center. A crude sign over the door with the club's name, and both *Private* and *Privado*. Plate glass windows blacked out and no way to know the interior layout.

"Any idea about inside?" I asked.

"A friend been there," Angel said. "Like a tavern, no difference. Tables and bar. Nothing special."

"Best we can do, I understand," I said. "So Angel, can you cover the bartender, make sure he doesn't call for help?"

"I can."

"What about the door?" Tony asked.

"I have two guns," Angel offered. "I watch the door too." He smiled, pulled back his bulky jacket lapels, showing crossed shoulder holsters, each with a big automatic in them. I thought again of the Shadow and his two .45s, smiled.

My Spanish is execrable, but Tony is fluent. "Tony and I will identify Perez or Santiago if they're there," I said. "Or Aguilar. We'll try to get something out of them, locate George Burgess. That's our main purpose tonight, find Burgess, maybe shake things up on the way."

"What if none of the guys are around?" Tony wanted to know.

I shrugged. "We just play it cool, scare the others a bit, leave."

Meierhoff had emailed me mugshot photos of the wanted men and I put them on the laptop screen, scrolled through. Perez and Aguilar were nondescript dark-skin guys of about forty, but Montalvo Santiago, maybe thirty, had a distinctive scar down his left cheek, a teardrop tattoo below his right eye.

"I'm not so focused on Perez as Aguilar or Santiago," I said.

"Why's that?" Tony asked.

"Perez is small change and he was a last minute sub anyway. If he's there, sure, we'll push him. But I'm really looking for the actual shooter or the guy who planned the thing. That makes Aguilar and Santiago our main targets. Okay?"

Everyone nodded. I looked to the Perdons. "Ricky, you can back us up, also help Angel, okay?"

"Sure."

"I've got my XD," I told them. "I hope there's no shooting but you never know. What about you, Ricky? And Tony?"

Ricky reached beneath his long coat and retrieved a monster revolver. "Casull four-five-four, mucho power."

I tried not to react humorously to Ricky's *mucho* but couldn't resist. Then the tension set us off and we all laughed a while. Afterward I felt less on edge.

"You, Tony?" I asked.

"The wonderful state of Texas still has my H&K man-toy, so I'm back to my spare Ruger, plus Sarah here." At which, Tony pulled his own coat aside, showing a custom holster holding a very illegal short-barreled pump shotgun with pistol grips.

"Sarah?" I asked.

"You had to meet her to know," he replied. "Couldn't name my Mossberg anything else."

* * *

We killed time by playing pool, none of us really into it, nobody trying too hard. Finally it was two in the thin morning and it was time. We made one last pass at the john and headed outside.

The Perdons had brought an old quad-cab Ford pickup as our go-to vehicle. Ricky was driver, Tony rode shotgun, literally, Angel and I in the back. As we got in I noticed that the ignition was jury-rigged, meaning the truck was stolen. "What if we get stopped?" I asked Ricky.

"Hey, *ese*, the license plates is differen' anyway. Don' worry th' small shit."

Don' worry th' small shit. Words to live by.

It took us about twenty minutes to get to the Fifth Ward, drive up Liberty Road and find Club Soledad. Traffic was busy for that time of night, a plethora of booze and drugs in the barrio keeping folks up wee hours. But the strip shopping center was nearly deserted, only a few cars and trucks parked. Good. Assuming our targets were there, the fewer extra people the better.

Ricky parked sideways across the stripes so we couldn't be blocked. Tony pulled out Sarah, jacked a round in the chamber, put her back in the holster. We all took a moment for inward reflection and went inside.

The place was surprisingly neat, clean, well-lit. Restaurant-style tables and chairs evenly spaced, two dozen men, no women. They were drinking, playing cards, dominoes. A jukebox squawking ancient and scratchy Latin music. Travel posters of Colombia on the walls. Bartender who looked up at us as we entered and fanned out by the door.

"Hey, privado!" the bartender said sharply.

"Hey, fuck you!" Tony replied, pulling Sarah and pointing her.

The bartender raised his hands. All the patrons turned, saw us, sat quietly, some unmoving, some put their hands up. They knew we meant business and thankfully nobody challenged us.

Ricky and Angel both drew guns, holding them down alongside their legs. Angel moved to the bar and stepped behind it while Ricky took the opposite corner of the room, watching.

The bartender frowned, switched to English. "Not much cash. You take it, leave, okay?"

"Not okay," I said. "Looking for Juan Perez, Castillo Aguilar, Montalvo Santiago. Everyone just sit quiet." I glanced to Tony. "Tell 'em."

Tony rattled what I'd said in Spanish while I scanned the room carefully. When he came to the name *Santiago*, a couple of customers inadvertently glanced to a table by the wall near the jukebox. Just what I was hoping for, because there sat our man, left cheek scar, ringleader of the men who murdered Kate Morley.

I glanced around to my partners. Angel and Ricky had everyone covered, as promised. They positioned themselves accordingly, having done this sort of job before. Nobody moved, no one spoke. We owned the room.

I drew my pistol, walked to where Santiago sat, and pointed the gun at him. "You hired men to kill my friend," I said. "Who paid you to do this? Where do I find him?"

He looked at me, and smiled slyly. "*No entiendo, señor.*"

"I know you understand English and can speak it well, asshole!" I put the pistol muzzle under his chin, raised it, and he followed my action, stood up and leaned against the wall, still smiling, unshaken. A serious, tough man, not intimidated by threats. I looked to Tony. "Explain it to him."

Tony came over, transferred Sarah to the left hand, drew his Ruger .357, cocked it, pointed it at Santiago's head, repeated what I'd said in Spanish.

"*No entiendo.*" The same. Unflinching and stubborn, not showing fear, especially in front of his pals and fellow gang members.

I was at an impasse. What was I going to do, shoot the man dead where he stood? I was contemplating just slapping Santiago across the head with the pistol and leaving when Tony took over.

"Fuck this!" he exclaimed. He lowered his gun barrel and shot Santiago in the left knee!

The blast of the Magnum round in the small barroom was immense and everyone except Tony and Santiago jumped. Tony didn't bat an eye and Santiago collapsed to the floor, screaming "Mieda! Mieda!" and rolled back and forth. Blood was splattered and I instinctively stepped back.

"Hey, asshole!" Tony yelled, cocking his revolver again. "Look at me, butt-fuck!" Tony leaned over, poked at Santiago's face with the gun, jabbing him with the muzzle until the man finally looked into Tony's huge glowering face. "Yell *shit* all you want, but the guy asked you a question and we want a fuckin' answer!" He repeated what I'd said, English and Spanish. "Well, motherfucker?"

Despite the immense pain, Santiago just glowered at Tony and said nothing. I'll give him credit. Few men could stay silent, but he did.

"Tell you what, dick-face," Tony said calmly. "I got five more bullets. That's one in the other knee, one in each elbow, one in each shoulder. Or maybe your balls?" As he spoke, Tony thrust the gun's muzzle hard at Santiago's body, signaling each point. Again in Spanish.

The room was silent, the only sound the old fluttery jukebox. Santiago was now breathing rapidly, face contorted, obviously in terrific pain. The bleeding had slowed, as Tony's shot apparently hadn't hit a big artery or vein. But the fact remained that Santiago's knee was ruined and still he kept silent.

Tony crouched over the man. "Y'see this dude here?" Tony spoke in a conversational tone, tilting his head in my direction. "He don't look it, but he's the meanest motherfucker you'll ever meet. Known as the Tiger. Hear what I'm saying?"

Santiago nodded, the first actual response from him.

"Now, dude," Tony went on. "I'm just doin' what Tiger tells me. I don't want to fuck you up worse, but I got to, account Tiger says to. Sorry, that's how it is." At that, Tony put the muzzle of the gun square against Santiago's right knee.

"*Esperar!* Wait!" Santiago gasped.

"Wait for what?" Tony said.

"Man hired me. Give me bug, tell me what to do. To shoot Tiger. El Tigre."

"Go on, pal. Who hired you?"

"Hombre blanco. Alto hombre."

"Tall white man. Go ahead."

"El cortador, el diablo!"

Tony glanced at me. "Calls him the cutter, the devil." He poked with seeming boredom at Santiago's remaining knee. "More, motherfucker!"

"No! Miedo de él!"

"Says he's afraid of him," Tony translated.

Santiago steeled himself, yelled in English, defiant and frightened at the same time, "I'm not talkin'! Fuck you! Shoot me!"

I gave it some thought. "We've sapped this well," I said. "Let's go."

Chapter 37

Two days passed. Sunday morning and everything was quiet. I'd just come back from a run, a light workout, shower.

I emailed my final Mid City personnel report to the clients, attached an invoice for the last chunk of work. I'd been living mostly on savings since Kate's death and the payout for my consulting would fill in the cracks.

It was also time to start some new jobs. I had a potential contract for a long-term consultancy with a small motel chain, providing them employee screening and guard services. Another joint venture with Jensen Security?

* * *

Alice Colhoun calling. "I've got a couple days off, going sailing tomorrow. Want to wet your landlubber toes?"

"Sure! What do I need to bring?"

"Yourself. Swimsuit. Change of clothes as we might stay on board overnight, light jacket if it cools off, hat for the sun. I've got major sunblock cream, seasick pills if you need them."

"Anything else?"

"Beer, two cartons of a good IPA."

"Done."

"And shoes. You need deck shoes, the kind with white soles. I don't want to be scrubbing black marks off my boat all next week, y'know." Alice seemed adamant about this, so I acquiesced without a smart-alecky comeback.

"White sole deck shoes it is. But what about shark repellent?" I joked, unable to keep that out of the conversation.

She laughed. "Unnecessary. Sharks smell a bloody Yank in the water, they head to the next ocean." Colhoun gave me directions to the marina, told me ten in the morning.

Hey, I thought. Pretty gal, intrepid private eye, a sailboat. Maybe I could emulate Travis McGee? I mulled that over, but since Alice was a surgeon, Lucas Davenport instead? He was married to a doctor. But no, gets too cold in the Twin Cities. And hey, I hate snow.

Another incoming call, Meierhoff. "Yeah, David?"

"Made an arrest, kinda. Thought you'd be interested."

"Sure."

"Security at Ben Taub ER found this guy at the entrance, someone dropped him off."

"Yeah?"

"Docs tried to save him but he lost too much blood, died from shock. We just ID'd him as Montalvo Santiago. You remember, guy that hired the gangbangers who shot you, killed Kate Morley."

"Dead, huh?"

"Yeah. Waited too long to come to the ER. Somebody had blown his left knee halfway off."

"Huh."

"That all you can say?" Meierhoff asked.

"Yeah."

"Don't suppose you know anything about how the guy got shot, who shot him?"

"Nope. Not a clue."

"Of course not," Meierhoff said. "Not that it's any great loss, but I thought you'd want to know."

"Thanks."

"Sure you don't know anything about it?"

"Nope. Sorry."

"Just sayin'."

"Just sayin'," I echoed.

Chapter 38

Next day, proudly wearing my new white-soled deck shoes, I drove down to the Galveston Bay area and east to the marina. Besides buying some nice shoes at Academy Sports, I decided to junk the flamingo motif and found a pair of comfortably baggy but stylish trunks with an abstract seashell design. At least I hoped they were seashells and not some weirdly perverted Lovecraft symbolism. Regardless, the new trunks I wore under my jeans, augmented by the shoes, an Astros T-shirt and my Montrose Beer and Gun Club camo ball cap. I was good to go.

Some marinas are lavish, have their own clubhouse with restaurant and bar, cater to the country club set who may not even remember in which slip they've moored their boat. Alice Colhoun elected the other variety, a genuine working-class marina with docking facilities, ramps, plenty of dented, hard-use SUVs and pickups parked all over, trailers attached. I checked the facility map at the office and drove to where Alice moored her sailboat. It wasn't slip F-18 like Travis McGee but it would do fine.

I'd of course surfed the Net for photos of the boat she owned but I wasn't prepared for just how graceful it was. A truly beautiful design, however not nearly so lovely as the woman standing on it, waving to me. Alice today wore tight navy Capri pants, an aqua pullover proclaiming her sailboat's brand *Beneteau* and of course, white-soled deck shoes.

I grabbed my overnight bag and the beer, locked the X3, and walked the few feet to the mooring. As I approached I glanced at the stern, saw *Suture Self* painted there. "Nice boat," I told Alice, politely deferring any mention of the sailboat's name.

"Nice car," she replied, gesturing to my new black Bimmer.

"Thanks. Just stole it yesterday. Permission to come aboard?"

"Granted! Let me show you around."

I stepped across the gap from pier to boat and managed to get on board without falling into the water, a minor victory. I stood on the small deck area just rear—belay that, mate—*aft* of the cabin.

"You can stow your gear below. C'mon." And Alice led me down a short set of stairs to the cabin. I was frankly amazed, the seeming space and roominess of this small boat. Precise design, of course, attention to how everything was stored in fitted lockers that lined the walls.

"Put your bag here, far from the hatch as possible, in case we get overspray." Alice pointed me toward an empty area just beyond two rolled-up sleeping bags. "Put the beer in the fridge next to the sandwiches. Hope you like ham and cheese. The fridge runs off batteries and we can fire up a generator to charge them if need be. And here's the porta john." She pulled aside a little privacy screen. "It flushes with this button."

Good to know, I thought. Best button to push I'd seen all day.

"Give me a second," I told Alice, unzipped my bag, reached back to my belt and pulled out the Springfield XD, put it inside the bag in a side compartment.

"Why I do declare, Mister Wayne," Alice said, affecting a silly schoolmarm accent. "That's one big gun you have there."

I tried to emulate Wayne's drawl. "I'm jes' a marked man, Missy, me bein' th' marshal and all."

Alice guffawed, hopefully at the humor and not derisively at my poor mimicry. "Understood. I'm simply not used to pistols. My uncle took me hunting when I was a kiddo, shotgunning for dove. Handguns aren't very common in New Zealand."

"Want to see it? Show and tell?"

"Certainly."

I smiled inwardly how we'd gone all gaga over Ranger Danforth's pistol, and thought it funny how even most non-gun people seem fascinated by them. So I took the pistol out of the bag, began a little safety course. "Always keep a gun pointed away from anyone. And never put your finger on the trigger until you're ready to fire."

"That I know, the same with shotguns. Proceed."

I ejected the magazine. "This holds thirteen rounds." I racked the slide, locking it back, letting the ejected cartridge fall onto a nearby cushion. "Plus one in the chamber."

Alice frowned. "Always keep it loaded like that?"

"Won't do much good if it's not. Takes too much time loading the pistol when you need it otherwise."

"All right, I'll give you that."

"Now the gun's safe," I told her, indicating the empty chamber and lack of magazine. Next I eased the slide shut and handed her the pistol.

She took it tentatively. "Heavy." Pointed the gun around the cabin, squinted along the sights.

"It's a large pistol, true," I said. "Caliber forty-five is about as big as it normally gets. There are plenty of smaller, lighter handguns."

"Would take getting used to."

"As do most things, Kiwi trauma surgeons in particular," I ventured. Thankfully she smiled and didn't threaten to keelhaul me. "Tell you what. Should you ever decide to buy a pistol, self-defense or simply for target shooting, let me know and I'll help you pick the right size and caliber."

"Sometime maybe, not now."

"No biggie," I told her. "Since we're on the boat, I'll leave the pistol unloaded, okay?"

"Okay. But we need to cast off. Let's go topside. It's my turn to show and tell," she said, smiling.

So I put the gun away again and emptied my pockets, put all my stuff in the bag. I shucked off my jeans to display the tentative seashells. "Let's do it, skipper."

"Skipper, my butt."

About that, I had no comment.

Chapter 39

A brief internet cram job on sailing terminology the night before gave me hope I wouldn't be too much in the dark. Or in the way.

I now knew that ropes were *lines*, pulleys were *blocks*, and that Alice's *First 20* had two sails, a squarish mainsail and a triangular *jib* up front. Excuse, at the *bow*. Regardless, both sails were *furled*.

"The boat has a small engine, we'll use that to clear the dock, then we'll deploy the sails, okay?"

"Just tell me what to do. Or more important, what not to do."

That got a smile. "Yanks. Always underfoot."

"I do know that port is left and starboard is right," I said. "I remember this because both *right* and *starboard* have an *r* in them."

"Correct," she replied, then a moment later, "Wait. Port also has…" and catching the joke, laughed. "Bloody smartass Yank."

I helped her cast off and secure the mooring lines and I sat a bit out of the way and next to her at the stern, in the cockpit. She started the engine and we slowly moved away from the dock. I watched how she worked the tiller to steer, wearing a pair of leather driving gloves. "Need to protect the surgeon in me, tools of the trade," she explained, wiggling her fingers.

Presently we were in open water although there were many other boats nearby, coming in and out of the docks. Alice stuck with the engine, maneuvering until we had some space, then shut the motor off and started the process of unfurling the sails.

The rigging was beautifully designed. All the lines terminated at points within reach of one person. There were two winches, either side of the cabin roof, several attachment points for other lines. I helped her crank the winches and we gradually let out the sails until they caught the gentle breeze coming from ashore.

"Right now we're sailing ahead of the wind," she said. "Which means the prevailing wind is behind us and all we do is catch the air and steer." She pointed to the jib mast. "See those little cloth streamers along the front edge of the sail? They're *telltales*. We watch them to know which direction the wind's from and estimate its velocity."

Alice gestured to a row of digital instruments glowing from a small control panel in front of her, and chuckled. "Or we can just look at the electronic anemometer and other gauges. The sensors are up there, tip of the main mast." She leaned back, pointed and as she did, she came against me and did not move away. I followed her fingertip but also focused on her body, hard and trim, muscular but slender, like her sailboat. Her scent was fresh, human, and I savored her sitting there, confident and at ease with herself. I also felt at ease in her company.

Presently she moved away, continued her lessons. "If there were a harsher breeze we'd perhaps trim the sails a bit, furl them a tad so the force is reduced, as we're in no hurry. But today we're forecast all gentle breezes and clear sailing."

"And what if the wind is coming from ahead, but we want to sail that direction anyway?"

"That's called *against the wind* of course, and requires tacking. Know what that is?"

"I think so. Sailing at angles, back and forth, port to starboard, working your way forward." I wiggled my hand side to side like an idiotic fish.

"That's it in general, and of course there are other methods, but yes, you're right. It's a technique that wasn't discovered for maybe a thousand years and the ability to sail into the wind was a closely guarded secret."

As is most technology, I thought. It's always the same, each step forward is sometimes treasured and protected, sometimes held in suspicion and discarded. Society in its varied fits and starts, trundling its way along the ages. Progress by inches.

That's how it is for people, too. Each of us advances through life, but we often only mark time instead. I knew all about this, as marking time was what I'd done for the past two years. Yet I'd resolved to change this, reset my lifestyle, regain the energy and drive which I'd lost.

All the time we were talking I noticed how Alice watched the sails, the rigging, and her compass as she steered. It was a delight, feeling the air and hearing the slap of waves and the rustle of canvas.

I could understand how she was attracted to sailing, the sheer joy of being on the open water. Despite my lack of boating knowledge, I was an okay swimmer and had no real fear. Maybe she would convert me. I certainly needed something new in my life, some pastime or endeavor or distraction from the vicious direction I'd turned of late.

I seemed to learn at a decent pace as Alice schooled me on sailing basics. I tripped over some lines and my own big feet a couple times, turned the windlass the wrong way once, but in the main, not too bad. She didn't yell at me and she even let me hold the tiller and steer a while, absolutely under her precise supervision.

* * *

We went quite a ways into the Gulf, with not much other sailboat traffic, being a weekday.

I didn't appreciate just how fast we were moving until Alice steered us near a huge container cargo vessel and we practically zoomed by. We waved at the crew, some of whom were leaning over the railing far above, waving back.

After a while Alice caught an inshore breeze and brought us about a mile from land. I could see people swimming and fishing in the surf, little mobile dots. There were marker buoys all around and seeing them brought back crisp images of last year, when David Meierhoff and I, aided by Ricky Perdon, chased the insane Paula Albertson to where she'd moored her family yacht at a huge deep-water buoy with plans to savagely murder the kidnapped Cheryl Stern.

But these buoys were small, friendly and not interwoven with blood and blood remembrance. I thrust the past away.

I looked at Alice Colhoun instead, reveling in her innate decency, stable mindset, humor and intelligence. She had an abundance of external beauty, too, a shag of bright red hair, intense hazel eyes, and the thrill of life in the very way she turned and moved and walked and breathed.

"It's shallow all along this sector," she told me. "That's why the buoys, to warn off larger boats with deeper draft. But ours is less than two meters." She smiled at me. "That's—"

"About six feet," I finished.

"Smartass Yank, you are for certain."

"Thank you for the semi-compliment, m'dear."

"Make yourself useful and help me furl the sails."

She showed me how to work the windlass again. I was particularly intrigued how the jib was pulled in, wrapped around a hollow cylinder that the jib's mast went through.

"That's known as roller furling," she explained. "Most sailboats use it."

Now that we weren't running under sail and were adrift, the boat rocked side to side from the waves, but I was okay with the movement, had no twinges of seasick or nausea. *Good.* "What next?" I asked.

"Grab us a couple beers each and some sandwiches while I drop anchor."

I retrieved the food and beer, and noticed that after Alice set the anchor, the boat's rocking was minimal.

So we stretched out on the deck atop the cabin and drank our beer, wolfed down the food. The surface area where we relaxed was about that of a king bed. Alice leaned against the mast, then sat up. "How about a swim?"

"Sure."

"Help me first." She went below, dragged out a hose with shower head attached. The hose snaked down into the cabin. "You're taller. Clamp this to the mast so it sprays down onto the deck. After we swim, we rinse with fresh water. The tank holds quite a bit but we'll still need to quickly jump in and out of the spray. Nonetheless, we don't want salt water in our eyes or skin too long, y'know."

As I attached the shower nozzle to the mast, Alice dropped a small ladder over the side, kicked off her shoes, slipped off her pants and shirt. She wore a black bikini and it fit her snugly, beautifully. Easily in her late thirties, she had the physique of a much younger woman, a bit thin but shapely, narrow hips and small breasts, skin tanned by the Texas sun to contrast her ginger hair. Lovely lady indeed.

Without hesitation Alice Colhoun dove into the water and began to swim back and forth easily, laughing, waving. "C'mon in! Water's warm and the sharks are tame today!"

I pulled off my shirt and shoes, joined her. We both splashed and frolicked, the burdensome world forgotten, distant and unable to reach us. I felt energy channel through me and emotional chains slip away, chains that had wrapped about me like those of Marley's ghost. But now those chains were sliding off, slipping into the water below, lost for all time.

As we swam near one another, I noticed Alice glancing at the scars on my left arm and shoulder. I didn't know whether it was clinical appraisal or just fascination.

"How's the recuperation proceeding?" she asked.

I raised my left arm, and was able to extend it most of the way. "Progress is on track and generally better each day."

"Some of those incisions are mine," she laughed. "You'd best ensure they're well cared for or I might sue."

After some time, Alice swam to the ladder, held a stanchion, reached down below her waist with the other hand. "Sorry," she laughed. "Had to go. The beer, y'know."

Why not? I thought. So I treaded water and did the same. After all, the Gulf of Mexico is considerably larger than your average backyard pool.

We swam a bit more, but were now tired. "Ready to call it quits?" she asked.

"Ready when you are, CB."

"CB?"

"A long and bad joke," I told her. "I'll explain later."

"Explain a Yank joke? That'll be the day!" And at that, Alice heaved herself up the little ladder onto the deck. I was close behind and watched her gamine body with growing desire. Thus far, however, the growth was all mental so I felt somewhat at ease beside her.

As we left the water, Alice reached to me, pointed at the fresh horizontal scar along my right side where the biker bullet grazed me, and the wide scars on my left where George Burgess cut me last year. "Now those, I had nothing to do with."

"Ran into some trouble here and there. Termites," I lamely joked.

"I don't think it's so funny, Mitch. I care about you and I don't want to see you hurt."

"I appreciate your concern. Honest, I do. But my lifestyle isn't that placid and there are some expected hazards to my profession. Believe me, Alice, I try to be careful."

"See that you do. Else I've wasted two ham sandwiches."

We stood on the cabin roof and Alice turned a small valve on the hose. We were immediately splurged by cold spray and gasped inadvertently, then stood there under the water, rinsing off.

As we showered we bumped into one another, competing for the water. It was fun and we giggled like kids.

Then a moment, a golden moment, when we were quiet. Alice looked into my eyes, smiled. She turned, facing away, and said, "Unhook me."

Chapter 40

I just stood there, dripping, silent.

Alice Colhoun glanced over her shoulder, and laughed. "C'mon, Mitch. Do I have to show you how that's done, too?"

No, I could handle this job just fine. I unsnapped her halter and she pulled it away, turned back to me. Her small girlish breasts were upright, white in contrast to her otherwise darkened skin, pink nipples prominent from the chilly shower.

"Turn off the water," she said.

As I reached up to twist the valve, Alice grabbed my swim trunks, slid them down. I kicked them free and embraced her. I felt her breasts against my chest, her lean body pressed to me.

"Are you—" I mumbled.

"I'm okay. The pill. And I've seen your medical records, remember. I know you're all right, no unwanted bugs."

"I didn't want to—"

"Bloody Yank," she laughed. "Stop talking and kiss me. You've been wanting to all day and I've been waiting, the same." She looked up at me, green eyes blazing with desire, mouth inviting. She was so much shorter than I that her neck was arched. Not that it mattered.

We kissed, and deeply. Our tongues touched, moved, exploring. She took my penis, began to massage, stroking. I slid her bikini bottom off, clasped her taut buttocks, pulled her close.

We embraced even tighter as I reached to her vulva, silken smooth, zone shaven. I slipped my fingers between the moist lips, found her clitoris, stroked in rhythm with her hand on me, back and forth, up and down, ancient motion but new and stunning each time it's tried.

I kneeled, my mouth against her pelvis. I began licking her, tonguing her. She moaned, stroking my shoulders, rocking against me. She came quickly, a yelp of desire, scarlet hair tossing. Then she knelt beside me, pulled me back, flat onto the hard cabin roof, trickles of water curling around. She lay atop, guided my penis into her. I pushed and she sat upright, writhing in ecstasy and passion.

I reached up to her body, gently squeezing her breasts, pulling at the erect nipples. She placed her palms over my hands, pressed harder. I took her cue and kneaded with more strength, cautious at first but as she kept pressing, I worked her small breasts outward, stretched them, rolling the nipples between my fingers.

Alice began to climax again, and I worked to synchronize with her movements, thrusting faster and faster until we shared a glorious orgasm, joined both in body and heart.

We lay side by side in the sun unspeaking, panting, my arm around her, bodies linked, sweat evaporating with the currents of air. We stared at the sky, birds circling randomly.

A few minutes and Alice raised herself on one elbow, reached out, grasped my penis again. As I responded she once more straddled me, this time reversed. She began to suck and massage me, stroking me to full erection as I tongued her inner lips. We took our time, slowly at first then rapidly, reaching another exquisite peak of uninhibited pleasure that enveloped us without reserve, without hesitation or caution.

Chapter 41

Finally we were spent and lay there, free, unencumbered by clothing or necessity.

"Want a beer?" I asked.

"God do I. But d'you have the energy to make it all the way to the cooler and back?"

"I'll try, may have to lie down occasionally throughout the pilgrimage, rest up."

Somehow I made it, but the beers didn't last much longer than the time it took to open them. I leaned against the mast and Alice against me, a perfect arrangement. My right arm was around her waist and I'd reach up now and then, caress her little breasts. She'd wriggle appreciatively.

I knew it might upset the moment, but I had to ask. "Why?"

"Why what?"

"Why me? We really don't know each other that well and I don't think you're... well..."

"Promiscuous?"

"You said it, I didn't."

She turned, looked up at me, made a little face. "No, I'm not. But it wasn't my decision."

"Huh?"

"We have a monthly lottery in the ER. All the surgeons play. We put the patient names in a bedpan, draw one. If both the doctor and the patient are the same sex and they aren't gay, we just draw again. Last time I got the name *Mitchell King*."

At that, I tickled her and she jumped. "We Yanks may be dense but even we aren't *that* slow," I said, and both of us laughed.

After a moment, Alice said, "Tell the truth, it was your pal David Meierhoff."

"David?"

"Yes. I don't know whether he's playing matchmaker or he simply considers you a friend, but he talked about you a lot, things that surprised me."

"Such as? If you'd care to say, that is."

"That you're actually a very nice fella. That you're maybe the smartest and most wide ranging person he knows. That you had things fall against you that weren't really your fault. That you needed a change."

"David said that?"

"He did. Mind you, he didn't suggest outright that we should become, ah, *acquainted*."

"I just hope this wasn't a… a…"

"Charity fuck? A pity fuck?"

"If you wish to put it in those terms, yes."

"Not a chance. I'm not that sort of girl. I make my own decisions and nobody pushes me into anything. So don't concern yourself about that."

"Okay," I said, acquiescent again. "I just wanted to know."

"What your friend said may've piqued my interest, but the decision was mine and mine alone. You and I spent some time together, I liked what I saw, decided that, well…"

"I know I talk too much," I admitted. "Sorry to have broken the mood, apologies."

"No worries. I would've brought it up eventually. I'm not one to leave people in the dark."

Awkward moment behind us, we snuggled a bit closer. She turned her head upward and we kissed. Kissed again.

Then a cellphone rang.

Shit!, I thought.

"Shit!" Alice snapped. She stood, stretched, headed to the cabin. "Got to take it. On call whenever, y'know."

Presently she returned, frowning. "Damn. Two major crashes on the I-10, they're pulling me in. We have to cut this short. I'm so sorry, Mitch."

"That's okay. It's been wonderful." I looked at her standing in the midday sun, naked, slender but shapely, precise high breasts and nipples, warm loins. I felt my desire growing again. As well as other things.

She looked down, smiled, came toward me, reached. "However, I suppose we might have time…"

* * *

And indeed there was time, to paraphrase Eliot's Prufrock.

Afterward, it was panic in Sailboat City. Alice and I quickly dressed, kissed again, passionate, rushed through the return, sails unfurled and motor aiding, we made it quickly to her slip without incident. I helped Alice clean up, secure everything, moor the *Suture Self* to the dock with a heavy steel cable. I accompanied her to where she'd parked. She drove a no-nonsense Jeep Cherokee, muddy and a bit battered, but eminently serviceable. *No wonder she likes me*, I thought. *I'm just like her car.*

We kissed again, reached for each other's neither zones, thought better of it, parted. "I'll call you soon, m'love," she promised, drove off rapidly.

Being called *m'love* in a Kiwi accent was the best thing that's happened to me in a long while. No, wait, *second* best thing.

When I got home I dragged myself inside, fed Kraze, fell atop my bed still clothed and slept in perfect abandon until morning.

Chapter 42

It was about ten and I was sipping my second cup of coffee while reviewing a set of proposed contracts when Meierhoff called.

"Got another one, Mitch. Remember that tweeker you interviewed, Eddie Macintyre, lived next door to Renata Martinez?"

I caught the past tense *lived*. "You're telling me that he… no way."

"Yep, way. Missed classes, a friend phoned, no answer, went to his apartment. Heard the TV blasting, nobody came to the door when he banged on it. Called the landlord, you can guess what next."

"Burgess?"

"Yeah. I'm at the apartment now, unit five. Appreciate if you'd come down, have a look."

"Jesus, David. I don't know if I've got the gumption for it after the last time."

"This one's not so messy, but Burgess did leave you a note."

"Okay. Give me a while."

"We'll be anticipating your arrival with baited breath."

"And David?"

"Yeah?"

"Thanks about Alice. Doctor Colhoun. What you said about me. We went sailing yesterday, had a terrific time. She's quite a woman."

"Thought so. Hoped you guys would hook up."

There was a lilt in his voice when he said *hook up* and I thought, *David, you devil!*

* * *

I flashed my HPD Consultant ID and was waved to a parking spot a half block from the apartments. The cluster fuck was identical to that of months earlier, cop cars, CSI vans, TV remote trucks. Bunch of homicide investigators at the apartment, this time centered around unit five instead of four. Otherwise the same. As if any vicious murder could be similar, human life blotted out, devastated and vacant.

Meierhoff was chatting with a medic when I walked up. "Mitch, this is Lee Chin Ho, just telling me about Sister Mary Frances. You know, lives in unit three. She was home when the Macintyre body was discovered. Didn't see anything this time, but with all the commotion, she's not taking it well, as you can imagine."

Chin Ho and I shook hands. "She okay?" I asked.

"No, she's not," Chin Ho replied. "Not at all. We wanted to take her in for observation, refused, said she had a class to teach."

I looked to Meierhoff. "You might call the school, make sure they keep an eye on her."

"Already did. Besides that, not a lot we can do."

"I have a fairly good rapport with her," I said. "I'll call her later, see how she's doing."

"Good. You do that," Meierhoff confirmed. "Ready?"

And so it was on with the booties and gloves and forward into the darkness of George Burgess' soul, into the bloodletting, the savagery.

Yet scant hours previous, I was making love to a beautiful woman. So does the great wheel again turn.

Chapter 43

Eddie Macintyre was sitting in a low and threadbare recliner, watching television in his equally threadbare undershorts. Except that his throat was cut ear to ear.

Macintyre's head tilted forward as if he'd fallen asleep. Rivulets of blood oozed from the throat wound to drip across his thin bare chest, pool on the seat of the chair and soak through the cushions. But there were otherwise no further indications of the violence that had been done to the young man until I leaned closer, saw a rag stuffed in his mouth, numerous cuts and stabbings all over his torso and legs, his face and groin as well.

"Time of death?" I asked.

"Per the liver temp, sometime Sunday evening," Meierhoff said.

"Don't guess there are any witnesses?"

David shook his head. "Nope. Was a big summer party at Saint Vincent, food and a band and all. As most of the folks who live here are connected with the school, apartments were deserted."

"He was tortured?" I gestured at his body.

"Sure looks like it. Coroner says none of the cuts were deep, just painful."

"So he bled to death when his throat was cut?"

"Don't think so. Amount of blood loss via the neck wound isn't copious, indicates his heart stopped first. Tweekers often die from heart attacks anyway, Burgess probably went overboard and Macintyre just zeroed out on him. Otherwise he'd have bled a lot more."

"So Burgess didn't find what he was looking for," I said. "Or what he wanted to know, either way, and cut Macintyre's throat in anger post mortem?"

"That's my guess."

I looked at the floor, saw other blood splatters, some that appeared to be leading away from the chair. "What's this?"

Meierhoff gestured to the CSI techs. "They picked up samples and will run blood tests to verify, but it looks as if Burgess was injured, no way to know how bad."

"Anything else? You said a note."

"Yeah. Over in the kitchen." David led me a few steps. "Looks like Macintyre used a crack pipe and smoked his meth, but he'd also been slamming—shooting up. Here's his rig. And the note. If you need to move the paper, be careful to just touch the edges."

Typical for the needle addict, Macintyre had a little alcohol burner and a blackened aluminum tablespoon. There was a film of residue in the spoon's bowl. Next to that, a 5cc syringe and a hank of rubber tubing used to tie off. And the note, printed neatly on a scrap of ripped out notebook paper.

Mitch no time to fix him like the girl so they would be bookends love George.

Taunting but icy, as was George Burgess. Just what I needed to round out my day.

CSI finished measuring and photographing the body and its surroundings. Meierhoff and I stood aside, watched as the coroner techies spread out a body bag on the floor, carefully lifted Macintyre's corpse onto the plastic, ran the zipper closed. They put the bag on a collapsible gurney and rolled it out the apartment door.

So long, I thought. You poor asshole, you somehow stumbled across the Slicer or he stumbled onto you, and that was all she wrote. *No more good time meth for you, kid.*

One of the CSI techs, a guy named Larsen, was checking the lounge chair, taking pics of the residual blood, when he reached down to the seat cushion. "Bingo!" Larsen exclaimed. "Found his stash!"

Naturally we went over to see. Larsen had pulled the cushion aside to reveal a mound of plastic zip lock bags, each containing small translucent blue pills. He took one up, looked closely. "*Crystal Blue Persuasion*, my guess."

"Which is?" I asked.

Larsen looked at me, smiling. "Ever since *Breaking Bad*, all the meth cookers dye their shit blue. It's just food coloring, but the junkies don't care, they want their boost to be blue." He held the packet so I could see, rattled it. "And this particular stuff I know. Size and color, even the bags they put it in. Street name Crystal Blue Persuasion. This is pure-dee BC junk. Premium shit, too."

"BC meaning Barrio Colombia?"

"Yeah."

I looked to Meierhoff. "There's no way a student like Eddie Macintyre would be into the BC gang for this much dope, is there?"

"Right. I used to work Vice but I've kept up on the news, since drugs and murder work hand in hand." He peered at the pile of bloody bags. "Has to be ten thousand street value. More than that. Macintyre would never have the money or trust to hold a stash this size."

"So what are you thinking?"

"I'm thinking this. We know Burgess has ties with BC. He's been running their meth to support himself, is my guess. But an older guy can't easily deal to college kids, especially since he's got wanted posters halfway to Thursday on every wall."

"So he subcontracts to guys like Macintyre."

"Exactly. But somehow Macintyre talks Burgess into a big loan of dope, or steals it, whichever, and Burgess wants it back."

"But Macintyre gives up the ghost before Burgess can make him tell."

Meierhoff nodded. "Looks like it."

"Hey, guys," Larsen called to us. "Any idea what this is? Found it down between the bags." He used small tongs and they held a scrap of paper, ragged torn edges. Blood stained but visible was a small circle, inch in diameter, divided into blue and yellow arcs, intertwined.

"Yin and Yang," I said. "I always thought it looked like two amoebas screwing. You know, sixty-nine."

"That's where you're wrong," Meierhoff came back. "*Soixante-neuf* maybe, but not with amoebas. Amoebas don't have eyes and both Yin and Yang have 'em. See the little dots?"

"Then paramecium, maybe? They've got those sensor spots on them, don't they?"

Meierhoff pondered my question. "I know they've got these squishy little pump things, pulsate in and out. And they're kinda crescent shaped, like the drawing here."

"But do paramecia… parameciums, whatever, do they even have sex?" I asked.

"They must, else there'd not be any baby paramecium."

"But are there actually baby parameciums?"

"Have to be. D'you think they just appear out of nowhere, like Athena springing full grown from the brow of Zeus?" Meierhoff was certain on that point.

And here we go again, I thought, sailing off into infinity at the scene of a bloody homicide, dissembling pure and simple.

Larsen interrupted in comic frustration. "I can see I'm not gonna get any help from you guys in ID-ing this swoopy thing." He looked over to the EMT medic Lee Chin Ho, who was just standing there, spectating. "Know what this is? It's Oriental, you oughta know, hey?"

Chin Ho snuffed. "The fuck you think, *Karate Kid* and I'm the mystical Asian philosopher Mister Miyagi? I got no damned idea what the friggin' thing is." He laughed. "Besides, you CSI guys have this huge database at your gazillion dollar lab, you just scan this and in two seconds it comes back with the answer, right?"

"Yeah, sure," Larsen said. "I'll tell that Caruso guy to get on it immediately."

He bagged the paper scrap and walked to his toolbox to stick a label on it, where it would soon join countless thousands of other carefully labeled pieces of forgotten evidence in some forsaken warehouse of catalogued oblivion, right next to the Ark of the Covenant.

Chapter 44

Alice Colhoun and I were lying across my bed naked. We'd just finished a vigorous lovemaking and were recuperating, panting like two dogs after chasing cars.

"Want to go downstairs, play some pool?" I asked.

"Is this a thinly disguised Yank ploy to trick me into having sex with you?"

"Yeah, that's it. One of those subterfuge things, ulterior motive and all."

She propped herself on an elbow, glared at me. "So you're using your private eye macho attitude to take advantage of this poor frail Kiwi lass?"

"You betcha."

"Then let's do it!"

Well, one thing led to another and we ended up competing in the first game of nude pool ever played in my house. I know it sounds silly, but we had a great time, laughing and poking at each other and decidedly not caring whether we made a single ball. Okay, maybe two. Mine.

* * *

Despite his ominous and murderous background presence, George Burgess had not encroached upon our growing relationship by killing anyone else. The bond between Alice and me was rapidly becoming transcendent and immune from external influences anyway. But the real world is there nonetheless and I therefore took precautions, always checking cars for bugs, always being particularly observant and always, always going armed.

Alice and I spent most of our spare hours together now, and I had rarely felt more alive. Of course, occasionally I thought about Kate Morley and her senseless death and each time it put a damper on my spirits, as the memory rightly should.

But I'd vowed to move from where I'd been so long, stuck on bottom dead center, always casting desperate glances over my shoulder to discover, like Satchel Paige, that my past was gaining on me. No longer. Nor would I waste my life with senseless plunges into the bourbon. Life inside me was again refreshed and I was filled with simple pleasures.

Nevertheless, I continued to keep my contacts open for any word of Burgess, although he'd gone quiet after the Macintyre killing and nothing more turned up. But hoping that he'd been cut severely enough to bleed to death afterward was fanciful. We'd never get that lucky.

Joe Duggan opined that Burgess had left Houston again but I didn't think so, that the man was still on the hunt for me, hoping for gaps in my defense. And consequently I endeavored to keep him at bay. I was also watchful for BC gang members, but it was quiet there, too.

Cops were still looking for Juan Perez and Castillo Aguilar, the two men who'd shot me and murdered Kate. But nothing. Word on the street was that they'd either gone home to Colombia or moved to L.A. and joined MS-13 there. But any productive leads had dried up.

I made a point of phoning Sister Mary Frances occasionally, chatting, and we'd become friends. Having endured the double trauma of two murders where she lived had changed her, made her more inward, reflective. But she still maintained a positive mindset and had thrown herself more into teaching. This at least was good, a working therapy.

She also told me that Ozzie had been hired by St. Vincent after graduation, working with Father Gibson as a liaison for disadvantaged students. I was happy for him, knowing that helping others would serve to heal his own wounds.

And despite Kate's terrible death and other murders, I somehow persevered. It was through the good graces of my friends and particularly owing to Alice Colhoun, her open demeanor and humor, her wit and spiky personality and of course her joyful, healthy and adult sexual attitude, that I'd climbed out of the swamp of my own self-flogging and was finally reaching for some degree of personal resolve and stability.

So it was that when Cheryl Stern phoned me one afternoon, told me that her father, gang lord Julio Cardozo, had passed away, I felt sadness for her loss, but felt this with a new degree of detachment.

* * *

The funeral cortege for Julie Cards was of course lavish. It was reminiscent of old time gangland sendoffs, cars and limos draped with enormous garlands of flowers, friends and associates bearing big photos of Cardozo, a band playing slow march intermixed with some strange flavor of back-country salsa. Julie Cards had been a figurehead in the community, partial saint, much sinner, a powerful force with whom to be reckoned. And now, as will eventually fall to each, become dust.

I rode in the main hearse with Cheryl, cousins Ricky and Angel Perdon and the ever-present and unsmiling Carlo, now firmly attached as bodyguard to Cheryl as he'd once been to her father, Julie Cards.

Cardozo had no immediate family, having outlived two sisters, neither of whom were ever involved in the gangs. So most attendees were business associates and other gang members. Or, as

Cheryl steadfastly promised to me the last time we'd visited, *former* gang members, as the Fifth Ward Apaches were now disbanded. This I'd never actually believe, even if it were proclaimed on the side of the Goodyear blimp or if Walter Cronkite were resurrected to announce this as fact on the *CBS Evening News*, but if Cheryl wanted to think it so, I had no objection.

Funeral mass was celebrated at Our Lady of Sorrows, a small Roman Catholic parish on the far east side. Cardozo had some connection with the parish, its former priest, now long deceased, a man who helped Julio when he was a starving ghetto castaway. The church was unused to a crowd this big, so Cheryl picked up the tab for the outdoor overflow, chairs in rows across the lawn, memorial ribbons everywhere, ubiquitous loudspeakers to hear the service. It went off well.

Reception was at a rented dance hall not far from Cardozo's auto parts headquarters. Depending on familial desires, these wakes can be solemn or festive. Cheryl and her advisors chose the latter, so food and drink were generous, the band lively, people dancing and laughing.

I sat alongside Ricky Perdon as we both ate carnitas and drank Dos Equis. A lull in the music and Ricky leaned toward me. "A sad day but a good one, *ese*."

I nodded. "Julio would've wished it this way. And he certainly didn't want to be as ill as he was, no longer vigorous or able to share time with his daughter."

"This is true, my friend."

"I am still in your service," I told him. "How you and Angel helped me that night."

"No mention. We are your friends, always."

"We all have to look after Cheryl now."

"True, true."

I leaned closer. "I'm sorry I was unable to visit often, say hello to Julio."

"I know that you and Julio had a problem," he said. "Julio was a proud man and he was not perfect. Perhaps he had offended you somehow, then wanted to find a way to set things straight again. Before he got sick he tried many times to see you." He shrugged. "Such is life."

"I'm sorry about that, Ricky. I tried to make up for it later, after his stroke."

"You were there plenty, *ese*. Not to worry. And each time you come, I think Julio knew you were there, wanted to talk to you."

I thought about this. "Do you remember the gesture, the movement he would make, like he was reaching for me or giving me something?"

"Yes, my friend. Every time you come, the same."

"Did anyone ever figure out what he was doing, what he was trying to tell me?"

Ricky shook his head. "No, *ese*. Now we never know."

Chapter 45

A good two months, no Slicer sightings, no killings.

No killings, that is, except for the dozens of random homicides rampant throughout any big city like Houston. But nothing close to home, at least.

Alice and I were dating steady now, but her surgery schedule was demanding enough that I got weary just keeping up with her. She had ten times the energy and stamina I could boast, but even she could be fatigued. She'd drive over to my house, we'd start a movie, but she'd be asleep in minutes. I'd just slip a duvet over her and slink to bed myself. Sometimes in the morning she'd still be curled up on my sofa, Krazy Kat nestled against her. Or she'd wake in the middle of the night, crawl into bed beside me, half asleep. Either way our lovemaking was in temporary decline, but that was fine with me. Simply having Alice in my life was sufficient. We did manage to find time to go sailing again, however, this time overnight, banging our heads on the cabin bulkheads as we made awkward love, laughing at our own distress. I was happy again for the first time in three years.

* * *

Morning and Joe Duggan calling, which bothered me. He was so engaged with his new supervisory duties that we rarely talked of late, so when Joe called, something critical was on the agenda. "Yeah, Joe. What's up?"

"Was a dustup over at the Burgess murder scene apartments last night."

"What the hell?"

"Remember Sister Mary Frances?"

"Oh, no! Not her!"

"Relax. She's okay. She's just major stressed out, admitted to Saint Joe's for observation. She's asking for you."

I heard chimes and a pager in the background of Joe's phone. "You at the hospital now?"

"Yeah. ER, room six."

"I'm on the way."

I double-timed it to Saint Joseph's, the big Roman Catholic Diocesan hospital just south of downtown, parked in the closest lot I could find. It took me longer to find the ER than did my driving to the hospital.

Joe was sitting in the waiting area, reading a book on his Kindle, which was a miracle in itself.

"Joe," I said.

He got up immediately. "C'mon."

I followed Duggan down the hall and into a small suite of four beds, curtains drawn between. Beepers abounded, nurses and doctors moving throughout, administering to patients.

Sister Mary Frances lay in a hospital gown, propped up, oxygen tube under her nose, IV in her arm and sensors all around. But she was conscious and seemed reasonably okay at first glance. She was attended by two men. One was Father Dan Gibson, the priest whom I'd interviewed at St. Vincent. The other was Oswaldo Lopez, the late Renata Martinez' boyfriend.

"Sister, how are you?" I asked.

She waved, shook her head either up and down or side to side, I couldn't tell. "I'm okay, Mitch, wanted to see you, tell you that I appreciate your friendship. I knew you'd be anxious about me." Her voice was slurry.

"Don't talk so much, Mary Frances," Father Gibson told her, smiling, patting her arm. "Save your strength." He looked at me. "They just gave her a sedative, help her rest."

"What happened?"

"Ask Ozzie here," Gibson said. "He was there. He's a hero, too."

"I'm no hero," Ozzie said quietly. "I just did what anybody would."

Mary Frances rejected that. "He saved my life is all," voice weaker now. "Fought him off. He was... he... so..." And she drifted off to sleep in the middle of her sentence. The sedatives had kicked in.

Duggan put a finger to his lips, gestured that we should all get out. So we left Sister Mary Frances Brookshire to her rest and quietly filed from the room, back to the visitors' area.

"Tell me, somebody," I said.

Joe Duggan pointed at Ozzie. "Sister Mary Frances is right. The kid here's a hero. He ran up against George Burgess and beat him!"

"Burgess? No!"

Father Gibson nodded. "Mary Frances' car was in the shop, distributor went out, something like that. So she got a ride home with Ozzie and that's what saved her life."

Duggan continued. "Mary Frances was ambushed. Ozzie here let her out of his car, then he saw she forgot some books. So he took them to her, was about a minute behind, and there she was, up against the wall at her apartment doorway, George Burgess with a knife at her neck."

"What happened, Ozzie?" I asked.

"I saw this guy, I thought he was just some drunk, you know. I didn't even see the knife at first." He shrugged. "He was mugging Sister, so I smashed him in the head with the books I had."

"Smashed?" I was delighted.

"Yeah. I musta hit him pretty hard, he went right over and dropped this knife. I saw it, picked it up."

"You're a big guy, Ozzie," I said. "You bash somebody, he stays bashed."

He chuckled. "I guess so. Anyway, he got up, all wobbly. I yelled at him to get lost, and he just ran away."

Finally, one for the good guys. "Mary Frances wasn't hurt?"

"Nope. But she was scared something terrible, got dizzy and threw up, so I called 911."

"How is she now?" I asked Gibson.

She'll be okay," he said. "Docs thought she had a mild heart attack but no, the EKG is clean. She was just stressed, needs rest."

I looked at Joe. "Certain it was Burgess?"

"We're sure. Both Sister and Ozzie ID'd him. He's gone bald on us, shaved his head, but it's Burgess."

"He got away."

"Yeah," Joe said. "Nothin' we can do about that." Then, smiling, "But Ozzie, tell Mitch what you saw. About Burgess."

"The guy had a bandage on his neck, another one on his arm and he was limpin' when he ran off."

Chapter 46

David Meierhoff and I were double dating to hear the Dave Alvin band.

Alice was of course my companion, she having become my main and only squeeze. And Meierhoff was hooked up with an HPD motorcycle cop, Monique Devereaux, who looked exactly like her name, over six feet tall and shaped like a James Bond movie girl. They'd been an item for two years now.

I realize it's expected that all Texans be passionate country-western fans, but I'd never cared much for that genre, with classical, opera, or progressive jazz my three standbys, classic rock on the side.

So it was with some personal surprise that I fell head over heels for Dave Alvin. And true, his music isn't what you'd call traditional country, more a new-wave California sound with heavy influence of hot blues guitar, but since Alvin is still labeled country-western, I'd overlooked him totally. Until, that was, one evening when I was glued to the TV for the latest episode of *Justified*, which featured a cameo of Dave Alvin and his band playing a tune written especially for the show, *Harlan County Line*. And as they say, it was love at first sight.

Tonight Dave Alvin was playing at a cozy dive bar, the Continental Club on South Main. The four of us got there early to stake out good seats, so we first shared a barbecue plate from the small quick-order restaurant at the back of the bar. Overly sweet, I thought, but okay for a blues club.

People all around were staring at Monique. She sported an intense platinum blonde hairstyle that only emphasized her striking good looks and seemed to add even more inches to her verified six-one. "I think she's twice my size," Alice whispered to me.

"Intimidated?" I asked.

"Not for one second, m'dear."

None of the others had seen or heard much of Dave Alvin until I began incessantly campaigning for him, so they were skeptical, but I knew they'd be equally enraptured when the music started. Unless, I thought in a furtive panic attack, Alvin was one of those performers who phoned it in during live shows, a throwaway habit that plagued even some of the best.

Luckily my suspicions were wrong. The band started with *East Texas Blues* followed by *King of California*, and I knew that I'd done good, sponsoring our foursome.

Alvin was in great form, a deep and elegant baritone, his guitar soaring in extravagant blues riffs. The sidemen (and female drummer) were perfectly matched as well and they poured out song after delightful song. I glanced to see that all three of my companions were entranced with the music. And when Dave Alvin played *Black Rose of Texas*, his plaintive tribute to a now-deceased blues singer and friend, I saw tears in Monique's eyes.

* * *

We stood in the parking lot next to our cars, chatting. Alice and Monique had stepped off a ways and Monique was smoking, holding her cigarette down and sideways, surreptitious as most smokers are these days. The two women were sharing something funny, glancing at us as they giggled. Women do that a lot, and although we men pretend to be irritated, we're in fact flattered to receive even scattered attention, however sarcastic it may be.

"How's the home front?" David asked.

"Best in ages. Alice works long hours at Hermann, but we still manage to get together fairly often."

"Same here. Monique has different schedules than I but we work things out. Tonight was great fun."

"Told you Alvin was tops."

"Agreed," he said. "But I need to change the subject. I checked yesterday with Juanita Hertza. You know, Hispanic gang task force?"

"Yeah. Hertza and I are this close." My arms widespread, both forefingers indicating the gap.

He laughed. "Regardless, she's a good cop. And I thought to ask her about Barrio Colombia, whether there was much action of late."

"And she said?"

"No action, no special stuff, just the usual. So apparently things have quieted down and I wanted you to know."

"Thanks. And thank her, okay?"

"Sure."

"But David?"

"Yeah?"

"I'm never going to let my guard down again."

"Be sure you do that. You know how I am about funerals."

Chapter 47

I'd taken the motel chain hiring and security contract, and just finished a set of employee interviews, maybe thirty people. I also ran background checks and most had come though fine. I was typing up my report to the motel management group when the doorbell chimed. I switched screens to the monitor and saw Ricky Perdon standing there, grinning up at the camera.

"Come in, my friend," I told him, opening the door.

As Ricky entered, he glanced down to the Glock 30 in my hand. "Nice gun."

"What can I do for you?" I asked. "Want a beer?"

"A beer, always."

So we sat in my office, facing one another in a pair of reasonably comfy chairs I'd scrounged from Mattress Mac's Gallery Furniture. We clinked our Bud bottles like we were in a commercial, sipped the cool brew.

"How's Cheryl?" I asked.

"Fine, fine. She manages the business so good, we make money and everyone is happy."

"Glad to hear."

"Of course, she is still sad about her father. She misses Julio."

"Julio is missed by many."

A quiet moment, more beer. "I don't suppose you were just in the neighborhood and dropped by," I said.

"No, *ese*, I bring good news and want to tell you myself, not the damn phone."

"Good news is always welcome. But what?"

"We talk to other people all the time, you know. Some in gangs."

"Yes, I know."

"I hear news from BC."

"Barrio Colombia?"

"Yes, *ese*. But good news. There is no more vendetta on you."

"What do you mean, no more?"

He waved his hands, crossing them like an umpire ruling *safe*. "After Montalvo Santiago die, the BC, they have no anger for you, they say he kill your lady, you kill him, equal."

"They're a gang, Ricky. They shoot people for fifty bucks. Why would they not still want to kill me?"

"You are not worth it, *ese!*"

That broke both of us up, and we laughed until we were out of breath. I grabbed two more beers from my little office fridge and we toasted my worthlessness.

"You're serious," I said.

"Yes, my friend, serious. Nobody pay them to kill you, they have other things to do."

"And bullets are expensive," I added.

At that we clicked bottles again, sat back, relaxed, reached down to pet Kraze.

Later, as I escorted Ricky to the door, we were still chuckling at the joke of my relative small worth to a vicious gang. "Thanks for coming by," I told him.

"Always good, my friend."

"Say hello to Cheryl and everyone else."

"I will, *ese*."

Ricky was on his way out when he turned. "Oh, one thing other. I almost forgot, small thing, you know."

"Sure."

"You remember Julio, trying to give you something, say something?"

"Yes, of course."

"When we bury him we want his best clothes, you understand. We have many other clothes to give to the charity, and we have this jacket he didn't wear much, when I check the pocket, I find this. Your name. Maybe this was what he wanted to give you."

Ricky reached to his inside coat pocket, retrieved a folded sheet of paper, handed it to me. I opened it.

A message from the grave and it dealt with death most certain, most absolute.

Preprinted invoice for a storage facility, all the spaces blank except the unit number, *15*, the fragment *burg* scribbled there and in the margin, *Mitch*. The form bore an address and the title *Mid City Moving & Storage*. At the top corner, their yellow and blue logo, circle halves of Yin and Yang.

Chapter 48

I thought about taking Tony Vee with me to the Mid City address, decided against it. I also gave consideration to simply alerting Duggan or Meierhoff, remembering Joe's anger a couple years back, when I'd held out on him and gone it alone where it wasn't advised.

But this time was different. I had a personal grudge to settle, Kate Morley's death. And since the facility was in Mid City, it was out of Duggan's jurisdiction anyway and that made things okay. Or so I persuaded myself.

I Googled the company name and address, but found no web presence. After surfing through various mapping sites, I finally located a rather grainy and distant view of the place. It sat on a wide secondary thoroughfare three blocks from Spencer Highway. The place was shabby and rundown, sign out front askew, paint faded, the dualist logo nearly invisible, but there nonetheless. I zoomed in to discern the layout, but only revealed rows of generic prefab lockers, roll-up doors, no details.

Some advance scouting was needed, so I phoned Ernie Banks across the street. "Hey, Ernie, what say we trade cars tonight, let me borrow your T-Bird a while?" Ernie owned a meticulously maintained '96 LX. *Satin black like my skin*, he'd joke.

"What? Your Kraut car fall apart on you? I told you to only trust American iron."

"Not so lucky," I told him. "But folks recognize my Bimmer and…"

"Say no more, my friend. The Blackbird is yours. Just make sure the tank is full when you bring her back."

"What is this, high school?"

"Hey, price you pay. Meantime I'll take your fancy-ansy Krautmobile and see how many chicks I can pick up."

"Deal."

"Deal," he said. "But you gotta show me how to run the stereo and radio and that computer stuff too."

* * *

Ernie's Bird was smooth and quiet. I made it to Mid City by dusk, passed the storage facility once to verify the layout, pulled into a franchise Tex-Mex restaurant that was diagonal across the avenue. I parked with a view to the facility but shaded beside a big dented van for cover. Traffic was light, still being early, so I hoped that nobody would see me and complain to the cops. I brought my Kowa 8x30 binoculars, good for the fading light.

I had zero idea of the number arrangement of the lockers but got lucky and could see straight back to a row of large sheds, each about the size of a one-car garage. Which made sense, as restoration buffs without requisite space at home often rent these for storing and working on their vehicles. I couldn't see unit fifteen, as it was blocked by a closer building, but sheds eleven through fourteen were easy to spot. All I had to do was extrapolate to fifteen and watch for George Burgess. If indeed he was there and I wasn't chasing wild geese.

Over the space of three hours I moved the car twice, once to hit the Burger King john and grab a Coke, the other simply because I didn't want to be sitting parked in one spot too long.

It was after nine and the entire storage facility was deserted. I was about ready to quit for the night when I saw him!

Burgess was dressed well, dark shirt and tan slacks like a thousand other ordinary people you pass on the street every day. And yes, he'd gone bald and at first glance wouldn't be recognized

262

in his wanted posters, but when he turned around, I knew the face and knew it well, ingrained as it was into my mind. I tracked him as he made his way through the pedestrian gate and sauntered toward unit fifteen. He was limping, too.

Contact!

* * *

No way I would get involved in a confrontation while using Ernie's car, nor was I yet prepared, so I headed home. When I pulled into his driveway, Ernie and Malcolm were sitting out front, Ernie in a folding chair, Malcolm his low-slung wheelchair. I got out, brought Ernie his keys.

"Thanks, pal. Tank is full, as promised."

"Not to mention, Mitch." Ernie reached in his pocket, gave me back my keys. "Me and Malcolm toured the whole east side, lookin' for chicks in your Bimmer. Brought a few gals back here, partied."

Malcolm grunted, smiled. "Truth told, we never even popped the lock. Your X3 is sittin' where it was before. We wouldn't be caught dead in that honky piece of crap anyway."

We all laughed at that. Ernie gestured to a cooler next to his chair. "Beer?"

"No, sorry, not tonight, got work to do. Take a rain check." I made farewells and walked over to my house to get ready.

First the small stuff. I fed Kraze, chugged an Ensure, did the bathroom thing, showered after. I dressed in dark, close-fitting clothes, tight black Levi's, a black pullover, Nikes the same, a hooded windbreaker. My car and house keys, no wallet, just my IDs and about a hundred cash, a Visa card. I wanted to be trim as possible.

Now came the weapons and other gear.

Some months ago I ordered a pair of tactical gloves from the 5.11 website. The gloves were for beat cops who had to get up close and personal with druggies, and the material had a special tough liner that protected the cop from body fluids. My thought was the reverse, that I wouldn't be leaving DNA evidence while wearing them, sweat perhaps. When I ordered the gloves I also bought an XXL pair for Tony Vee, just because.

Tony wanted to show his appreciation, borrowed my gloves and later brought them back, pointed out what he'd done. "Call 'em enhanced, okay? Lookie here." He indicated a small flap stitched alongside the palm of each glove. Inside, a thin, flexible blade, slender knife with a short grip, a miniature scalpel. "For emergencies."

I thought it gimmicky, but hey, gimmick or not, the gloves went on my belt, along with a small LED flashlight.

Next, my gun safe. Deep in the back, a thick plastic bag. Inside, a Czech rip-off of the venerable Browning Hi Power, 9mm design that had seen service in countless wars and other skirmishes. I acquired the gun from a friend of a friend, no questions asked. Yes, it was undoubtedly stolen and yes, impossible to establish the provenance.

I had fired the pistol in several range trips, found that it was fairly reliable and reasonably accurate enough for close range. I had trouble with the safety, however, and no manner of lubrication would fix it. I don't have the requisite skill to fully disassemble a pistol, especially one without an owner's manual, and I couldn't let someone else work on it either, because they'd likely jot down the serial number and I wanted no backtracking, ever. I finally blamed the balky safety on shoddy workmanship and got it to function, albeit stubbornly and needing a firm push from the thumb to disengage. Better, at least, than a blunt object, I suppose.

So after establishing the pistol's cranky but marginal workability, I field stripped and scrubbed the gun of any fingerprints or other tracings, same for the spare magazines and especially for the hollow-point cartridges themselves. The fully loaded pistol, round in the chamber, plus two spare magazines also went onto my belt.

Once more into the breach, but this time not for England or St. George. This time for Kate Morley.

* * *

I got to Mid City Moving & Storage just after eleven, parked in a nearby used car lot, squeezing the BMW between two big pickups. Hopefully nobody would sell the car while I was gone.

As I walked toward the facility I thought back about the last time I'd engaged in a solo mission, that terrible night at the trailer park nearly two years ago. I resolved for this to have a better outcome and with luck, I'd be home early tonight, the alternative being to never return home again, ever.

There was a chain link fence around the property but the pedestrian gate was unlocked. I looked for cameras, saw none. I nevertheless pulled the hoodie tight around my face, also kept my head down, just like I was robbing the local Stop-N-Go.

Unit fifteen was about halfway through the property. No movement anywhere, no barriers, no delay. Fifteen was at the end of the row and now I saw what had been blocked from my earlier surveillance—on the side of the building, a regular metal door, second entrance to the unit.

I put on the gloves, drew the pistol and stood quietly, watching, listening. A thin line of light beneath the metal flap against concrete, faint sound of music. George was home.

Conventional storage operations offer electric service and allow renters to spend time inside on a temporary or daily basis, but forbid overnight occupancy, as this infringes upon residency ordinances. In Mid City, however, a blind eye was turned by the property manager. It was evident that Burgess was living here, if only occasionally.

I leaned against the wall, thinking. How could I surprise him? No way I could force a metal door without a big pry bar and plenty of time. I'd be shot dead within ten seconds. I'd just have to camp out till he emerged.

But I got lucky! The music quit and a rattling at the door. It was being unlocked! I quickly dodged around the corner to the rear of the structure, peeked to see whether Burgess would emerge.

Nothing. No movement, no sound. I waited two, three minutes.

And then, behind me, a small noise, a scraping. I half turned and I was struck! A burst of bright inward light.

Blackness.

Chapter 49

A growth of perception mixed with intense surges of dizziness and pain, nausea.

I was sitting on the concrete floor, hands pulled behind me, legs out in front. As I regained consciousness, I squinted against the bright overhead light, saw George Burgess seated on a folding chair, holding my pistol and smiling.

"How you feeling, Mitch?"

I didn't answer. Couldn't really, as I was still too woozy, my vision pinching in, blurry, fireworks exploding in my head. I recalled only pieces, never totally unconscious, just stunned. I remembered Burgess hitting me several times across the head. Dragging me, my feet stirring dustmarks on the floor. Tape around wrists. His reaching for my gun and my thinking it was over.

But here I sat, alive, at least for now. Eventually the numbness dissipated, gradually I began to feel my own body and became aware of the surroundings.

"Thought you'd fuck with me, didn't you?" Burgess asked. "I spotted your sorry ass this afternoon over at the restaurant, knew you'd come back later. Don't know how you found me, but what the fuck."

I said nothing, tried to focus my vision and mind, fought to stay awake and maintain awareness. As my eyes began to work better, I saw that Burgess had small bandages on his right arm, the left side of his neck.

Burgess laughed. "I guess you thought you had me cornered, stuck away inside fifteen, nowhere to go." He gestured to the side and I saw that the area was much larger than I'd anticipated. "I rented out fourteen too. They even cut down the prefab wall between. I saw you through a peephole, went out the back door of fourteen, came up behind you, caught your ass!"

Burgess waved the pistol around, sometimes aiming it at me, otherwise just randomly at imaginary targets. I was still groggy but it seemed he wasn't as rational or studied as I remembered. Whether he'd been sampling his crystal meth or was going slowly berserk, I didn't know, but the more he talked, the more obvious it became. Not that it made a damn. Crazy or not, he would soon kill me.

"Y'know, Mitch, I planned it all but things went sour. That fuckin' Macintyre kid, he got in my way, busted in here one day, stole my whole stash. That's gratitude for you, my fronting him to a shitload of blue, his making good bucks selling it at the school. But he rips me off! And when I go to his place, get him to tell where my stash was, the fucker fights back. I got cut up some, my damn kneecap dislocated. But I fucked him over anyway. And then he had the damn bad luck to die on me before I found my dope! Asshole!" Burgess was getting wound up.

I stalled. "So you never found your meth?"

"No. And me owing the BC boys with no way to pay. Lucky they didn't know about this place. But I had to skip out on the nice little house where I was livin', up in Fifth Ward, lost my guns and all my best knives." Burgess reached over to a small table, tilted it so I could see an array of cutlery. "But I got new stuff, Mitch, new sharp blades and we're gonna have a real fun time tonight."

When he said *blades*, something bubbled itself up into my forebrain. Something about knives… something… and with instant clarity, I knew! I gently moved my bound hands, pulling against the thick tape. Burgess had left my gloves on!

"Barrio Colombia, right?" I said, trying to draw him out, prolong things, keep him talking.

"Yeah, BC, like I said. I was a good customer of theirs from the start, Mitch. Way before I got fired, way before you killed Ray."

"Your brother killed himself. And you kept him addicted to that damn asphyxiation rig of his instead of getting him professional help."

"Fuck you, pal! I'm gonna make you regret saying that!"

I strained carefully at the tape, not wanting him to know, so I squirmed at the same time, stretched my legs and thumped my heels to direct his attention from my hand movement. I pulled and I could just feel the hidden blade inside the left glove. I kept moving slowly, testing the limits of the tape and trying to retrieve the teeny, gimmicky blade. But I'd never distrust gimmicks again and so I prayed good things about gimmicks, prayed hard. And again, banged my heels, a distraction.

"Feet gone to sleep?" he asked. "Don't worry. I'll soon relieve you of any worries about your feet. Or toes, or hands. Or balls." Burgess picked up a long, slender stiletto from the table, admired its shine, smiled.

I felt the blade slip free from its little scabbard! Now I had to turn it, cut at the tape. But I needed more time. "Tell me about Renata Martinez. Why her?"

He shrugged. "Why not? I didn't want to bring attention to the apartments, Eddie Macintyre living there, but one look at her, quiet little student, she was so very inviting, so luscious. You got no idea, Mitch, how wonderful it feels, that first cut."

"Cops say you ate part of her."

At that, he laughed aloud. "All a joke! I took some special things, slices of liver, you know, just to fuck with their heads. I guess it worked."

The blade was now turned in my fingers, rubbing at the tape. I had to concentrate on holding it, not dropping it and keep my mind alert as well. Hard to do, dizziness still splashing around me. But I finally felt it start to cut, razor sharp.

"So you didn't eat her?" I wanted to keep him talking, bragging.

"Okay, maybe a little, just to give it a try. But not a lot."

"As if that makes a difference," I said.

"Difference or not, you're fucked and I think I'll do the Hannibal thing on you. How's that sound, Mitch?"

"I don't suppose I'll know." I was halfway through the tape. "Being dead when you do."

"Oh, don't be too sure of that. I'll start small and work my way up, take a snack break, let you watch."

I tried not to think of that, so I took him back to the killings. "You murdered the Martinez girl just because she was there?"

He shrugged. "Had to, I guess. I knew it brought the cops and I knew that Macintyre would be checked out, but sometimes the urge is too much. It's hard to describe, a blessing and a curse."

"It's not much of a blessing, you ask me."

"Don't be too sure of that, Mitch. I even did you a favor last week."

I kept sawing at the tape, trying to make my motions small so he wouldn't notice. "Favor, you say?"

Burgess swung around, gestured across the small room, and while his head was turned I cut more vigorously. Propped against the wall where Burgess pointed were two thick rolls of plastic sheet, something large inside each roll. "See there?" he said.

"What?"

"Juan Perez and Castillo Aguilar. All gift wrapped. No ribbons and bows though, but like they say, it's the thought that counts."

"Perez and Aguilar? Guys who killed Kate Morley?"

He nodded, smiling. "And shot you. Can't have any loose ends, can we? So I told them I had more money to keep them quiet, got 'em to visit." He chuckled. "Now they're very quiet. You should thank me."

Just a little more time. "But Eddie Macintyre outwitted you, didn't he? Stole your meth."

"I wouldn't say outwitted, but I can't be in all places at the same time, no matter what the news says about me."

"And the security guard at the school vigil?"

"Just for show, Mitch, just for show. You woulda been disappointed otherwise."

The little blade cut through the tape! I carefully worked my hands free, but kept them together so Burgess wouldn't suspect, once again wiggling my feet as a feint. *Bless you, Tony Vee*, I thought. *And bless your gimmicks!*

"What about the nun? Why did you attack her?"

"For fun, Mitch! I was just gonna mark her a little, leave you another message. No way I'd kill her. Shit, I'm Catholic!"

"Catholic and you'd cut up a nun?"

"You just don't understand how it feels, Mitch. Nobody does. You have to be there, know how exciting it is, almost as good as fucking. Maybe even better."

Now that my hands were free I needed to taunt him, get him close enough for me to get in one good kick, reach out for him and grab hold. His having the pistol, it would essentially be suicide, me seated on the floor, legs in front. But still I had to try. *No other options left, Mitch. Go for it!*

"Know what, Burgess?" I said, adding sarcasm to my voice, sneering. "You're a miserable, fucked up loser. You think you're a hotshot and scary bastard, but you're pathetic! All the cops know this, laugh about you. Always have, laughed behind your stupid, pervert back!"

"Shut up!"

"Fuck it! No wonder you like to kill people, you can't even get goddamn laid! And you tried to hurt a nun, for Christ's sake! But when you did, some big fat clumsy schoolkid busted your sorry ass! You worthless piece of shit, letting a fatty kick your butt, ha!"

He stood up, pointed the pistol. "Shut the fuck up!"

"Or what? Gonna kill me? Go ahead, loser! You couldn't even keep your fucking idiotic self-strangling loser brother alive! Hell, you were an enabler for him! You're just a piece of crap! Shoot me or use your stupid knives. I don't give a shit."

"You asshole! I'll take my time with you!" He quickly strode over to me, let loose a vicious kick to my side. The pain was sudden, intense, and my ribs snapped!

Burgess reared his leg back for another kick, and it was then I spun, swung my legs, swept them under his feet, and he went crashing to the floor.

Hands free, I pushed myself up as quickly as I could. Burgess was regaining his balance, standing now, leaning toward me, raising the pistol. My legs were numb and I slipped, fell back, then once more raised myself, but it was too late. Burgess had the gun aimed and he jerked his hand in a firing motion. I could almost feel the bullet hitting me between the eyes.

But nothing! He jerked the pistol once more, again. That damn balky safety was stuck!

And then I was on him, the pistol sliding away, across the room.

Burgess was police trained in physical combat, but I knew the same drills, plus four years of Shotokan karate. Both of us were injured, but I was stronger than he, younger and fighting for my life.

Burgess caught me with a good left hook and I was momentarily staggered, but when he moved in, I slammed him under the chin with a palm thrust into the larynx followed by a side chop to his neck, right onto the bandage and the nerve bundle beneath. He felt it, I could tell, but he still put up his fists, kicked at me. Too slow! I blocked the kick with my thigh, turned and drove a knee into his groin. He gasped, frozen. I caught him with two stiff-finger strikes into his solar plexus and he was down! I finally put him out with a chop to his neck, hard, all my strength, where the carotid artery runs and the surge of blood pressure will temporarily stun the opponent.

He lay on the floor, groaning.

I kicked him under his chin for good measure, quickly looked around, found the roll of glass fiber tape he'd used to handcuff me. I wrapped him with a few turns, arms firmly to his side, then his knees and ankles. I used Tony's little knife to cut the tape, then tucked the blade back into the glove, like I did this every day.

A moment of dizziness pushed its way into my brain and I sagged against the wall. I was still feeling the effects of his earlier beating.

Burgess started to hump awkwardly across the floor, knocking over his tray of knives. They went bouncing everywhere. He saw the long stiletto near where he lay, wiggled to grab it with his left hand. I pushed myself away from the wall, none too steady, put my foot on the knife and scooted it aside. "Naughty, naughty," I told him.

Still staggering, I found the pistol, saw that the safety had become jammed against the frame, bent out of true. Whether this happened when he first attacked me or when the gun went flying, I didn't know, but still I silently thanked the gods of cruddy workmanship. I put the gun on the floor and turned to him again.

"Now what?" Burgess said. "What you fuckin' gonna do?"

I squatted beside him. He tried to raise himself, but I pushed him down. "Stay quiet or I'll hit you again."

He had a sarcastic grin on his face. "So you win, motherfucker."

"I don't consider it winning, all those people you murdered."

"Hey, it's what I do."

"You're an abomination!"

Burgess was still smiling. "So call the cops. Fuckers convict me for murder one and sentence me to the drip. Or else they stick me in some psych ward. Either way, they lock me up the next twenty years while my chickenshit lawyers appeal. So call 'em."

"I don't think so," I said. I reached over, picked up the stiletto. "This is for Kate Morley."

I grabbed his shoulder for support and rammed the blade straight into his eye, to the hilt, gave it a good stir.

He screamed and thrashed around a while, but eventually went quiet.

Chapter 50

I put off seeing Alice, claiming that busy consultancies were grabbing all my free time. I had to stay away from her until my bruises and scrapes healed. I didn't want questions.

And recovering from being knocked unconscious isn't as it's portrayed in the movies, the tough hero shaking his head and coming to full cognizance in six seconds. After all, it's a goddamn concussion. During the shaky drive home, I pulled over twice and vomited. And for days afterward, I had recurring spells of nausea and disorientation. It wasn't until a couple weeks that I felt okay.

Medical help would have been good, but unlike fictional private detectives, I didn't know any backdoor unlicensed sawbones. I could have called Tony Vee or the Perdon cousins, I suppose, but I didn't want to be owing them either, especially regarding a capital crime.

So I stayed low and didn't get out much, kept alert for any mention of Burgess on the news. Thus far, nothing. All I had to do was keep busy and not make waves.

Good, in a way, that I in truth did have plenty to keep me occupied. The motel people renewed my services for another six months. And their referral landed me another job, this time with a string of locally owned convenience stores. Plus more work from the fledgling Mid City restaurant and bar chain. All the personnel interviews and screening kept me hopping, but the work was mostly office related, none too physical, which let me lope along and mask my injuries.

It was likewise fortunate that my entire work ethic and enterprise philosophy has undergone a change for the better. No more lurking around bars to catch wayward hubbies or wives, no more slinking under wraps to video a guy on total disability playing the back nine. Let Bugsy Binton take those jobs. He needs the dough.

I'd also forgone my boozing and disruptive lifestyle. Earlier this year I compared my indulgent and destructive behavior unfavorably with my pals David Meierhoff and Joe Duggan, how they'd made progress while I lagged. I was trying to be objective now and not self-aggrandizing, but I do think I cleared personal hurdles that had restrained me too long.

* * *

I was kicking back after a workout and shower, lounging in my upstairs study and listening to Beethoven's violin concerto, a remastered RCA release featuring Isaac Stern, likely the finest player of double stops in our era. I was still a bit stiff in the side but everything else had healed, thankfully without need for obtrusive medical attention.

Speaking of obtrusive, the front door chimed.

I clicked the stereo off, went down, saw Joe Duggan, impatient as always. I laid my Glock on a nearby table and let Joe in.

"We got to talk," he said, walking to the kitchen, helping himself to a beer.

"What is it, Joe?"

"HPD had a call this morning from Mid City major crime, asked us to come down, help ID a puffer they found in this ratty storage shed. You know, puffer, bloater? Body that's been sitting a while, kinda ripe?"

"Bloater. I know."

Joe took a deep swig from the bottle, looked askance at me. "What? You not drinking?"

"Not so much as before. Got to watch my girlish figure."

"Girlish figure? That'll be the fuckin' day."

"I'm mostly off the sauce of late, Joe. Occasional bourbon, glass of wine, beer now and then. Moderation is better for the insides, better for the soul."

Joe quickly downed the rest of the beer, dumped the now-empty bottle in the trash, got a fresh one, drank about half. "Speaking of the soul…"

"What, Joe? You don't normally chug two beers in two minutes. Tell me."

"Bloater was George Burgess. We ID'd him but the pathologist still has to verify dental records."

"You mean…"

"Burgess is dead. Squishy meat balloon blown up dead. Piñata ya don't wanna bust open dead."

I tried to say something, but Joe waved me to silence, continued. "But wait, there's more. Two more."

"Two more what?"

"DBs, two more puffers. Besides Burgess, that is."

"Two?"

I could see that Joe was frustrated by my nonchalant attitude but he kept on. "Yeah. We think they're Aguilar and Perez, the guys who shot you and Kathryn Morley. Both of 'em was carved up, sliced and diced, stuck inside two big plastic bags, stacked against the shed wall like ol' King Tut. We're guessin' that Burgess didn't want any links back to him on the shooting, jumped them both. And with Santiago dead too, there's nobody left to say he hired them. Dead skunks in the middle of the room, stinkin' to high heaven."

A flicker of a grin passed over Joe's face but I forced myself to keep it straight. "So Burgess was also dead, a bloater? Been dead a while, right?"

Joe squinted at me, set the bottle on the kitchen counter, started the patented process. "Count 'em off." He raised his hand, pulled down the little finger. "One, yeah, we're glad he's gone." The ring finger, and Joe was now more abrupt. "Two, he was layin' in a shed of some jerkwad storage yard where it looks like he'd been hiding, crapped out for at least a month, smell brought the cops." The middle finger, and voice tinged with anger. "Three, they found this big knife stuck in his head, through the eye socket." Forefinger to form a fist, a stern voice. "Four and out, you killed the fucker and I know that you did!"

"Joe, I don't—"

"Can it!" Joe was intense now. "Remember when me and Meierhoff saved your sweet ass, that shooting on South Main, down by the old Astrodome?"

"Sure. But that was another me, another person."

"Bullshit, Mitch! People don't change!"

Sometimes they do, Joe, sometimes they do. I spread my hands, gesturing ignorance. "Joe, I—"

He didn't wait for me to say anything more. "Crime scene people found zero evidence as to who killed Burgess. Most think it was comeback from Barrio Colombia for taking all that meth, not paying up."

"That's pretty likely," I ventured.

Joe took up the beer, drained it, tossed the bottle into the trash where it clunked against its empty companion. "Likely my ass."

"What can I say, Joe?"

He looked at me, eyes intense. "Don't say a fuckin' thing, pal. Not one fuckin' goddamn word."

I shrugged.

"Hey Mitch, chill," Joe said, more restraint in his voice. "I wanted to rattle your cage, see what you would say, make sure we're straight on things. In sync, okay?"

"Okay, sure, if you say so…" I was tentative, not knowing where Joe was going.

Joe reached out and for a moment I thought he was going to punch me. Instead he buffed me on the shoulder, friendly like, smiled. "Remember after the Martinez murder, we were in James Coney Island, talkin' about finding Burgess?"

"Sure, Joe. You had two chili dogs but I could only manage a Coke."

"More. Remember I said if there was vigilante stuff, I didn't want to know?"

"Yeah. But—"

"Take it easy, Mitch," he remonstrated. "Also remember I said not to fuck it up this time?"

"I remember."

"Just came by to tell you that you didn't."

"Joe, I—"

"Didn't you hear me? Let it drop. Done is done."

Chapter 51

After Joe left I was shaking. I poured myself a jigger of Maker's Mark, sipped, dumped most down the drain. I sat quietly, thought a while. I checked some things online and next called Alice, whom I knew was getting off work soon.

"Okay for dinner tonight?"

"Absolutely. I'm starved. I'll change and stop by your place, okay?"

"Okay. Fresh fish, Goode Company Seafood?"

"Perfect!"

"Also," I said. "You told me you had a weekend off soon?"

"Yes. The ninth, tenth."

"I know we were going sailing, but ever been to San Antonio?"

"No. You asking?"

"I am. There's a jazz festival that weekend, all along River Walk."

"I've seen photos, videos of the River Walk. Looks inviting."

"So I'm inviting you. We fly there, maybe rent a car, maybe not. I've got a room booked at the Hyatt, overlooks River Walk. We can also tour the Alamo. It's nearby."

"I accept, absolutely."

"It'll be fun, I promise."

"Do I get a money back guarantee on the fun promise?"

"You know it. We'll talk more at dinner."

"Looking forward to it," she said. "But Mitch?"

"Yes?"

"Any special reason? Celebrating anything in particular?"

"Freedom. I'm celebrating freedom!"

About the Author

Photo by William Hebel

Sam Waas has been a writer throughout his adult life. He began by editing an underground newsletter while in college at the University of Kansas, and has freelanced ever since. He's written book reviews for major dailies, strung for newspapers with sports car racing coverage, and has written articles for gun magazines and local newspapers, varied pieces for slick monthlies, and short stories, screenplays and essays. He's also written numerous book reviews for the online mystery website *Over My Dead Body*.

Recently, Sam's concentrating on his Mitch King private detective novels, based in Houston and the surrounding Gulf Coast region. There are three novels thus far: *Blood Spiral*, *Blood Storm* and *Blood Vengeance*, and he's now writing his fourth Mitch King novel.

Sam worked in science, technology, and research for many years. He was involved in polymer physics, programmed for structural engineering firms, worked with high tech computer ventures, and has also edited petroleum exploration and production specifications as a tech writer. Sam believes that his science and engineering background augments his fiction, in that it provides insight into meticulous details which lend texture and flavor to his mystery novels.

Sam is a longtime fan of classical music and opera, and as a classically trained baritone, sang in opera, chorales, and Episcopal church choirs. He also enjoys classic rock and progressive jazz. A voracious reader, Sam's favorite book is James Joyce's *Ulysses*, which he's read several times and of which he's made a personal study. He also enjoys books on Imperial Roman history, quantum physics and cosmology, science fiction, biographies and of course, mysteries. Besides Joyce, his favorite modern mainstream authors are Cormac McCarthy, James Dickey and Joseph Heller. His favored mystery writers are Bill Pronzini, Robert Crais and John Sandford. Sam enjoys attending opera and classical concerts, pistol shooting, playing chess and pool, and just hanging out at the local pub. He makes his home in Houston. More info on Sam and his Mitch King novels is available on his website at www.sam-waas.com

Blood Betrayal

Sam Waas

Chapter 1

After ten on a mild November evening, I was driving west on Cavalcade and decided to be thirsty. The little Asian quick-mart with the insanely cheery name Happy Nice Day Here came up on my right, serendipitous timing, so I pulled into the lot to snag a Coke.

I spotted a Houston police cruiser parked alongside the store, recognized the officer inside, tacked my Bimmer in that direction, and parked nearby to chat.

Corporal Carl Dixon, known to all as Cool Carl, was slid way down in the seat, barely visible, huge opaque Polar Optics sunglasses despite the hour, duty cap tilted low on his forehead. Carl cultivates his nonchalant persona, works it to the max. In fact an excellent police officer, he nevertheless projects an aura of indifference, a ploy that everyone, police and citizens alike, tease him about, knowing it to be a sham. But he perseveres and takes pains to display no anger, surprise or any other emotion. Carl could give cool lessons to Steve McQueen.

I walked up to his open window. "Hey, Carl, what's the buzz?"

"Mmm." Carl didn't move a muscle.

"Quiet shift tonight?"

"Mmm."

"Seen any movies? How 'bout them Texans? Beat up any innocent citizens lately?"

A reaction of sorts. Carl slowly turned his head toward me, lean face impassive as always. His fingertip raised the cap brim half an inch. "What's your main pain, King? Wandering the streets, scraping through gutters for new clients?"

"We private investigators need to stay alert, solving crimes, rescuing maidens, cleaning up messes that you cops leave."

"Mmm." Dixon turned his head forward again. I always relish my conversations with Cool Carl. So enlightening, so vigorous.

Carl's partner Tonya Arrondo was coming from the store, carrying a cardboard tray overflowing with certified cop nutrition—two large frozen slushes, bags of assorted chips, two greasy hot dogs, and a box of those little chocolate donuts made from a tasty blend of kindergarten paste and artificial flavoring.

Tonya's the opposite of Carl, exuberant and outgoing, always upbeat. She's a pretty young woman of mixed Hispanic and African-American ancestry, solid build, cascades of ropy dark hair, lovely deep eyes, an engaging smile. Tonya and I'd dated a couple times last spring, nothing serious, just hanging out for pizza, chatting. It had been a while, though, and I could kick myself, being so thoughtless to not keep up our friendship. Tonya had even come by to see me in the hospital after the shooting, brought me a get well card.

But during my recuperation I'd pared my personal contacts to the minimum because I needed to focus on rebuilding my own self, both inside and out. And more recently, my newly beloved New Zealander trauma surgeon, Dr. Alice Colhoun and I were, as my pal Joe Duggan in Homicide would say, a hot ticket, and in an exclusive relationship.

Tonya grinned when she saw me. "Why, if it's not Mister Mitchell King in the flesh, my very fave-o-rite private eye. Come here to pick on my poor little partner?" She peered into the car.

"Cool, this man botherin' you? Want me to jam 'im up? Tase him mebbe?"

Dixon's tacit response was to reach over and open the passenger door for Tonya. She handed the tray to Carl, strolled over to me, leaned back against the cruiser's hood, smiling, flirting. "Ain't seen you in a buncha Sundays. Tryin' to avoid me, huh?"

"Busy lately, Tonya."

She squinted. "What, you seein' somebody else?"

"Well—"

"C'mon, don't you be lyin' to your friendly local po-leece gal."

"Yeah, Tonya. I sort of have this person in my life now."

"Don't mean we can't be pals, right?" Tonya winked.

"Nope. My bad. Actually, I'd like you to meet my new lady."

A small frown. "Hmm... maybe."

"Hey, we're friends, like you say, right? Mexican food, my treat. You bring a pal too, okay?"

"Talked me into it."

"Great. I'll give you a call later this week, we can all hook up for lunch and a beer."

"Or three," Tonya joked.

"Sounds good,"

Dixon interrupted us, leaning out his window, voice calm as always. "Hate to put a crimp in the love affair, but Tonya and I've got rounds to make, baddies to arrest, private eyes to shoot at."

Tonya and I both turned to Cool Carl, surprised he invested more than a dozen words into a sentence. She reached out to me, we hugged briefly, a little air kiss. "Stay safe, Mitch. See ya around." She pantomimed a phone held to her ear, thumb and little finger protruding from her fist.

She was getting into the passenger seat when the scream came soaring across the night air.

Chapter 2

The cry was a clear high note, climax of a sick, twisted soprano aria, purity of tone but birthed in terror. We all looked toward the source, the empty alley behind the Vietnamese buffet restaurant next door. Nothing.

"Dammit!" was all that Tonya could manage before the scream came again, and as if propelled by the sound, a slender, sixtyish Asian man stumbled toward us from the alley. He wore a white apron, a peaked white cook's cap, and his face was filled with anguish.

"Come!" he gasped. "I see police car, run to you. Come! Terrible!"

Carl instantly discarded his detached persona and jumped from the cruiser, clutching a big patrol flashlight, other hand on the butt of his pistol. Carl and Tonya ran forward to help the man and I was a couple steps behind. The Asian guy himself looked all right, no visible injuries. He grabbed Tonya's arm, pulled. "Come see, very bad, you see!"

Carl shined his light down the alley but still nothing. Tonya gently detached from the man and transferred his grasp to me. "Keep him out of this, okay?"

I nodded, patting the man's hand to convey calm.

Tonya called for backup on her lapel mic, then joined her partner. The cops drew their pistols, held them down to the side, began to walk into the depth of the alley.

I reached inside my jacket, felt the .45 in its holster, then let my hand drop. The police would do their job just fine without me sticking my nose in. Instead I held onto the man and we both followed in the officers' wake, keeping back a ways. The man was frail but he still kept pulling me forward with an energetic surge. "Terrible!"

"Okay, okay," I reassured him.

The screams had ceased but it seemed their echo lingered, an ominous drifting presence. The alley between the store and restaurant was short. It t-boned into a parking lot and driveway of sorts, defined by a high chain-link fence along the back. There were a half dozen bulky commercial garbage bins in a row, some cars squeezed in nearby, not much else. Illumination was minimal but everything seemed fine.

The service door to the restaurant was open. A young Asian man poked his head out, saw the police, and stepped outside to stand on the concrete steps, cellphone in hand. The guy was dressed identically to the older man at my side.

"Police!" Tonya called out. "This is Houston police. You okay?"

"Yeah, I'm fine," his English perfect, unaccented. "I just called 911. You guys are fast."

"We were next door, sir," Carl replied. "We heard a scream, this man came running, asking for help."

"That's my dad. My mom is inside, needs a medic right now. She hollered, then I guess she fainted and fell. She hit her head." The older man left my side and rushed toward his son. They exchanged a few words I couldn't understand, then both were silent.

"Ambulance on the way, sir," Carl assured the son. "We'll have a look at her. But why was she screaming? She get burned in the kitchen? Cut herself?"

The young man shook his head, irritated. "No, hell no. She was taking out the trash, saw it and started yelling."

"Saw what?" Tonya asked.

"That! You guys friggin' blind, or what?" He pointed out his back door, across the alley and a few feet down the way, where it was darkest. Carl shined his flashlight toward what was hanging on the back fence.

It had once been a man.